LYSISTRATA COVE

What Reviewers Say
About Dena Hankins's Work

Advance Praise for *Lysistrata Cove*

"A very well-written book with excellent, hot scenes. ...Unapologetically queer and kinky."—*Patrick Califia*, author of *Macho Sluts* and *Public Sex*

Blue Water Dreams

"...when Lania and Oly set their differences aside and embrace their sexual chemistry, the scenes are graceful, sure, and spicy. This debut shows promise."—*Publishers Weekly*

"It is refreshing to read a love story where there is no jealous triangle, just people working out changes in their individual visions of their futures. ...Lania and Oly's sexual encounters are described in detail that goes on for several pages each time. The author uses the reality of what current medical treatment offers trans men to allow her characters to become quite inventive sexually."—*GLBT Reviews*

"Not your typical romance. ...It has some extremely hot sex—something I neglected to mention in the original review because I was so blown away by how well-drawn its characters are and how naturally they interact. An absolutely terrific first effort by a novelist I'll enjoy reading even more from in the future."—*Out In Print*

By the Author

Blue Water Dreams

Heart of the Liliko'i

Lysistrata Cove

LYSISTRATA COVE

by

Dena Hankins

2016

LYSISTRATA COVE
© 2016 By Dena Hankins. All Rights Reserved.

ISBN 13: 978-1-62639-821-4

This Trade Paperback Original Is Published By
Bold Strokes Books, Inc.
P.O. Box 249
Valley Falls, NY 12185

First Edition: September 2016

CREDITS
EDITOR: CINDY CRESAP
PRODUCTION DESIGN: SUSAN RAMUNDO
COVER DESIGN BY SHERI (GRAPHICARTIST2020@HOTMAIL.COM)

Acknowledgments

Partnership thrives on the water. James Lane and I have been together for 20 years as of October, 2016. We've been sailing and traveling together for 17 years as of September 2016. The years, with their ecstasies and adventures, living in wee little environments that run on sun and wind power, have comingled our thoughts and dreams and dovetailed our strengths.

When sailing Down East through Maine, we broke the toerail, a fifty-five-year-old piece of teak, just south of Mount Desert Island. We limped over the Bass Harbor Bar, past Great Cranberry Island, into the seven-mile long Somes Sound fjard, and put the hook down in Somes Harbor so that we could effect repairs.

James and I created this book at anchor, surrounded by glorious forests and tiny Maine towns. Between the first cup of morning coffee and the last, we roughed out the entire plot. By lunch, these two people were quite real to us, and I had to write their story.

I couldn't have done it without James. His unapologetic and passionate creative ethics and his reminder to, whenever at a loss, do something horrible to my characters shaped this book as much as my keystrokes.

Thanks, James. I love you.

Dedication

To James

Chapter One

A s the anchor chain rattled off the junk-rigged sailboat's bow roller, Jack checked his depth on the electronic chartplotter.

His deckhand, Marie, let out chain as fast as she could, hand over hand. She was young—just out of undergrad and trying to figure out which marine biology master's program she'd enter—but her baby softness was melting away under the labor on board. She hollered, "Anchor's on the ground," and slowed her pace.

"On the ground, aye." He marked the spot on the chartplotter. Ten feet of water at high tide. With gentle winds predicted and high-test chain rode, five to one scope would be sufficient. "Fifty feet."

"Fifty feet, aye."

As he backed slowly away from the big Bruce anchor, Marie let the boat's gentle bucking pull the heavy anchor chain out of her bare hands a bit at a time. Jack had trained her not to drop it in a big pile, and she was as conscientious about this as everything else he'd taught her.

The only passengers on this trip, an adventurous lesbian couple from the Midwest, marveled at the clear water, pointing out the frilly octocorals he had avoided when setting the anchor. Visibility remained good because the prop on his electric motor, turning slowly in reverse, wasn't powerful enough to kick up any sand.

Marie called out. "Fifty feet."

"Fifty feet, aye." Jack poured on the power and sighted on a rock in front of a solitary Buccaneer palm. She settled onto her anchor like a champ, and he patted the old wooden wheel, salvaged from a turn-of-the-twentieth-century cargo schooner. When the rock and tree stopped moving relative to one another and the boat held position, he turned off the motor. "We're hooked."

"Hooked, aye." She snapped the rope bridle onto the chain and let it take the weight of the boat, giving them the equivalent of a shock absorber.

The usual eighty-five-degree Caribbean breeze wafted through the cove, and his boat, the S.V. *Lysistrata*, pointed her bow into it. The February water was a wintry seventy-three. He monitored the boat's position on his chartplotter a bit longer, while Marie named the specific types of damselfish, beau gregory, and parrotfish for the couple peering over the midships railing. Amy and Melissa held hands and ran from side to side like teenagers as *Lysistrata's* ornately curved double bow swung around.

Marie slipped by the women at the railing and climbed the two steps to the cockpit. "Want me to check the anchor or cover the sails?"

"Cover the sails. It looks like Amy and Melissa are going to hit the water, so keep an eye on them while I check the anchor."

"Sure thing. I bet they're going to want to lounge on the beach. It's too perfect." She waved at the gorgeous cove.

Jack eyed the strange island. He had tucked them into a small unnamed cove, just broad enough for two or three mid-sized boats to anchor, bounded in a narrow crescent by straw-colored sand, fine-grained and pristine, or so it appeared from three hundred feet away. A stubby little wooden pier thrust into the crystal clear water across the cove, and a broad deck disappeared into shade that probably hid a shack under the Jamaican dogwoods. "I can't believe this place. My electronic chart just shows this as a rocky area, but check it out. The old paper chart has the whole island right where it ought to be." It would have given him a shiver, otherwise. How many sailors really wanted to find Serendib?

"That seems dangerous. Not everyone carries backup charts."

He tipped his head at Marie. "You know me. Backups for my backups."

"A decade of experience, but you still don't take anything for granted. Best skipper ever."

He ducked his head and fiddled with the chartplotter. His face warmed, but he didn't think she'd see the blush through his dark tan. "Well, if they want the beach, we'll give them the beach. I don't want to launch the yawl boat for such a short trip. See if you can talk them into swimming over. You can float the cooler over with towels and the umbrella and get them set up." Marie nodded. "Feel free to hang out on the beach or in the water. Leave them the conch shell if you want to come back to the boat. We're chillin' until it's time to make dinner."

"On it." She pulled the sail cover from the deck box. Good memory on her. Much as he wanted whatever was best for her, and that probably meant going back to school soon, he hoped she'd keep crewing with him right up to that point. They savored most of the same foods and alternated cooking duties. They both adored light roast Ethiopian Sidamo coffee, and she got the same kick out of hand-grinding it as he did. Little things that lubricated their fused lifestyle. The lack of sexual tension between them was another crucial boon—Marie went for femmes. Even living together on opposite ends of the sixty-three-foot boat didn't strain their working relationship. She nested in the cozy fo'c'sle, and the aft cabin was his kingly abode. Passengers took the guest cabin, which could sleep two in a wide bottom bunk and one above, and overflowed into hammocks in the main salon, unless they opted to sleep on deck under the moon and stars.

He walked to the bow, sharing a few words with Amy and Melissa on the way, and eyed the fractured image of his chain as it curved below the water and stretched toward the anchor. Too many tiny wind waves in the water obscured his view from the deck. He slipped off his deck shoes, stretched his toes on the warm teak deck, and arranged the boarding ladder over the side, amidships. These folks hadn't checked any of the boxes on his accessibility form, so the hoist would remain stowed.

The couple had stripped to bathing suits—Melissa wore a brand-new-looking halter top bikini, very pinup, and Amy wore swim shorts and a ratty old tank top—and he reminded them of the rules. "You can jump from anywhere but the sail and the yawl boat. If you stand on the railings, hold on to the rigging. Varnished wood can be slick. We're only in ten feet of water, but you should be fine for shallow dives. Most of all, drink lots of fresh water and have fun."

"How could we help it? You brought us to paradise." Melissa's eyes gleamed with unshed tears, and Amy wrapped an arm around her waist.

Jack's chest tightened. Best job ever. "Vacations are meant to be life squared, right? Everything in excess, even love and beauty."

Amy nestled Melissa closer. "And freedom and release. This place is out in the middle of nowhere, as far as I'm concerned. I'm usually a control freak, and that should scare the shit out of me, but you're so…well, methodical, I guess. It feels good to let go and trust you to take care of us."

Melissa adjusted the strap on her bathing suit. "I couldn't help watching you while we were sailing here. When we got going nice and strong, with the waves rolling us along, you got this look on your face. Like someone praying."

Amy offered a word. "Transfigured."

Jack bit his lip, shrugged, and grinned. "You caught me. I love it."

"You won me over, for sure." Melissa stroked Amy's hand where it gripped her hip. "Our conservative little town copes with us living together because we're both locals, born and raised, but we don't push buttons. We always vacation where we can hold hands or kiss in the street and no one cares. Provincetown, Rehoboth Beach, or cities like Chicago, New Orleans, Austin. But this?" She waved her hand at the boat and the beach. "This is all the exhilaration without the trumped-up confidence."

"I know what you mean," he said. "I stayed in the schooner trade for six years after I realized I was transgender. I had a good thing going as first mate and watch captain, but I couldn't see how to transition at my own pace on the job. When I moved to Miami and started going by my new name, with new pronouns, I was proud but defensive. It was exhausting sometimes. Then getting out here." He looked around at *Lysistrata's* lines and curves. "I know exactly who I am out here, and I don't have to fight for recognition. Just another being in the universe, loving life."

"Transfigured." Amy repeated her word from earlier. "I guess the trick is bringing this state of being back into the real world."

"Amy, this is the real world."

She looked taken aback. Melissa cocked her head and looked at Amy. They stared at each other as though the world had just slipped sideways.

Lives changed; job done. Jack leaned over the rail and looked into the water. "I'm going to change so I can check the anchor. See you when we're wet!"

His light tone brought the fun back. He left them egging each other on about who would go first. He'd bet on them jumping together, holding hands.

He modeled good behavior by turning to face the ladder as he climbed down into his aft cabin, but he jumped the rest of the way as soon as he was out of sight. His cabin boasted a cozy fore-and-aft-oriented, twin-sized berth across from a built-in armchair, a private composting head, and dozens of tidy nooks and crannies and cabinets and shelves. A place for everything and everything in its place.

He stripped and pulled on his rash guard and boardshorts, swarmed up the ladder and to the side deck, swung a leg over the railing, and let himself fall in sideways with a yell and a splash. Amy and Melissa were laughing, still on deck, when he sputtered to the surface and waved before stroking away.

With such clear, shallow water, he hadn't bothered with a dive mask and fins. He regretted that almost immediately when a school of peppermint basslet darted out from behind a clump of speckled cup coral. He would have loitered if he could see them better, but he was supposed to be working anyway.

He heard a double splash and looked back to see Amy and Melissa in the water, then he dove to the bottom. The anchor's flukes were buried deep in the sand and the shank lay flat on the bottom.

There was no pull on the chain near the anchor, so his scope was sufficient to keep them from pulling the anchor from its bed.

Jack surfaced and tossed his head, blowing stinging brine from his nose. Melissa splashed Amy playfully and turned to race away, but Amy caught her ankle and pulled her back to dunk her. Water games they could play just as well in their nearby lakes, but the Caribbean speared its way into the minds and bodies of visitors. Most eventually yearned to come back, which meant repeat business and extended relationships with folks who made regular trips. Again, best job ever. It would be an honor and a pleasure to watch Amy and Melissa grow into each other over the years.

From the deck, Marie caught his eye with a gesture at the beach. They must have asked to go ashore, as she'd expected. He nodded and dove, this time for the pure pleasure of streaking through the water. He wished, as he always did, that he felt comfortable stripping bare on top. The rash guard made him look like a surfer, but he'd rather feel the water on his skin.

Amy and Melissa slogged out of the water onto the beach, holding hands again. Melissa pointed to a bird in the pomegranate trees and Amy looked. They turned to each other and embraced.

Jack smiled. He couldn't help it.

He was living the dream.

❖

Eve strolled out onto her silvered wooden deck, humming an esoteric melody she'd been playing with. She wasn't going to be able to force it out, though she'd spent a couple of hours at the piano trying. Perhaps the sea breeze on her bare skin—she worked best nude—would release the jam. The evasive tune looped and folded in her mind, vibrated in her throat. She needed to change the key, get it lower where it would rumble for a more sensuous effect. She sipped her chamomile tea and hummed low.

The furious sun defied the end of day with golden light against mackerel clouds. Eve opened her arms wide to the sky and warmed her face, her back to the deck railing. She let her arms drop, and a practical wing of her mind said bugs.

Eve bowed to necessity and lowered the long screens that protected the open wall of her house. The seas were hurricane free, so she could leave the wall raised and positioned as a deck roof. She wrapped the screen lines around a little cleat and stroked the wooden post that ended the open section.

She never thought, when she retreated to Anne Bonny Isle to lick her wounds and plan her revenge, that the house she built would charm her so thoroughly. She needed climate control for the bottom two floors, for the electronics and musical instruments, but her living space could be completely open to the world. Block and tackle systems raised entire walls high enough that they simply shaded the spaces underneath while allowing the Caribbean breezes to freshen the whole. And when the lashing rains came, securing her home was a simple matter of paying out a little line. The walls came down like big shutters and no deck roof remained to catch the fierce hurricane winds.

The deck looked over the long crescent beach and peaceful cove, and she spent productive hours reclined on a deck lounger, composing in her head or working on her computer. When she sang, though, she never sat. She stood, upright, and mustered the strength and flexibility of her whole body to project her voice out over the water.

Motion on the beach caught her eye, and she went to the rail. There was a boat in her cove! People on her beach! She threw her mug of chamomile tea at the water.

"Harmonie! Harmonie!" Her powerful voice should have raised the dead, but she'd last seen Harmonie in the sound booth. Fine, she'd take care of the invaders herself.

She spun around and grabbed her sarong from the deck lounger. She wound it around her body as she stomped down the deck's steps and onto the soft sand. A knot behind her neck fixed it in place. As she passed the driftwood folly she'd crafted just above the high tide line, she grabbed the jade Buddha by the head and hefted him over her shoulder.

The additional weight hampered her progress through the thick sand, hot on her bare feet, and she headed for the harder area at the waterline. Her anger flared—not only an invasion but an imposition as well—and her vision narrowed.

She couldn't have random people showing up and making themselves at home. Hacking the databases of every electronic chart maker had been a huge undertaking, involving hours of painstaking coding to hide the hack and rewrite the backups as well as the main charts. Getting rid of an island was no joke—and highly illegal—but it had been the only way to protect her work.

Harmonie had thought the effort futile. Deleting a feature on a chart didn't hide the physical reality of the island, and they'd agreed not to take the risk of hacking the governmental databases at NOAA to get the island, which cartographers yawningly called Decker, off the official charts. Their hack had been completely successful to that point, though. Few boaters used NOAA's paper charts in the age of electronic chartplotters, to the point where they didn't even print them anymore except on demand. On the open water, power boaters tended to head from one island to another, or toward the mainland, and Anne Bonny Isle wasn't on the tourist routes. Others, the fishers, weren't as interested in land features as water features. The tradewinds that had made Florida and the Caribbean so wildly popular in the age of sail also drew most sailors right past her.

Three people lay on colorful towels in the sun, and a white umbrella shaded a small cooler. Sparks sizzled down Eve's bare arms at the thought of their nonchalance. How dared they?

They'd claimed a spot most of the way around the cove, but the long slog only gave her anger time to blaze. In moments like this, throughout her life, she'd never bothered to conserve fuel, only burned as bright and high as she could. As she neared them, she drew on the thousands of times she'd stood on stage and poured herself at an audience that screamed back in delirious joy, whipped her fury to its peak, and pulled air into the enormous cavern of her chest.

CHAPTER TWO

Jack sat on a towel at the mahogany navigation table below decks, tracing the inlaid curly maple and purpleheart compass while he pondered their return trip. The weather might give them time for sightseeing before they went back to Miami.

A wave of sound brought Jack's head up. Someone out there was screaming.

It didn't sound like Marie or his passengers, but he leapt up the companionway steps and scanned the beach. Someone stalked the beach, a person in a fluttering wrap of some sort, wielding a short, broad object like a fat bat. Marie stood between this person and the passengers, hands raised in front of her as though saying hold on a minute.

Jack dove. He kicked underwater until buoyancy pulled him to the surface, then stroked for shore. The clear saltwater burned his open eyes, but he kept looking for the spaces between coral outcroppings as he approached the shallows. When his fingers touched drifting sand, he pushed to his feet and waded farther in against the suck of a receding wave.

Marie must have pointed him out, because the furious woman bore down on him, walking straight into the water. The hem of her dress darkened where the next small wave washed over it, but she kept coming in water to her calves.

Her intimidating charge slowed Jack's approach. The golden late afternoon light saturated her long black hair, too thick for the breeze to lift more than the edges. The locks flowed over soft bare shoulders as richly colored as aged varnish and showed hints of curl under her full breasts. The dress was just a big piece of fabric. Each side folded over her breasts and disappeared behind her neck. Her round hips pressed against the bright, thin cotton, and thick thighs flashed into view as she moved.

Water weighted the bottom edge of the sarong and drew it back from her legs as she stalked forward. The curtain parted, higher and higher, exposing more and more skin until skin stopped and fur took over.

Jack stumbled to a halt, shocked by the unexpected peep show and his even more unexpected painful hardening. Nipples, clit, and muscles alike throbbed suddenly.

Just a body. Just a body.

Her skin was rich brown all the way up, with a yellow undertone, her cunt hair as black as the hair on her head.

He looked up, desperate to move his focus.

Her eyes flashed. He shook his head, certain that eyes did no such thing. What a cheesy thing to think, but there they were, black and liquid and full of light. Her arched brows and narrowed eyes gave her the look of a wicked queen, but she didn't have the smug smile of a movie nemesis. Her dark, well-defined lips parted, and she took an enormous breath.

"What the fuck do you think you're doing here?"

Jack quailed and nearly fell to his knees. Her voice cleared his head of thought with sheer volume and a rich timbre that seemed to use every cubic centimeter of her voluptuous body. He wanted to beg her for punishment, to learn her every desire and fulfill it before she even had to ask.

She used her hands wildly, shaking a heavy jade statue in one, pointing with and waving the other. Her breasts swayed and bounced with the force of her fury.

Yeah, yeah, she wanted them to go away. He'd gathered that.

Her voice dropped to a threatening rumble. "You can't anchor here, kid. Get your boat and get the hell out of here."

Who are you calling a kid? At twenty-eight, he was probably older than her. Jack shook his head, thought returning in a rush. "Like hell I can't." If he knew anything after the last year of battling the Miami-area homeowners' association, he knew that the right to anchor was protected by maritime tradition as well as United States law.

"This is my island and my cove, you brazen trespasser!" Her voice penetrated even deeper, though he would have sworn it was impossible.

"You've got to be kidding me." He stepped up to her, almost eye to eye, and leaned close. He scented warm sandalwood and amber over the light stink of sea wrack and the omnipresent salt. "If this is your island, the most you can do is make us move down the beach, below the high tide line. You most certainly can't make us pull up anchor. Your land. My water." He did a little hand waving of his own to emphasize that statement.

Her breath rushed in and out in her rage, her abdomen swelling with each fast inhale. At such close range, he smelled chamomile on her breath.

She bared sharp teeth and he flinched instinctively. She inhaled one more deep breath, bigger than the rest, and screamed in his face.

Jack staggered at the frontal assault and braced himself several feet away. This was no movie scream, no ingénue attacked by a shadowy murderer. This was the full-throated roar of an enraged beast.

And he knew her.

Holy shit, the virago was the singer, Eve La Sirena. He knew her work intimately, loved all three of her albums. He'd fucked to "Rogue's Gallery" more than he was comfortable thinking about all of a sudden, and her first album, *Fit to be Tied*, didn't have a weak song on it.

The indie scene adored her, though her popularity and notoriety went far beyond bar venues and college radio stations. He'd fallen for her music through a late-night radio DJ who had been obsessed with her, as so many were. Jack had even won a ticket once to see her live in concert. She'd come to town the day he started rebuilding

Lysistrata and he'd been too exhausted to go. He'd given the free ticket to a former crewmate and regretted that ever since. She never played another real concert, only popping up now and then in clubs to steal the spotlight from the scheduled performer. She went behind the scenes as a producer and finally disappeared altogether after the lead singer of one of her bands died. When she dropped out of sight, she should have fallen off the pop culture radar, but instead her mystique took over, and barely a month went by without her face on the cover of a tabloid. Usually wrecking a marriage—lesbian, gay, or straight—or dying of a rare disease.

Suddenly, the whole conflict, the whole island, took on a different cast. This was a superstar throwing a tantrum, a prodigy who'd never learned what no meant. There was no argument against the blind confidence of the gifted, insulated by fame. The visceral reality of her notorious body arm's length away, pumping heat at him, hazed with the sudden, incontrovertible knowledge that she was not just out of his league.

Eve La Sirena lived on another planet.

Still didn't mean she owned the water, but he figured she had reasons to cultivate privacy. She'd been dogged by paparazzi throughout her late teens and early twenties, even her overt and loud-mouthed outness failing to quell the fervor over her celebrated bisexuality. He'd even caught kinky references in her songwriting.

Holy shit, he thought again. She really was his dream dominant. Literally.

❖

The handsome young captain morphed into a different creature. Their posture, their expression, their very smell altered when she screamed at them.

Recognition.

Eve clenched her hands around Buddha's neck and wished she could crack his ass upside this person's head. Her own fault, of course, for coming out here to begin with. And then to vocalize like that. Damn it. She was supposed to be on the down-low here.

The new precariousness of her position modulated her anger. She was a creature of her passions, but she prided herself on knowing when the tide turned against her.

She tossed her hair at the captain and slogged out of the warm water. She pulled her wet sarong with her free hand, bunching it in front of her as she approached the freaked-out baby dyke who'd tried valiantly to head her off in the beginning.

That one, adorably ginger and using her coloring well in a russet bikini, was smarter than the captain. The small cooler was packed, the towels and umbrella fastened to the top with shock cord. The whole lot floated in a rectangular air tube, which struck her as damn clever.

The other two, a butch/femme couple, stood wordlessly staring with their hands intertwined and their shoulders touching.

She addressed her comments to the couple. Baby Dyke had called them her passengers. "Folks, I'm sorry I came out with my metaphorical guns drawn. My privacy is crucial to my happiness, crucial to having any kind of pleasant life at all, and I didn't give the situation time to soak in. I'm sure you can sympathize and, now that I've taken a moment to calm down, I understand that you're not here to make problems for me." The passengers stopped clutching each other so hard. A self-deprecating smile finished the job.

The femme in the cute halter pushed her glamorous sunglasses up on her hair. "We had no idea we were imposing, and I'm so sorry to have upset you."

The butch had tried to speak, but let her lover go first rather than talk over her. Too charming. Damn it. She didn't want to like these people. "Really, the boat is wonderful and we're perfectly happy to hang out there."

Neither blamed the captain, and Eve warmed to them further for that. Most people spent an inordinate amount of time looking for others to blame.

"You don't need to apologize, really, just enjoy the rest of your vacation. Shall I bring out my canoe to get you back to the boat?" Not her most subtle moment, but if it worked…

They moved as one toward the water. The femme dropped a step behind her lover and turned back to say, eyes direct and open,

"You've changed my life more than once. I live a life I love in part because of courage you helped me find. Thank you."

Eve's eyes filled with tears, and she went to the other woman. She dropped the jade Buddha and filled her arms with warm, trembling femme, pungent with sunblock and brine. "We help each other every day. Courage and love, sister."

They clung a moment, then let go. The lovers held hands as they walked into the softly heaving sea and then dove one after another to swim for the sailboat at anchor. Eve watched them go, wondering about their story, making up a half-dozen in a flash, each one possible, beautiful or painful or both.

She turned to see Baby Dyke standing shyly nearby. Eve brushed aside her hand and drew her into a quick, rough hug. The bright red girl and the cooler contraption started for the boat.

Eve bent to the sand and picked up her Buddha, a gorgeous statue that she would have regretted breaking. She cradled him in her arms. She turned back to the captain, pulling a regal veil over her bearing. "You may or may not have the right to be in my cove, but I warn you. If you bring even one iota of attention to this island, to me being here or having a house here, I will end you. Don't speak my name to a single soul."

Head high, Eve sauntered away down the long curve of firm sand at the edge of the water. As she rounded the cove, the setting sun gleamed on the black and gold lettering streaming across the red boat's transom. *Lysistrata*.

❖

Harmonie waited on the deck, arms crossed. She might as well have been tapping her palm with a ruler.

"I know. Stupid." Eve diverted from the walkway and headed into the sand.

"I know you know. So why? Why would you reveal yourself to a bunch of strangers?"

Eve retrieved her mug and mounted the deck steps. She stalked past Harmonie restlessly. "I thought we were safe here. Alone, getting our revenge and crippling the industry, opening music up to the people who want it. Need it. Funding the musical revolution." The tagline to the movie of her life. Gross.

Too distracted to work, she went in to the bar, left her mug in the sink, and filled two glasses with a Sangiovese from Abruzzo. She raised her voice so Harmonie, still on the deck, could hear her. "We changed the shape of the planet to hide this place. What else can I do to get some damn privacy?"

Eve brought the wine out to the deck and handed a glass to Harmonie, who took it with pursed lips. Eve leaned against the deck rail so she could better glare at the beautiful boat. In Boston drawing room furniture, Chinoiserie seemed hopelessly exoticizing and Western imperialist. Floating on the water, the strong and elegant Chinese-looking lines had a sense to them. The boat had three masts with red, folded sails lying at the bottoms and wooden buttresses at both the front and the back. Rather than hugging the water like a racing boat in the Hamptons, structures rose along its length, starting low at the front and getting higher toward the back in what struck her as an old-fashioned design, something she'd see painted on rice paper at the Met. Red lacquer accents—probably paint—insisted on the Chinese theme, and the bronze dragon stretching along the back reiterated it. Instead of black to complement the red and gold, the bulk of the boat gleamed with dark wood varnish.

Harmonie snuggled close beside her and stroked her cheek with a soft fingertip. "Let me take care of anyone else who shows up." Harmonie touched Eve's lips when they twisted, running her sharp nail across the top. "Please, Eve. That's what you can do."

"Hide, because my fame and power are weaknesses."

Harmonie didn't have to smile. Eve could see her amusement. "I know this isn't a word you're very familiar with, but how about acting with some discretion?"

Eve sipped her wine, casting her witchiest gaze at Harmonie over the rim, who laughed and shook her head. Eve sighed. "Fine. I accede to your request that you handle trespassers from now on. But we need to know what our rights are."

"You mean whether or not people can be on the beach?"

"Or at anchor. The captain of the sailboat says there's no way to keep boaters from anchoring in the cove."

"I'll email the lawyer."

Eve leaned on the deck's railing. "Let's see what Shonda can find on the captain, too. The boat's called *Lysistrata*."

"What an intriguing name." Harmonie's eyebrows rose. "A man who knows where the real power is?"

"I don't know the captain's gender. They're probably transmasculine, or maybe butch. If they're a trans man, they may be new. There were little tits under a tight swimming shirt—what's that called—a rash guard, and no sign of facial hair."

"Even stranger. A person who may or may not be a trans man choosing to name their boat after a story about men's weakness in the face of female sexual power. Why change teams in that case?"

"This one must see relations between the sexes as inherently antagonistic. Ridiculous, of course." Eve sent Harmonie an arched look. "Antagonism follows sexual attraction for any combination of genders, especially when the yen is one-sided. It's embedded in the process of deciding whether or not to fuck."

Harmonie swallowed her wine and rolled her eyes. "Tension and antagonism aren't always the same thing."

"They are to me." Eve leaned in and took a sharp little bite of Harmonie's bare shoulder. Salt and lime body scrub. Yum. When Harmonie's eyes closed, Eve put her hand on Harmonie's soft throat. "And you like me this way."

"Yes." Harmonie sounded breathless, and her voice box barely vibrated as she spoke. "I do."

Eve smoothed her hand across Harmonie's collarbone to her shoulder and rubbed the little indentions she'd left with her teeth. "I think the captain is a bottom."

Harmonie's deep brown eyes opened, soft-focused. "Everyone's a bottom around you."

Eve laughed and enjoyed the answering smile that revealed Harmonie's strong teeth. "Would that it were true. No, before they recognized me. I charged into the water when they swam up, and I thought they were going to fall at my feet."

"Your fame isn't the source of your power, Eve."

Eve pushed away from the railing and brushed aside Harmonie's insightful reassurance. "Whether or not you believe in the concept of a natural bottom, they worked hard at not giving in to my fatal allure." She vamped it up, dropping her voice to a devastating purr and pulling the sarong back to reveal her hip. "Of course, I'm sure it helped that the water dragged the sarong apart and they got a full-bush eyeful. Clutching at my sarong would have ruined the raging goddess effect, so..." She shrugged, insouciant.

"You've got to be kidding me." When Eve shook her head, Harmonie's rolling laughter filled the air, ricocheting from the low shores of the cove. They probably heard it on the boat.

She had the best laugh, holding nothing back, and Eve wallowed in the sound. When Harmonie started gasping for breath, wiping her eyes, Eve took her hand. "Seriously, though, if they're a bottom, maybe that has something to do with their focus on powerlessness."

Harmonie had pulled herself together, for the most part. "Maybe it's about the boat being stronger."

"Or the sea?"

Harmonie sighed, the breath catching in her throat with the last scrap of laughter. "What's this person look like?"

"Think of the brunette in a boy band."

"Oh, not that again."

Eve adopted an affronted look and descended on her assistant, her lover, her friend.

CHAPTER THREE

Jack sat in the bootblack's chair and let Tigger work on his boots while they caught up. He'd gone for dapper, with a soft button-down shirt and slacks, twisted toward leather by the boots and his favorite bondage belt. Another thrift store outfit, only a little wrinkled from being folded in his small cabinet. The crowd at Puss'n'Boots sported the usual array of clothing, from street casual through high-femme and fetish wear to nothing at all.

Now that he'd arrived, the urge to play had gotten stronger. Maybe his chest harness and jeans would have been better advertisement.

The club's main space spread out before him. The black walls soaked away the light of the bright spots where the furniture stood. He'd been on the committee to repaint and had never dreamed it would be so hard to find a color that didn't look either garish or hospital-industrial in the type of lighting required for tops to see what they were up to. Back to black. The rectangular room boasted the usual St. Andrew's cross, spanking and fucking benches, slings, stocks, cages, and padded hobbyhorses, but it also had open spaces with rings that dropped from the ceiling for suspension play. He couldn't quite see into the side rooms: a medical room, a schoolroom, an orgy room, and a playroom for the littles that looked like a day care.

By the horse, a collared sub in a waist cincher and gartered hose laid out the implements of her torture, handling each item reverently while her top stretched her shoulders for the work to come. A bantam rooster of a dominant checked herself in each mirrored surface as she strolled around the room greeting her friends. No-nonsense fucking proceeded in the nearest sling, where the wearer of the dildo harness jackhammered the jiggling woman splayed out in front of her and occasionally glanced around at the folks watching.

The bootblack chair was a throne, really, a big wooden platform with a densely padded seat. The boot rest thrust out at a convenient height for Tigger to kneel on the floor or sit on her little stool while shining shoes. That also put her well below Jack, who enjoyed the view.

"That shirt makes your tits incredibly distracting."

Tigger spread the blacking over his leather. "It's not the shirt. It's the bra. You've seen this shirt before in less strained circumstances."

"Huh." Jack considered. "Okay. Regardless, it works."

She looked up through her green Bettie Page bangs. "Thanks." She swept one sparkling fake eyelash down in a slow wink.

"Damn, you're good."

"You too, handsome." Tigger massaged blacking into his boot leather with a strong hand, rubbing his toes somehow. "I thought I'd be all alone until Daddy arrived. I hope you keep coming to the women-and-trans nights."

"They certainly bring all the people I'm attracted to into close proximity." He gave her an exaggerated leer.

"You don't take it as an insult to your manliness?"

"My limited manliness is pretty robust." She kept looking at him and he dropped the flirtatious tone. "I'm not such a man as all that. I'm still tussling with the idea that I may be at my best gender right now. I don't want to join the boys' club, but I feel like the girls' club isn't a great fit anymore. Actually, I appreciate not having to pick a binary gender just so I can get into a party."

"And even the womyn—" she pronounced it whoa-mine "—dig your vibe."

"Lucky me. Masculine enough but not too masculine."

She must have caught the bitter edge. "Do you work at balancing there?"

He laced his fingers and watched as her hands moved slowly across the leather. "I try not to, but it's like code-switching."

She hummed. "You mean you get more or less manly depending on who you're around?"

"More like I think of my behavior as gendered more around some people. It's like there's some piece of me that believes it's outside of gender, that represents the truest me, and it gets refracted through these gendered lenses. So sometimes I'm just being me while other times I'm being manly-me and other times I'm manly-me-lite."

"Sounds like a gender studies master's thesis."

"Know anyone who would want it?"

"Maybe. I'm still thinking about going back to school."

Jack shuddered. "I barely escaped high school without burning the place to the ground. Give me a good library over a school any day."

"I don't want the debt, but I miss the academic environment sometimes. Not as much when we get together and talk sex and gender theory." She changed the subject again. "I haven't seen you around."

"I took a bright-eyed lesbian couple on a two-day sail. Good people, really enjoyed themselves."

"Did you get any action?"

Jack rolled his eyes. Tigger thought everyone should have sex with everyone else, and voila! World peace. "No, they're a pretty traditional butch/femme couple. I would have gone for a night with Melissa, but Amy didn't do it for me. And they smelled monogamous. On the other hand, I got into a fight."

Tigger rested her blackened rag on his toe and looked at him, her eyelashes making sparkly circles around her wide eyes. "Seriously? How did you manage that out in the middle of nowhere? You don't usually take people to crowded spots."

"Yeah, not my specialty. But I found an island I'd never been to and we anchored in this glorious cove. Turbinado sugar sand, tall palms, clear water, coral, fish. Exactly what folks want from sailing in the Caribbean. The passengers went ashore with Marie—"

"Oh, the delectable deckhand. I just want to eat her up."

"—and they got attacked by a wild woman wielding a jade statue."

"Are you kidding me?" Tigger propped her wrist on his knee.

The person on the St. Andrews cross screamed, and he looked over. She was being whipped with a singletail. Ouch. Nice technique, though. Tigger poked him, and he resumed his story. "Well, verbally attacked. I dove in and swam ashore—"

"What a hero!"

"—and she screamed at me. She was trying to kick us out of the anchorage, but you know how I feel about that."

"Nice boy turns to stone killer." She pretended to machine-gun the crowd.

"Not quite. But I stood my ground. Anchoring is never at the discretion of individual property owners along the shore. Sometimes municipalities control anchoring for various reasons, but—"

"Get back to the fight."

"Fine. Sure. So we went back and forth a little, but not until I'd gotten myself under control."

Tigger waited a moment, mouth open. "What does that mean? You went Hulk on this person?"

"No, I went nonverbal. Tigger, she was amazing." Jack's eyes lost their focus as he remembered how she'd looked wading into the water to meet him. The noise level in the club rose as the party picked up steam, but he heard only Eve's voice. "A goddess on bare feet with a fat Buddha as a weapon. She rushed toward me, right into the water, and her dress parted up the middle."

"What kind of dress?" Tigger inched closer like a little kid at story time.

"Not a dress, really, just a piece of fabric wrapped around her torso and behind her neck."

"A sarong, then."

"Okay, so her sarong got caught by the water. The bottom edge flowed back until, honest to God, I could see her cunt hair."

"No way." Her eyes and mouth were equally round.

"Yes way. She is huge. Her presence, I mean. And big-bodied, round and full of motion. I'm telling you, a total goddess."

"So you..." Tigger bounced on the edge of her seat.

"Told her we wouldn't leave. I'm tired of being kicked around by landowners who think they can dictate my life. After the fiasco with the harbormaster and his brother-in-law..." He shrugged. "She turned away from me and had some sort of moment with one of the passengers. She hugged her and Marie both and then just left." He hadn't decided whether or not to reveal her identity until just that moment. Eve La Sirena. He was practically bursting with it, but he chose to obey her in that one particular.

"That's it? Are you going back?"

Tigger's enthusiasm for the idea pulled the truth from him. "Definitely. I have a point to make." Though seeing Eve again both drew and frightened him. Jack raised his chin at the tanned brunette rolling through the door in a tricked out wheelchair, sleeves turned up to show off bulging arms. "In the meantime, there's fun to be had right here. Your Daddy just arrived."

Tigger lit up. "I'm going to finish you up real quick, okay?"

"Of course." He didn't bother to offer that she not finish. She was rightfully proud of her shines.

She pushed the stool aside and knelt, got her back into it, wiggling her ass in the air. Jack enjoyed the show while he cruised the room for his next thing. Tigger would bottom to Jane for the rest of the night and they wouldn't get another chance to talk. He pushed aside the pang of loneliness. He had other friends who'd be at the party, sooner or later.

When Tigger stood and curtsied, her green panties glowing under super-short white crinoline, he inspected his boots with sober ostentation and declared them perfect.

Jane rolled up with her usual impeccable timing. "Nice boots, Jack."

"Thanks to your girl. New wheels?"

She did a three-sixty on two wheels and stopped on a dime. "Sport model."

"Sick." The skater compliment echoed uncomfortably in Jack's head. "Is it for basketball?"

"No, I have a different chair for that. With this one, now there's no way my little girl can get away from me." She grimaced at Tigger, who giggled. "Have you been a good girl?"

Tigger nodded. She pulled her fist out of her mouth and said, "Yes, Daddy." Her voice was lighter, breathier. Jack didn't get age play, but it worked like a charm on Tigger.

Jack excused himself and left them to their fun.

A circuit of the play space showed one of those strange pauses, when all the players were doing aftercare, packing up, or setting up. A quiet time between scenes, with no one cruising him back as he walked around. He went into the den, basically a break room with food, drink, and casual seating. At the snack table, he got a soda and sipped at it. He sat on the arm of a couch and made conversation for a while.

Cynthia appeared in the doorway, hair teased high and small breasts smashed higher. Her latex minidress gleamed with hard light that rippled with her sinuous walk. He scoped her perfect fishnets and wondered whether she was wearing thigh-highs with a garter belt. He sure did love garters.

They'd played before, friends with benefits, and when she walked over to him, he straightened.

"My cock is so hard it hurts," she said without bending close or keeping her voice low.

A few of the conversations around them paused and interested gazes fell on them, but Jack kept his eyes on Cynthia. "How can I help?"

"I want you to suck me off on the stage. If you do a good job, I'll cane you as a reward."

Jack felt the smile spread slowly over his face. "Sounds like the perfect night to me."

❖

Eve lay, full-length, on Harmonie's back. They both struggled to catch their breath after the energetic fucking they'd done. Sweat dried on her shoulders and her legs.

She rose onto her hands and knees over Harmonie, who moaned at the tearing apart of their sticky skin. Her tits hung, her belly just visible beyond. She'd long since stopped trying to maintain the shape and weight of her youth, but occasionally, she saw herself with the camera's eye, with the tabloid eye, and knew that they would be vicious about her fat.

She slipped to the side and draped an arm and leg over Harmonie to anchor her through the aftershocks.

So be it. She felt good, she looked good, and it was no one's business but her own. When there'd been an industry built around her voice, her looks, her performances and appearances and interviews, she'd let others sculpt her body into the expected. Or nearly that. She'd always, even at uncomfortably low weights, been termed Reubenesque. She'd been called a dark Marilyn Monroe to her face, live on camera, but the discretion everyone thought she'd long since abandoned kept her from shredding those vacuous talking heads on the spot.

She turned her pillow over, seeking a cool spot, and pulled away from Harmonie's heat. She maintained the connection with fingertips and knees. Harmonie tended to get overwhelmed after play unless Eve shared the punchy energy they'd built together.

The charge of holding Harmonie down and making her come dissipated in memories of struggling for self-determination. She had beaten the music business on a personal level, damn it. She'd kept the power and the money and the control, enough to change her career when the constant scrutiny became oppressive.

Songwriting and cameos on other artists' work had eased the transition. She missed performing regularly, ached for it sometimes, but clubs and bars were so much more fun than stadium tours anyway. Showing up for an hour at a roadhouse in the country gave Eve the contact she needed, let her shine enough that she didn't burn herself up. Harmonie understood. Second-hand, though—as a studio musician by choice, being on stage was no part of her dream. Harmonie set up the shows, booked the travel, and got Eve through the door so that her imagination, her ear, and her voice could flourish.

Producing other acts should have let her create publicly, but she couldn't go on, drawing artists into the industry that wanted nothing more than to exploit them. Not after Audion lost everything. Not after Marc Fern killed himself in helpless despair.

Eve believed in what she and Harmonie were doing. Freeing music from the artificial boundaries of copyright and dead tech. But it wasn't creating, and she was a songwriter first.

She played and sang her grief, but she wasn't sure she wanted to share those songs. Under the name Kitten Caboodle, she'd self-produced and self-released seven albums, all beats and cuts and manipulated vocals, since the last one as Eve La Sirena. Music sculpted for sex, paced and flowing to bring out the sybarite in the listener. Maintenance sex was fine, like anything that gets a body through the day, but she wanted to inspire listeners to linger, to dive deep into sensation and duration and extend the frenzy that took over at the end.

And look at her, taking her own advice. Eve ran her hand down Harmonie's soft flank.

Harmonie turned onto her back, groaning. "I think you broke my cunt." She stretched on the light cotton sheet, her dark brown skin fading a little under her breasts and a lot at her palms. Eve loved to trace those frontiers, and the rich sunlight angling under the raised wall of Harmonie's bedroom brought out the rosy glow under the color.

"It'll heal." Eve propped her head on her hand and ran a finger, sticky with lube, around Harmonie's soft nipple. It never disappeared, like Eve's did. Poking out a little even in the most humid heat, her nipples were the first thing about Harmonie that had wetted Eve's cunt.

A breeze flowed unimpeded from the water, over their drying bodies, and into the living room beyond. Armoires lined the side walls, most of their doors open and spilling glorious fabrics onto the floor. Harmonie didn't care a bit about shoes, but her collection of gowns, sarongs, and headwraps brought fiery rainbows indoors.

"Yeah." Harmonie's agreement came out breathy on the end of another stretch. "You're wonderfully distracting."

"Glad you like it." Eve nuzzled Harmonie's shoulder and cupped her tit lightly. "I love your body like this. Soft and relaxed, hot and steamy."

They fucked most often in Harmonie's bed, when they used a bed. The third bedroom was the playroom, with their BDSM gear and a daybed for those times when they wanted a soft surface while playing hard. Eve's bedroom was densely decorated, rich with color, more of a cuddle room.

"You do a fine job of getting me this way." Harmonie slid her eyes to Eve's. "You're still not feeling it, though?"

Eve shrugged. "My cunt doesn't want to open up. I don't know why." She squeezed Harmonie's tit. "All my sexual energy is in my hands right now."

"Okay. Let me know when that changes. I'll eat you up." Harmonie rolled on top of Eve and bit at her eyebrow and nose and chin before settling into a deep kiss. Harmonie's hundreds of long, thin locs spilled onto Eve's shoulders and around her head.

Eve loved their connection. No pressure, even when desire waxed or waned. Just an almost sisterly closeness.

Harmonie dropped back beside her with a sigh. "I tracked you down to talk about something."

Eve closed her eyes and let her muscles go lax. "I had a feeling." She took a long, slow breath through her nose, absorbing the ever-present sea salt and lime, a hint of coconut oil, and the light sandalwood incense Harmonie favored, all overlaid with the sharp tang of pussy. Sea birds screamed and water lapped at the sand of her cove.

"Nothing terrible. I heard back from the lawyers about anchoring law." Eve stiffened and opened her eyes to the whitewashed ceiling. "The right to anchor is considered a safety issue. Safety for the boat, that is. The right has been protected and reinforced over and over. There's generally a two-week limit on how long a boat can stay in one place, but that's not a matter of law so much as precedent. Plenty of towns and cities and especially gated communities, and especially in Florida, want to control who can anchor or whether boats can anchor. There have been big battles between homeowners' associations and boating groups, plus a never-ending stream of boaters getting harassed. The people on land bitch about their property values and claim folks at anchor use local resources without supporting them by paying taxes."

Eve held herself still, but she was squirming inside. "These are the people on our side? Gross."

"It gets worse. The city-by-city rules on anchoring were deemed an unreasonable burden on boaters, and now property owners are lobbying for draconian restrictions on anchoring that would apply to every waterway in the state."

"Authoritarian pigs."

"Yep."

"So we don't like them, but we need to use their arguments to keep that boat away?"

Harmonie grabbed the burnished bronze bars of the headboard and her triceps tensed. "Do we? Maybe you already won."

"The captain went from brainless to self-righteous so fast that they'll have to come back. It would be giving in to stay away."

"Wouldn't hurt to try talking. Make some sort of deal. They already know who you are. You should be able to bulldoze them." Harmonie's tone was matter-of-fact, a sure sign that she was trying to wheedle Eve into doing what she wanted. Whatever the lawyers had said, or maybe Harmonie had done more research after she'd talked to them, she wasn't feeling the hard line with this issue. Eve had trusted Harmonie with far more important decisions. She leaned toward going with Harmonie's gut on this as well.

Eve plucked at the soft cotton sheet, thinking it over. "We have to keep this place a secret. If we get caught, we're looking at decades in jail and millions of dollars in fines before we even get hit with the civil suits."

Harmonie lay in silence. Finally, she sighed and settled one arm behind her head. "I still don't see the huge change we're working for. Too many people want to get paid every time one of your songs is played. There's constantly a bill in Congress to go nuclear against peer-to-peer networks, and we've won those fights so far. But the artists need more from us than a platform and a few pennies. They need support and legal aid and proper recording equipment."

The distance between them gaped.

A few pennies directly from someone who loved the music and wanted to support it was light-years better than a few pennies squeezed past the tight sphincter of the record label accountant.

Artists were sucked up, used up, spit out. Those poor, stupid fucking idiots. Lining up for the opportunity to sign everything away. Everything they created became commodities, items traded for their market value rather than their artistic value. All their passion and all their venom—simple products. As producer, she'd ended up feeling like part of the machine. She was like a union member who took a management job with the goal of changing working conditions, only to find that she couldn't, that she could only make excuses for her weakness. That she'd become what she hated.

But she'd already said that a thousand times in a thousand conversations just like this. The well-worn argument was going to push them apart. It was happening as they lay there, sloppy with sex. She and Harmonie had set up their operation together, studied coding and programming, split the plan into individual parts so they could job the complicated stuff out to anonymous programmers they found on the Net. After a couple years of spending extended periods of time on the island, sinking large money and larger time into their work, Harmonie chafed to get in front of the problem and take it by the throat.

Eve finally responded to Harmonie's question. "The danger is a musical version of what grocery coops have been through. They start out scrappy. All they have to do is stop handing their power over to an uncaring system. They put all their hopes and dreams and desires into a new system that grows and takes on its own momentum under the rules of capitalism. It turns into Whole Foods, union busters with dissatisfied employees and customers that feel ripped off. It's hard to stay small without disappearing, but it's even harder to pool your power as consumers or workers or citizens without setting up exactly the kind of system that invites the power mongers to take control." Eve stared at the ceiling. "Capitalism is a system for stealing value as a commodity passes through multiple hands. You want to change the hands. I want to remove them."

"Digital systems *can* remove them. Open-source value-moving systems don't have to skim. Of course, you can skim. The companies trading in Bitcoins are proof of that. But it doesn't have to be that way."

Eve turned her head and looked at Harmonie, who continued to stare at the ceiling. "Idealist."

"Cynic." The tinge of bitterness in her tone was softened by the slight curving of her lips.

"Yep." Eve sighed. They'd gone yet another round, and they were far from done.

CHAPTER FOUR

When the wind built suddenly, Jack signaled Marie to reef two sail panels. The junk rig—a two-thousand-year-old style of boat—was a slow goer into the wind, but it performed beautifully with the wind aft of the beam, and nothing could be easier than reducing sail area in a strong blow.

A process that would have required the full crew on most schooners, including the cook, was an easy job for Marie. He could have done it himself, but why have a willing deckhand aboard if he was going to do everything anyway?

Tony held the wheel firmly, but his wiry, liver-spotted wrists and forearms looked relaxed. Letting passengers take the helm thrilled them more often than not, and it was a crucial tool in the fight against seasickness. Tony was an old hand, though, and wanted a turn at the helm for the pure pleasure of it.

His husband Dan watched Tony as well, brand-new sailing hat pulled firmly down on his tender bald head. Spry men in their seventies, Tony and Dan had been together for over forty years, most of them spent closeted as housemates. The opportunity to marry had pushed them to have the last of their coming-out conversations over the past year or so, and they'd married once everyone they wanted to invite understood their relationship.

The wedding pictures Dan flourished showed their big families rallied around them to celebrate. Tony had bent Marie's ear about the few people who had boycotted the joyous event just past, but

Dan, the bigger talker in general, hadn't wasted much of his time on those "putzes."

Dan turned to Jack, who sat across from him on the other side of Tony. The cockpit was a perfect conversation pit. The seating made a broad semicircle around the wheel, and Jack had seen nine people at a time squeezed onto the long bench. The angled back was comfortable under heel on either side, and the curve let folks look at one another without having to crane their necks. Dan crossed his legs. "Have you sailed all your life?"

"I learned to sail as a kid on Optis and other tiny sailboats."

Tony nodded, his eyes sharp on the horizon. "Same here. Dinghy sailing on the lake."

Dan shook his head. "Too wet for me. I like this size boat. Bigger is better, believe you me."

"I went straight to schooner work from there. A lot bigger and not nearly so wet, except in the rain. When sailing's a business, it takes a big bad storm to make them call off a trip."

Dan shuddered. "I'm glad it's not like that today. Do you go out in storms?"

Jack reached across to pat Dan's thin, speckled knee. "Don't worry, I take a different approach. I wouldn't take you out if you weren't going to have fun. Of course, schooner work was more than just sail handling. We entertained the passengers with call-and-response routines and flamboyant hand signals and storytelling. Sometimes we had chantey singers aboard. I loved those trips. The sail handling and chores, well, those became second nature."

"Even second nature can be brutal." Tony kept his eyes on the waves, but a little smile played around his mouth.

"True. The routine was exhausting and rewarding by turns. What I loved was how the passengers were a little different every trip. Some crew members called them cargo behind their backs, but I got a kick out of watching folks. That moment when the boat picks up speed and starts to heel—"

"Make or break time." Tony glanced at him in amused understanding and looked back up at the sails.

"The big schooners never really lay down on their beams, but with all that sail area and those long waterlines, they can really move. And yes, some passengers learned they didn't like sailing right about then. But lots of people got it. The water sliding along the hull and the timbers groaning as the sails filled." Jack shrugged, unsatisfied as always with his attempt to express the core joy of getting under way under sail. "Anyway, I became a schooner rat, sailing and living aboard season after season, doing repair work and maintenance over the winter."

"Same boat the whole time?" Dan's bright eyes were fixed on him. Either he was really curious or just a kick-ass listener.

"No, I moved around a bit. I got to know dozens of casual crew members in it just for a season and made some close friends. It's a small community, spread out, and not without its drama."

"Oh, the good part." Dan's wrinkles only emphasized the pixie nature of his smile.

Jack grinned back. "The crusty, punk rock boats and crew, with their nonprofits, household paints, and accidental dreadlocks, versus the pomposity of the privately-owned polo shirt and ten coats of varnish types."

"Which type were you?"

"I was comfortable enough on both types of boat, but I enjoyed the middle range best. Middle class passengers and the occasional educational cruise—my favorite kind of season. Much as I'm attracted to the crusty type, I couldn't handle having children around constantly and hustling for that nonprofit cash." Jack signaled Marie to sheet in the main and watched as she worked the sail a little closer in. She went back to gripping the rail, face raised to the spray. They both got plenty of that kind of exhilarating rest while underway. She would take over entertaining the men later, if Jack wanted a break. He liked these two, though.

"But you left the schooner life and got your own boat."

Jack obediently went back to his story. "I saved all my pathetic pay for six years. I didn't come out as trans on the schooners. I felt that a fresh start would let me navigate my transition at my own pace." Dan nodded, but his expression didn't show any great understanding. With guys that age, Jack was happy to settle for respect and proper pronouns. He didn't need to go off about gender theory. "I'd wanted a small schooner for the familiarity and because everybody looks when a schooner sails into port, whether it's gleaming with varnish or streaked with rust. A schooner is its own advertisement. The only problem was crew."

Tony said, "What, you don't yearn to order people around?"

Jack chuckled. "Exactly. I never envied that part of a captain's responsibilities, and I kept my eyes open for alternatives to running a crew of four or five."

"And then you found her." Dan's dreamy tone made it sound like Jack had found his dream lover. He wasn't that far off.

"*Lysistrata* hit me like a brick and turned into an obsession. She had all the benefits of a schooner, with a twist. Junk-rigged boats are unmistakable under sail, and most people think there's something strange about them at anchor. The placement of the masts, the way the sails sit at the bottom—there are little differences that show even with everything stowed."

"Once the sails are up, even a 'cocktails in the cockpit' queen like me can see that this is not the same old sailboat." Dan looked up at the full sails and put a hand on Tony's hip. They did a lot of that—little touches that warmed Jack's heart.

"I studied junks while I kept sailing schooners. I learned the parts of the rig—parrels, sheetlets, sail panels, and a bunch more—and found a junk-rig missionary on a Web forum who was willing to take me out for a sail."

"Oh, that's ingenious." Dan clapped. "No stakes that way."

Jack rested his arm along the rail behind the bench seat. "The boat was big, plenty big enough to charter, and the guy ran it himself as though it were a daysailer while proselytizing the joys of the rig. He was the type of person who couldn't love something without trying to make everyone else love it too."

Tony said, "And if being preached at didn't turn you away, you must have really liked it."

"Right?" Jack nodded.

Tony's smile was abstracted. He was concentrating on taking each wave at the perfect angle. Nothing wrong with concentrating at the helm, but working that hard would tire him out. Jack looked back at Dan, who was also studying Tony, and picked up the story. "A visually interesting rig that didn't require a large crew but could push a heavy boat at a decent pace downwind. Perfect. The upwind performance was worrisome, but my pride made me think I could handle being tossed back onto my seamanship rather than powering through every difficulty."

Tony's increasing fatigue disrupted Dan's relaxation, so Jack handed Tony a tube of sunscreen. "Your ears are getting crispy." As good an excuse as any to take the wheel from Tony for the last part of the trip.

Tony moved over closer to Dan and spread on the sunscreen. Dan rubbed away the white streaks on Tony's jaw and they shared a tender kiss.

The wind didn't abate, so they swept through the water toward what Jack was calling Lysistrata Cove. Bursting waves misted the boat with glittering salt. They sailed into the cove well before dark and Jack, showing off for Tony and Marie, set the anchor elegantly under sail. Marie cheered along with the men and turned to coiling lines and covering the sails.

A fresh breeze flowed over the low island, ruffling the water more than on his first visit. He arranged the fruit and cheese he'd cut up earlier on a small silver platter and opened a light rosé wine. After he left the guys with their snack and some citronella candles, he dove in to check the anchor. He'd stuck it deep without raking it over or through any coral.

Back on the boat, he dried off and changed into light cotton pants and an even lighter long-sleeved shirt. He anticipated a buggy kind of night.

Marie had prepped the yawl boat by filling it with everything they'd need for a beach picnic and releasing the gripes, which held the boat close to *Lysistrata's* stern. Amy and Melissa had been fine swimming ashore, but he wasn't going to suggest it for the guys. He surreptitiously checked that she'd plugged the drain hole—she had—and called her over to help launch *Lysistrata's* tender. Getting the yawl boat up and down using the davits was much, much easier with another set of hands.

Marie stood next to him and started to speak, but she bit her lip instead. She looked at Tony and Dan, seated close together only ten feet or so away.

"What's up, Marie?"

"What are we doing here, Jack?" She untied the fall on her side and left one turn of the line on the cleat for leverage. Jack did the same.

"Lower away." They eased the falls, letting the weight of the boat pull it down. He turned toward her when the boat hit the water. "What do you mean?"

Vertical lines dug in between Marie's eyebrows, and she spoke quietly. "She doesn't want us here."

"Eve La Sirena isn't named on the title to the property. If she's nothing but a guest, I won't let her run me off from such a perfect, deserted cove. If the owner is around, let them tell us we're unwelcome." Either way, the beach was public property and his plan was to rub it in her face while giving his passengers a honeymoon they'd treasure.

"I'd be more comfortable if we didn't push the issue."

Jack climbed over the aft rail and down the stern ladder into the yawl boat. He didn't answer.

Marie leaned over the high stern. "I wouldn't mind some private time on the boat this evening."

He released the hooks from the rings on the yawl boat, freeing it from the falls. "No problem. I'll ferry them over and get the bonfire burning, then start their dinner. We'll probably be a couple-few hours."

"Thanks, Jack." Marie hauled the falls up far enough to stay dry and out of the way.

"It's nonstop work having overnight passengers. I know that a free hour is a wonderful thing." And it would give her a little distance in case there was another confrontation.

"No joke." She tossed him the painter, turned away, and disappeared toward her cabin.

Dan came to the stern and looked over at where Jack stood in the yawl boat, holding himself in place with a hand on the stern ladder. "There's wood in this adorable little boat," he said, clapping in his excitement. "I love a fire."

"So do I. And there's nothing like fresh conch cooked over an open fire, served in a coconut with lime juice. Of course, that's what comes after the caviar and champagne."

Dan mimed a swoon. "After you served all my favorite fruits and cheeses with such an excellent wine? If I hadn't just spent ten thousand dollars getting married to this big lug, I'd beg you to run away with me."

Jack spread his hands wide, well balanced in the sturdy little boat. "You're giving me more credit than I'm due. How do you think I knew all your favorites?"

Dan turned and melted. He held his arms up and Tony walked into them, wrapping himself around his husband like he'd never let go.

Pulling himself along, Jack brought the yawl boat around to the boarding ladder on the side of the boat—Marie hadn't missed a trick—and checked the contents of the cooler. Everything present and accounted for. As the lovers had themselves a little cuddle in the cockpit, Jack settled at the oars and watched the sun drop behind the palms, pumping orange and red through the black, backlit fronds.

Never been a better reason to get a little behind schedule. Besides, Jack sold cruises on the concept of throwing away the very idea of an itinerary.

He'd have been perfectly happy sitting right there all night if it weren't for his nagging desire to see Eve La Sirena again, but Tony and Dan appeared above him before long. Jack let Tony descend without help, but he offered a hand to Dan when he wobbled on the last step.

As he set the oars in the curved bronze oarlocks, he wondered what Eve would do. A series of day-sails had kept him plenty busy since his first visit. He didn't know if he could have stayed away as long as he had otherwise.

The sleek yawl boat started through the water at the first pull of the oars. Jack settled into the pleasant work of rowing ashore.

Her behavior seemed inexplicable. Storming down the beach to get rid of them, only to withdraw when he'd recognized her. Why not just stay in the house if she didn't want to be seen?

If she was using the island as a retreat, he could see her protecting her peace and quiet. She'd acted like there was more at stake than that, though he wasn't sure why he thought so.

Was she hiding something more than her identity?

❖

Holding her binoculars to the opening in her gauzy mosquito screen, Eve watched the older men join the captain in the little boat and head toward shore. The baby dyke remained on the big boat. The long sweep of the oars surprised her, but it made her think of hard, sweaty muscles. Hot.

They'd stayed aboard long enough that she'd thought there would be no need for a scene. She would have been disappointed had they stayed off the beach. She'd girded her loins for battle, and she hated to waste a good girding.

She moved to the mirror and practiced her most predatory smile. That young captain would never know what hit them.

The yellow cotton, block-printed sarong with repeating patterns in orange, red, and black, wrapped around her in generous folds. She laid the edges more carefully this time so she would stay covered unless she chose otherwise but draped the back farther down, framing the profound curve at the top of her ass with swags of fabric. The light shorts she often wore to combat thigh-rub came up too high for the effect she was after, so she pulled them off.

She studied the sarong in the mirror, shaking her shoulders to see her tits move under the cotton. Lascivious and precarious. Perfect.

Bold ankle bracelets with silver bells attracted the eye to her dark red toenail polish, while her bare arms spoke for themselves. She tumbled her hair on top of her head. The effect would be perfect with a heavily decorated silver chain running through and around the mass. She tugged and twisted until she was satisfied. A heavy clip actually held the hair in place, but it seemed to stay by magic. Dangling earrings finished the Gaia look, and she made quick repairs to the dramatic makeup she'd applied when the boat had arrived.

She skipped shoes but brought her driftwood staff. Twisted mangrove, polished by uncounted time spent tumbling in the surf, it shaded her look from harem girl to priestess-queen.

When she stepped onto the deck, she smelled the tang of a fire, though the wind carried the smoke away across the water. Maybe she would sit awhile by their beach bonfire after she sent them scurrying away.

She advanced on them with a measured tread, not sneaking but silent, not hiding but hard to see in the gathering dark.

What a fun role.

She'd gotten within a hundred yards of the fire when the captain looked over with a jerk of their head. They'd just served the two men something in coconut shells and the gasps and praise carried over the snap of the fire. The one she'd come to see froze, then walked away from the men with an absent pat on one's shoulder.

The young captain moved smoothly, their hands loose at their sides as though mesmerized. She stopped and allowed them to approach.

At a distance of several arm's lengths, she mustered her richest tones and spoke. "You dared return."

The captain's throat moved. "Yes."

"This is not acceptable behavior, Captain." She strolled toward the water, forcing the captain to turn their face toward the firelight.

"Jack. I'm Jack, I mean. Jack Azevedo. That's my name."

"And your pronouns?" She relished the surprised blink.

"He, him, his. Please."

Oh, too delicious. He'd been well trained by someone. She could feel him cut off the honorific after the please and wondered which he would have chosen for her. Ma'am? Mistress?

"Jack, I require that you and your passengers leave this beach. You may not use it again."

He frowned and she could tell he'd been a bit lost in the atmosphere of it all until then, as she'd planned. "I'm sorry…"

"You may call me Eve."

He swallowed again. "I'm sorry, Eve, but I won't leave. The beach is public property and as such, you don't have any right to make us. Also, this land isn't yours, or at least it's not in your name, and so you don't have the authority regardless."

Respect sparked in her, but his refusal brought her eyebrow up in what she knew to be her haughtiest look. "There are thousands of islands. Choose another one."

He didn't lower his eyes, but his hands twitched as though he was controlling the urge to fidget. "No. Anchoring and beach rights are important and need to be defended."

She tried a more threatening approach. "Do your passengers know that you're trespassing and creating what might very well be a significant hardship for someone who only wants to be left alone? Would they appreciate knowing they are pawns in your meaningless protest against privacy?"

Jack looked over his shoulder at the men sitting close together on low folding chairs. Their champagne flutes flashed with reflected firelight when they met. He turned back to her and she could just *see* his resolve harden along with his jaw.

"Repeating the word trespassing doesn't change the fact that we're not, and this is about protesting exclusive access, not privacy. Those men have been together for decades and they just got married. Are you going to fuck up their honeymoon? Are you going to make them pawns in your meaningless quest for perfect ownership?"

Eve's gaze flicked back to the couple, though she knew she was revealing a weakness. Some people oohed and ahhed over kitten pictures. For her, it was images of enduring love, especially between non-traditional couples. Whether it was the wedding of those Texan lesbians in their nineties right after the Supreme Court decision came down or a creaky septuagenarian kneeling to her dominant, old folks in love melted her right to the core.

She tried to bring back the persona she'd created to dominate this creature from a safe distance, but she'd cracked. Her heart wouldn't let her spoil a single moment of the couple's night.

"What did you serve them?" She tried to keep some hint of gruffness in her voice, but Jack must have heard the softening as well as she could.

He grinned, the impudent wretch, and said, "Conch in coconut and curry with lime."

"Sounds delicious."

He hesitated, the smile fading into a new tension that arrested her attention. "There's plenty more. Would you like me to bring you some?"

Eve tipped her head to the side and considered the person she'd thought was so young. Trans men could fool a person like that, seeming far younger than their real age. She would never have expected such a bold offer and gave it due consideration.

Sharing a meal was no way to get rid of someone, unless...

His tension continued to build while the silence stretched. Perhaps she could make this work.

"Yes, I would."

He tensed further as though surprised by her answer and excused himself with a nod.

Eve waited, leaning on her mangrove staff. Jack said a few words to the men, who looked over at her and waved. She waved back.

Maybe she could seduce him into obedience, but not if she got caught in a conversation with the honeymooners. Besides, Harmonie would kill her if she talked to another group of passengers.

Jack returned with a brown, hairy coconut in each hand, a blanket over one arm, and an open bottle of wine held against his side with one elbow. "Would you take the coconuts, please, Eve?"

"What did you tell them?" She took the rough husks in her palms, her thumbs dipping inside where the meat of the coconut was slick and wet. She breathed lime and curry, and a hum vibrated in her throat.

"That you'd come to see what we were up to and that we'd leave them to their private celebration. They'll wave when they're ready to go." Jack spread the thin quilt as he spoke, spilling a little wine in the sand. He reached for the coconuts and she let go in order to settle herself on the soft cotton. "I didn't bring enough glasses for four, but I'm game to share the bottle if you are."

Eve assessed Jack with renewed surprise. His mix of vulnerability and confidence could very well seduce *her*. In the last hints of sunlight, his features looked soft and nearly monochromatic, Euro-something in shape, but she remembered the dark, deep eyes, blue as the cobalt sky above them, that contrasted beautifully with his mahogany skin.

His even features lent a deeper sense of innocence to his general good-boy vibe. A small, dark mole drew her eyes to his neck, right at the best biting spot. His body was slim and strong as a swimmer's, but she imagined he dressed carefully to avoid enhancing his curves. When he knelt to push the coconuts into the sand under the blanket, she glimpsed a little curve in the open neckline of his light cotton shirt. If she knew her subject, and she prided herself on it, he would have sensitive, responsive, perhaps even orgasmic nipples. A fleeting sadness caused a twinge at the thought that he might have dysphoria around them and make them off-limits.

Not that she would ever find out. Right?

She picked up a coconut and looked into the hacked-off top before turning quizzically to Jack.

"I fish the conch out with my fingers and sip at the juice." He demonstrated, licking coconut water off his long fingers.

Eve stuck two fingers into the warm fluid in the coconut and found a sliver of conch. She pulled it up the soft side and took a quick look before popping the dripping mollusk in her mouth. A low moan eased from her throat as she moved it between her teeth, using her tongue to test the firm, slick texture before biting down and releasing a flood of flavor.

Jack ate another piece. "Caribbean spices, Indian influenced, plus a good squeeze of fresh lime. Easy, but unbelievably good. It's not ceviche because I pressure cook the conch beforehand, but it has some features in common."

Eve soaked up the sensual experience of the richness, the brightness, the spark all surrounding the firm flesh of the conch. Sexy food. She sipped the spiced coconut water, the hydrating fluid rushing down her throat.

"And when we're done, we can break the coconuts open and eat the meat."

"Wine?" She held out a hand and Jack gave her the bottle. A sniff and a sip let her know that he'd chosen the pairing thoughtfully. "Oh, Jack. This is so good."

"Am I forgiven?"

She blinked slowly and let her eyes focus on the near stranger who was feeding her as sensually as she'd ever been fed. That endearing look probably worked more often than not, but all she saw was a bratty bottom thinking he could charm his way out of a rightful punishment. She hardened her expression and waited until his grin faltered.

"Good and bad behavior don't cancel each other out. This is wonderful, but you're not off the hook for coming back when you knew you weren't welcome."

He perked up a bit. "Weren't?"

"Aren't." Frustration moved through her. Damn it, she liked him. "You trapped me with this whole honeymooning thing. You've improved my mood with this amazing meal, but don't press me."

His face fell again. "What's wrong with just being here, anyway? Are you using the island for something illegal?"

Eve used her hard-won control to keep her reaction a secret. She'd lived in a boarding school for performers, for Pete's sake, from the age of eleven. She'd learned long ago to keep someone from knowing when they'd picked up a real weakness.

She didn't want to think about why she'd revealed her soft spot for old lovers.

Her laugh was calculated to a T. "Why would I bother? Do you think cops like tangling with someone like me?"

Jack's eyebrows rose. "Guess I hadn't thought about it that way. I was trying to figure out why you'd be so fired up to get rid of us and I thought you might be running drugs or something."

Eve's laughter was real this time. She shook her head. "No." She sobered and gave him a bit of the truth. "I don't think you understand how many otherwise wonderful people would sell me to a tabloid without a second thought. My problems are so different from theirs that they have no empathy, no sympathy for what might hurt me."

Jack grimaced. "You don't have to greet us with open arms. You don't have to greet us at all."

Temper flooded her and pushed her to her feet. "You don't have to come here. Just go away and don't come back." She leaned over for her mangrove staff without putting down her coconut and, on a whim, grabbed the wine bottle. She tucked it under her arm and stalked away down the beach, complete silence behind her.

Brat. She was too busy to mess around with Jack Azevedo.

For one thing, her old record label had put out an insultingly bad mix of a great song. She liked the band, thought they had real promise—though they'd given in to the pull of an establishment career. The engineers had fucked them over, though, and they'd never see the success that should be theirs if she didn't get back to her little studio and remix the tracks she'd stolen from the recording studio's backups.

She'd rework it and release it on Integrated Music. Her lip curled, an involuntary response. Fuck that record label's cut. She'd pass along payment for the improved mix, and the musicians would see that they could do better than paying the industry to fuck them over. She knew her site's visitors better every day, and she anticipated at least a two percent payment rate. If two out of every hundred people who downloaded the song chose to pay for it, she'll be able to pass along more money tonight than they'd get from the label in a year. If they ever managed to pay back the outrageous production costs and get ahead of the avalanche of fees.

Though she filled her head with her next project, Eve couldn't help wondering if Jack was watching her walk away.

❖

Jack finished his conch and drank the juice, but he didn't have the energy to break open the coconut. He watched Eve all the way back to her house, a dim figure whose ankles and hair flashed in the moonlight. She rose onto the deck he'd spotted on the first visit and disappeared.

Eve La Sirena. What a perfect name. He knew it was a stage name and that her real name was Turkish, but he couldn't remember what it was.

He was in the right, damn it, but her angry gales buffeted him. Did the right to anchor need to be defended right then, right there? She was being straightforward, at least, rather than calling on family and favors to get him hassled like last time.

Depression settled over him. He didn't like the compromises he'd made in the past, and the idea of giving in poked a bruise. Long battles with marina owners who saw boats at anchor as lost revenue…condo owners who saw them as ducking property taxes… city officials who couldn't stand the disorder of it all…the brother-in-law of the harbormaster who hadn't hesitated to use his family connection to get Jack pulled over and inspected every time he weighed anchor.

No one could cite him a law that said he wasn't allowed to anchor. No one could fault him for unsafe conduct. Almost all of the people living at anchor were hassled, and they worked together to try to get some protection.

Eventually, complaints from his passengers convinced him that he'd have to give in. No one liked spending an hour of their vacation being questioned and searched by water cops, and it was only a matter of time before the cops found some illegal substance on a passenger. He could lose his boat if they did, but what was the alternative? Searching his passengers' luggage as he carried it aboard?

The people not trying to make a living aboard kept up the long, slow protest while Jack started paying for a slip behind the house of a friendly acquaintance and using the public pier for meeting passengers. He and Justin got along okay, enough to have a beer together now and then, but Jack wished to be back out on the hook.

Privacy, independence. The process of ferrying passengers to *Lysistrata* in the yawl boat had been part of the experience, and pulling up to the pier didn't have the same panache.

Giving up still chafed, and the soreness added to his intransigence.

As he sat, silent and still, the fire crackled and warmed the bones of the snuggling couple. The cessation of all human noise allowed him to hear the arrhythmic music of the planet. Fire, water, wind. Thought slowed with his breathing and his mind turned back to Eve.

Winning the argument was only part of why he'd come back. The island was perfect—easy to get to, gorgeous, secure—but in the Caribbean, those things weren't in short supply. Nearly deserted was harder to find, but he had a handful of islands he could visit instead of returning to Lysistrata Cove.

When Eve had softened, looking at Tony and Dan, his infatuation had come roaring back. He could see himself clearly now and knew that he'd come back to burn in her fire.

He hadn't expected, not even in his secret heart, to sit with her and flirt. He'd fed her the most sensual food he knew how to make and she'd reveled in it. She looked as though she spent all day being washed and massaged and oiled by slave girls, and in his fantasy, they were willingly bound to her.

She was beautiful, smart, impulsive, and dominating. She'd also treated him like a human being, an equal, instead of pulling that peon crap she'd tossed at him last time.

He absorbed the starlight. The moon formed a capital D shape, and it fell precipitously toward the horizon. He was pretty good at going after what he wanted, but she was undeniably intimidating and he was amazed that he'd opened his mouth and offered to feed her.

Sitting together, sharing food had given him a new perspective on her, though. He got a glimmer, again, of a realization he'd had over years of hauling passengers. Folks were folks, from the richest to the poorest, from the most easygoing to the most petulant, even including Eve La Sirena.

Eve.

He was almost glad she'd stormed off. He'd been wound up too tight, too raw and sensitive. If she'd have stayed, he would have exhausted himself just remembering to breathe. It would have been worth it, he intuited, but he didn't mind taking it more slowly.

He would be back.

CHAPTER FIVE

A zevedo is a Portuguese name, if I remember right, a
variation on the Spanish Acevedo. He's Anglicized the
pronunciation. I wonder how many generations away from Portugal
he is." Eve took a heaping bite of her omelet and was muzzled a few
seconds by a full mouth. "God, Harmonie, you do the best eggs."

Harmonie stared at Eve across the breakfast table. "I know that
tone."

Eve widened her eyes. "Of course you do. I praise your cooking
regularly."

Her mouth twisted. "Don't play coy with me. I know this look.
You're building a fantasy around your sea captain."

"Who better? Inconsistent, absent, adventurous, and bold."
Eve laughed when Harmonie rolled her eyes. "He's not exactly your
type, but I think you'd dig him too."

"That's not the point. This started with trying to frighten off
some trespassers with your favorite statue. How did it turn into
thinking about this guy between visits and wondering about his
ancestry?"

Eve toyed with her next bite, rolling the Muenster cheese
around her fork. She put Harmonie's question out of her mind to
enjoy the dense egg, smooth avocado, and spicy sriracha. "Mmm."
She swallowed. "Really, perfect."

Harmonie tipped her head to the side in a silent, *Seriously?*

"Darling, you know that I can keep it in my pants. I admit that I'm getting a kick out of the whole thing now. Whenever faced with two equally good options, I believe in choosing the one that makes the better story. But being attracted isn't a weakness, and I know that getting close to him isn't much of an option. I can both spin the yarn and coil it away."

Harmonie leaned back in her chair, her plate clean. She sipped her coffee, then warmed it from the insulated pot. Finally, she said, "That's a great image. You should put it in your lyrics."

Eve reached across the table, palm up, and Harmonie put her hand in Eve's. "Believe me, Harmonie. I know what's at stake and I'm not going to prison. I'll never allow myself to be caged. It would break me."

Harmonie shivered and pulled her hand away to reach for her coffee.

A flat sadness descended, one which had come to visit her more and more regularly. How would their transition go? Would they go completely separate ways when they decoupled or keep working together? Eve wanted to keep Harmonie in her life, somehow. She'd lost everyone she'd ever loved, and always due to her own intensity. Harmonie was the only person who had enjoyed the hard-to-love aspects of her. Her brashness, her impulsiveness. Her uncompromising vision and voracious need to create and control and share.

Even though she and Harmonie were on diverging paths, they were still on the same side. Compatriots, accessories to one another's crimes. That would continue to bring them together.

Injecting naughty glee into her voice, Eve said, "Let's figure out how we're going to get rid of him, for once and for all."

A faint smile tipped Harmonie's lips. "Intimidation didn't work. Seduction didn't work."

Eve snorted. "Had I been going for seduction, things would have ended differently."

"Okay," Harmonie said agreeably, "mysteriously dominating ancient authority symbol seductiveness didn't work."

They were back to working together. The glow was real and strong, as real and strong as the earlier sadness. "So what's next?"

"Well, we could go with my strong point."

Eve bypassed the trap easily. "You have so many."

"How about driving him off by being completely obnoxious?"

"Tell me more."

Their plan took shape quickly, and Eve kept an eye on the *Lysistrata* website over the next few days. He never came to the cove when he had short sails scheduled, only for the multi-day blocks. He had one on the calendar a little ways out, and Eve settled herself to enjoy the expectation.

Her remix hit the site like a hurricane and surpassed her expectations. Almost five hundred thousand downloads with a seven percent payment rate meant she had thirty-five thousand dollars for the musicians. That was orders of magnitude more than they'd ever see from the craptastic version the record label had released. Of course, those kinds of figures gave her nervous chills. Harmonie hadn't been able to ease her fear at handling large sums. Money acted like chum, drawing sharks from far and wide.

She worked hard on samples, practiced studiously on piano, guitar, voice. She played hard with Harmonie, leaving welts and bruises that she later got to poke and prod—sadistic double duty.

She watched the calendar.

❖

Jack clenched his teeth as he hauled one of the brats off the railing. The mothers couldn't be bothered to keep their kids on board, and Jack wondered if they were hoping to lose one or two at sea.

He considered letting it happen.

The kid shrieked and kicked at him, but Jack had learned the hard way that the tap shoes he'd tried to confiscate left small, dense bruises. When he explained how they were likely to damage his deck, the lawyer mother had waved his words away. "Bill me."

He dropped the child. The useless mother lounged on a deck cushion as though exhausted. "Honey, did you almost fall overboard? You must have been scared."

The kid dove for her stomach and she grunted at the force of a hard little skull meeting soft tissue. Jack turned away from the sickening sight and almost ran into the pacing lawyer mother.

"Don't you fucking tell me what we're going to do next. You got yourself caught with your hand in the cookie jar, so we already know the caliber of your thinking processes. Listen to me—"

Jack shook his head unconsciously in refusal, but she'd turned to pace the other way. After hours of being bombarded by her voice, he knew more about her law clients than anyone should. What happened to confidentiality? He rushed to the helm, calm water and light winds the only saviors on a day that was already the worst in his six years of chartering.

Marie held the wheel grimly, her eyes darting back and forth. "One of them got behind me—I don't even know how—and was inside the yawl boat, rocking it back and forth. By the time I realized what I was hearing, the monster had it going almost hard enough to hit the transom."

Jack peeked over the transom into the yawl boat, which was empty except for a red puddle. Too thin to be blood, which meant it was one of a bewildering variety of sugar treats the mothers kept shoving at the kids.

At least that would clean up. He stared harder. What were the lines under the red?

"Don't stick that knife into the wood, honey."

Jack stiffened and spun around. Useless mother hadn't moved from her deck cushion, but she waved her hand at the kid gleefully hacking at his deckhouse trim. It was some of the last of the original teak.

Jack yelled, his voice breaking high in his distress. Liberating the knife from the creature took courage, but he found it welling up right alongside outrage. He turned to Useless. "You have to keep your children under control. I've already made it clear that they're not safe running around like this. Now they're doing real damage to my boat, beyond the scratches in the deck I've already shown you. This is not acceptable."

Useless wasn't listening and Jack turned to see what she was looking at just in time to catch the next act in the nightmare carnival. The other kid was arguing with Marie, tugging at the wheel against Marie's attempts to steer. Marie looked over, and Jack could feel the call for backup in his spine. He started over, but before he reached them, the kid set its feet and threw a determined punch into Marie's gut. Jack stopped short at the righteous fury on Marie's face. She held the kid by the fist for a long moment and Jack held his breath. She said a few quiet words and let go.

He took a slow breath. The kid ran to the still-lounging useless mother. "Baby, it's not nice to punch strangers." The horrible creature punched her in the tit.

Jack couldn't tell the kids apart. Hell, after hours of torture under sail, he wasn't even sure how many of them there were. They were like gremlins, new monsters popping up all over. He swiveled in place, looking for the others, while the lawyer mother continued to ignore the entire scene in favor of starting a new phone conversation.

They were on a line for Lysistrata Cove, but second thoughts plagued him. He'd planned to go there all along, but he didn't hate Eve enough to bring this nightmare down on her. What if the kids went to her house and fucked with something?

A loud crack rang across the deck and the boat jolted.

The mainsail flew upward along the mast. The main sheet tightened with an abrupt twang.

Jack jumped for the kid. It blubbered in the path of the whipping downhaul line, freed by the explosion of the block. When Jack grabbed the kid, he got an agonized scream for his effort. The kid squirmed away from Jack, toward the base of the mast.

Jack put the kid down behind him and snatched at the line. He caught it quickly, thankful again for the light winds, and reeved it through the broken block's shackle. He pulled hard, lacking the mechanical advantage the block would have given him, and drew the sail back down into place. Marie—quick thinking as usual—

eased the main sheet so he wouldn't have to struggle so hard against the full sail.

By the time he had the rig squared away, he'd put together a clear picture of what had happened. He held the corpse of a block he'd built himself in one hand and a small metal car in the other. The monster had used the mahogany downhaul block as an anvil and a heavy teak pin as the hammer. The small metal car had survived, but the block had broken apart and the pin was pitted and cracked.

He showed Useless the wreckage.

"Now what have we agreed about smashing your toys?"

Jack turned away, numb, and walked to the helm. Quietly, he said to Marie, "I could rig something to take the block's place, but I want them the hell off my boat."

Marie nodded, mouth tight. He had a flashing image of what she'd look like when she was fifty. "We're too far out to get back before dark."

Lysistrata Cove was right there. He flipped open the waterproof paper chart book to get a wider view than his electronic screen could provide and considered his options.

They could swim anywhere he could anchor, but he really wanted to send them all to a beach. The nearest islands had fishing villages. He couldn't offload this family where folks were trying to scrape a living.

Damn it.

Lysistrata Cove was the best choice.

The lawyer mother screeched. "No signal?" She turned on her wife to Jack's dismay and relief. "You just had to have a vacation in the middle of nowhere."

He didn't especially want to insert himself into the fight—apparently, he had Useless to thank for the booking—but he had to tell them what was going on.

"The block your child broke is essential equipment. I'm going to have to anchor to effect temporary repairs." He thought about giving them a sense of how expensive these repairs would be, but he stopped.

Jack's contract stipulated what kind of damage was the responsibility of the passengers, and he would be billing them for a significant amount of wood and woodworking. Of course, with a fucking lawyer involved, it would probably be too much to expect they would just pay.

The lawyer mother waved him off and went back to berating her wife. At least she couldn't keep up the vitriolic monologue forever.

Could she?

Chapter Six

O n the deck, Eve plugged in the last XLR cable for her DJ rig and crowed with satisfaction when *Lysistrata* sailed past the cove's entrance and tacked to make its way into the protected waters. "Harmonie, check it out. Right on time."

Harmonie came through the gauzy mosquito netting holding two glasses of wine and looked over the water. The crescent of her cheek shone in silhouette. "Cheeky bastard."

"I should wait until late. It doesn't matter as much if I'm not disturbing their sleep."

"You are such a bitch."

"I know, right?"

Harmonie edged closer and looked up at Eve, a good trick since they were close to the same height. "What are we going to do in the meantime?"

Eve had planned to keep an eye out while pretending to ignore them. It seemed prudent to make sure they didn't come close to the house at least.

She looked out at *Lysistrata*, packed with what seemed to be a lot more people than usual, then back at Harmonie. Fuck it. "I'm going to tie you down and rub my cunt all over you. You're my favorite sex toy."

Harmonie turned and put her hands behind her back. Eve grasped her wrists and folded them together in the hollow above her ass. They both loved this game.

Eve pushed Harmonie ahead to their playroom. She shoved Harmonie's hips into the repurposed massage table and pushed her crossed hands higher up her back to force her to bend over it. The hard thump in Eve's cunt proved that this was a great idea. Eve kicked Harmonie's feet apart, more for pleasure than need, since Harmonie had automatically taken an open position. Draped over her long back, Eve absorbed Harmonie's ease of muscle and banked the need. She rocked her hips back and forth, pushing the bones of her hips against the giving muscles of Harmonie's ass. Eve couldn't bite her neck from there, so she pulled her upright and tenderized the slim muscle roping her neck and shoulder.

"On the table, face up."

She devised rope cuffs with a half-dozen wraps around Harmonie's paired wrists. Eve lingered over this part, relishing the increasing openness in Harmonie's body. When she pulled the wraps tight with frapping turns, Harmonie's elbows drew closer and her upper arms plumped her breasts. Eve kissed her curled pinkie fingers and stared into Harmonie's eyes. The utter ease of Harmonie's lips and heavy eyelids fomented a contrasting tension in Eve's belly.

"I'm going to enjoy myself so much. You're going to please me however I want."

"Yes, please, Evrim."

Eve's Turkish name—her birth name—sounded strange in daily life, but it fit her perfectly in moments like this. She thrilled at the sound of it, knowing it meant that Harmonie was hers to command, Harmonie's body was hers to feast on.

Eve took one of Harmonie's fingers between her teeth, delicately rolling it back and forth. She bit harder, knowing that the pain was sharpest where bone pressed against skin rich with nerve endings. The whole time, her eyes and Harmonie's maintained their contact, and tiny twitchings of Harmonie's eyelids and forehead gave away the twinges of pain.

Sadism lost to the hot smell of Harmonie's cunt. Eve's original plan came back to her, and she drew the free end of the rope binding Harmonie's wrists through a sturdy ring in the wall at the head of the bed. She hiked herself up to sit on Harmonie's belly, rope in hand.

Harmonie rested her hands between Eve's breasts and checked for permission to play with them. Instead, Eve pulled on the line, and Harmonie's muscles tensed against the loss of Eve's skin.

"As I please."

Harmonie's lips twisted and relaxed. Her resistance melted, and the rope drew her arms past her head and straight out beyond.

"Are you going to resist me? Sex toys don't fight their users."

Harmonie's muscles tensed against the rope and Eve tugged on it hard, jerking Harmonie's arms tight over her head. "No!" Harmonie held her breath, waiting for punishment, but Eve stared at her until she explained. "No, I won't resist. I want to be what gets you off. I want you to come all over me."

Eve smiled, not kindly, and brought her torso to Harmonie's. She pressed a hard kiss to Harmonie's lips, pushing lips against teeth, then pushed her fingers at her cheeks as though convincing a horse to take a bit. Eve pushed her tongue inside, where Harmonie's flexed just a little. As hard as Harmonie tried to be slack, her lips pursed. Eve pulled away.

Eve dismounted and tied off the line. She bound Harmonie's ankles the same way she'd done her wrists, then did as she'd promised. She teased Harmonie and herself until the hunger overtook her, then launched Harmonie into multiple orgasms while grinding on Harmonie's mouth. Oh, she enjoyed getting her cunt back into the action after a while of feeling closed up down there.

Focused on using Harmonie's entire body to stimulate her own cunt, Eve hadn't done more than grab her hard. She didn't expect to see any bruising, but she discovered while untying her that Harmonie had created her own pain pulling against the ropes. Before they made dinner, Eve ministered to Harmonie's chafed wrists and ankles, spreading salve over the red skin.

Harmonie seemed to linger in subspace, cuddling and then giving Eve's feet a light massage, so Eve allowed her to set up their dinner. Floating around the kitchen, Harmonie made hummus, poured extra-virgin olive oil over zatar, set out olives and dolmas, and warmed some pita. Eve settled herself into the thick cushions that circled her lounging room.

"Harmonie."

"Yes, Eve."

"Come here." Not in scene, but Eve didn't give up command easily.

Harmonie put the last of the dishes on the low table in the lounge and dropped to her knees in front of Eve. Eve pulled her into a hug and Harmonie climbed onto the couch, curled up sitting next to her, face to face, draped in Eve's arms. Harmonie nestled close, her head a welcome weight on Eve's breast.

"I love you, Harmonie."

"I love you too, Eve."

"The future is a mystery, but we know each other's hearts. Whatever comes, we will never be strangers."

Harmonie stroked Eve's breast, squeezed it as though she were going to nurse. Their sexual chemistry and musical ties had brought them together, but this, the sharing of need, the providing of emotional sustenance, had held them together. Eve wondered if they would always come back to one another over time. She hoped they could reconnect after splitting up, that they could maintain the space in their hearts for each other with sufficient brightness to allow fleeting reunions to bring them back to this feeling.

They snuggled for a long time, until the grumbling of Eve's stomach made Harmonie stir. It had gotten dark, and Harmonie lit candles throughout the room. The pita was cold, but it didn't matter.

❖

Jack tried to tune out the belowdecks brouhaha while he tacked into Lysistrata Cove. When he told the family they were almost at the destination—and that there would be plenty of time to spend on the beach—they trouped below to get ready. That process sounded as fraught with tension as every other thing they did together.

He only hoped they didn't bust up the boat's interior.

Marie stood by and dropped the sails once they were in protected water. They came down gracefully inside the jack lines with a dull clatter from the battens. He used the electric motor to find his spot and set the anchor, but the sudden silence from below put him on edge in a new way.

He descended to the abused deck along the side, cataloging the damage on the way to the bow. The anchor nestled in the sand, clearly visible, leaving him no excuse to dive in and leave the passengers to Marie. He turned back, determined to get them off the boat as fast as possible.

Marie must have been on the same page. She had the yawl boat ready to lower away and a monstrous pile of beach gear piled around the cooler on the side deck.

When he saw the conch shell on the pile, he gave her a questioning look.

"I'll take them in and drop them off. They've agreed to sound the conch when they're ready to come back."

Jack grinned. "Are you hoping they won't be able to blow it loud enough?"

"Why, Jack. That possibility never occurred to me." Marie's innocent look was good, but a smile lurked.

They lowered the yawl boat together and Marie climbed in to pull it around the side. He passed down the cooler, the blankets and umbrella, then started heaving the mothers' bags over. What the fuck were they carrying, gold bullion?

The creepy silence shattered when the family came back up. "Stop sniveling. Act like a barbarian and I'll treat you like a barbarian." The lawyer mother's acid tone reinforced the threat, and Jack flicked his eyes over the kids. No sign of violence, which horrified him suddenly. Such a terribly low bar for whether or not they were okay.

Marie held the yawl boat against *Lysistrata's* side while Useless passed children to Lawyer. As Marie let go and headed for the beach, Jack waved them off in his gladness to have them gone. Not ten feet from *Lysistrata's* side, the kids tried to fall over the bow of the yawl boat, but Marie pulled on the oars hard enough to jolt them back on their asses.

Good work. Now Jack could estimate the damages thus far. Instead, he sat on the cockpit bench and didn't move for several quiet minutes. The utter stillness in the cove made it all too easy to hear the resumption of battle when the family hit the beach, but he tuned them out and listened to his boat move. Why estimate damages when they were sure to commit more crimes against his woodwork before he ejected them in Miami?

Instead, he spent the time worrying that Eve would come out for round two. Anticipation of their next battle had buoyed his mood for days, but all he had on his side at the moment was the strictly legal right. His passengers handily demolished any courtesy argument he'd thought to wield. Not that he should have to be a "good" neighbor in order to exercise his right to anchor or use the beach.

Yeah. No. True as that might be, it didn't dislodge the guilt he felt for bringing the horror show to Eve's doorstep. His tension abated as time passed without that round figure stalking from the other side of the cove.

Marie didn't return for almost an hour, and she immediately changed into a swimsuit. "I have to wash those people out of my hair."

"No problem. I'll keep an eye out."

Over the next several hours, the conch shell blew seven times. Each time, Jack rowed in to learn that they'd forgotten something essential. Earbuds so one monster could watch a movie on a tablet. A cell phone charging backup battery. An aromatherapy candle.

Marie lay under a canopy on the deckhouse, soaking up the warmth and relaxing without sacrificing her light skin. She tensed every time the conch shell horn sounded. It wasn't right. Neither of them needed the kind of treatment that put them so badly on edge.

Eve remained a no-show. Jack juggled his unfulfilled yearning toward her and his absolute relief that she wouldn't meet the family. Reason reinforced the second feeling but proved helpless against the first.

❖

Harmonie cleaned up after dinner while Eve turned on her gear. The amps activated the subwoofers with a low thump that electrified her hair follicles. Powering up held a pleasure like bathing before a hot date.

The deck, usually clear enough for Tai Chi, was crowded with her mixing console, her turntables, her sampler, and synthesizer. The vinyl records she planned to use stood in a rack like racehorses in their starting sheds. Little red and green LEDs came to life, blinking or steady, and anticipation overcame her.

She and Harmonie had hung her studio monitors from the eaves facing outward, over the cove. She hit play on the sampler and listened to the sounds she'd been working on while she set up a dozen tracks on the computer and set it to record. She had plenty of server space. No reason to do any mixdown at this point.

She built her music, experimental beats that she overlaid with recordings of animal sounds. She slowed and sped the animal language until it sounded like a chorus of voices singing in the desert, small and overwhelmed but insistent. She looped the background so that she could focus on the manipulation of the animal voices. She got a good melody going and went back to the beat, giving it texture and dynamic. Maddening repetition, beats that settled in only to break off and start again, hits and misses in her manipulation of needle on vinyl. Through the mess, through the attempts and awkwardness, she heard the pure call of the song.

She'd put on and taken off her headphones dozens of times by the time she felt satisfied. She started the song from the beginning so she could listen to it for monotony or inappropriate changes. She vocalized along with the recording, hunting out the missing frequencies, looking for opportunity and balancing fullness with the purposeful use of void. She bobbed her head as she sang. Her hair had been piled on top of her head, but locks had fallen to line her neck and irritate her. She swept the headphones back and started to use them to catch and lift the hair.

Motion caught her eye. Someone stood at the steps from the beach walkway to the deck, and she knew, without turning, that it was Jack. She remembered the plan, suddenly and completely ripped from her musical trance. She'd forgotten her purpose.

On the other hand, she'd created a brilliant club song.

Too professional for something as simple as surprise to trip her up, she kept singing. She pulled the headphones off altogether and let her hips pick up the beat. Smoothly, without acknowledging the presence at the edge of her vision, she pulled an album from the Lucite case on the ground, slid it out of its cardboard cover touching only the edges, and put it on a turntable. Pressing one side of the headphones to her ear, she matched the beats between her last Kitten Caboodle album and her work-in-progress. She slid the fader slowly across, bringing the two to parity and then letting the older stuff take over.

She dropped the headphones and turned. Jack stood where he was, where he'd been for who knew how long. His dripping wet shirt and shorts clung to his body, slender ribs showing, slight chest caressed and hard nipples poking against the fabric. His dark hair rose in short spikes at the front and lay like seal fur against the rest of his scalp. Eve wanted to smile and tease him about the bitch handle, but his hands were tight fists.

She gave in to half the urge, the tough smile at home on her lips after topping so many brats. Yes, I enjoy you, the smile said, but don't push your luck.

Or do. That could be fun too.

CHAPTER SEVEN

In order to draw out Marie's time off, Jack decided to serve dinner on the beach as the sun set. Lawyer flipped through a foot-high stack of magazines—*Attorney at Law* and *The American Lawyer* among others. The aromatherapy candle seemed to have worked on Useless, though it was hard to tell the difference between her exhausted-and-put-upon look and her rested look. They surprised him by eating without complaint and requesting to go back to the boat. Perhaps terrorizing each other had worn them all out. He could only hope.

The moon peeked over the horizon opposite the downed sun. Colors piled like sediment on the horizon, the entire rainbow compressing into ever-narrower bands as stars began to pop. Jack took them right back, without packing up. He returned to the beach for the gear and took his sweet time stowing it all in the beached yawl boat. The post-sunset light confounded him, with the water finding an impossible light source and acquiring the mercurial sheen that never failed to fascinate him. Hard sun on waves dazzled the eye, but this slippery glow under a violet-black sky hypnotized the mind.

As he put the last bag on the pile, a blast of sound crossed the cove from Eve's house. A dark mass covered her deck, gleaming at the edges from strings of multicolored lights hung above. What the hell was she doing?

The sound modulated and gained a beat, then twisted, stopped, and started over.

Oh no.

Jack fretted on the way back to the boat, sunset's spell broken by the surety that there would be trouble.

Marie met Jack at the side of the boat and hissed, "Your girlfriend is waking the animals. The kids just went to sleep in the saloon."

The calm Jack had pieced together while cleaning up the beach detonated in the next set of screeches that crossed the water. "What the hell is she doing?"

"I don't know, but if she doesn't stop, this could get ugly."

Marie was right. The mothers came on deck and stared at the source of the sound. He couldn't call it music; it was too raw for that. It didn't follow any rules.

Useless looked across the water. "You brought us to a club?" Her whine signaled a return to the put-upon attitude she'd copped before spending hours on the beach ignoring her kids.

"This has never happened before." He kicked himself for using such a weak excuse as the sneer blossomed on Lawyer's face.

"It's happening now," Lawyer said. "What are you going to do about it?"

Some part of the noise regularized and got louder. The rest kept starting and stopping, swooping and diving. "Why don't you folks try to get some sleep? She can't go on forever."

Lawyer grasped his slip. "She who? If you know this woman, call and tell her to stop."

"I can't call her. I don't have her number." For one thing.

"Who is it? I'll have my assistant track it down." She pulled her cell phone from her pocket.

"No." Jack went with his gut and braced himself for the blowback. "This is her island and we don't have the right to tell her what to do here."

"Are you kidding? This is sound pollution. There may not be noise ordinances out here in the middle of nowhere, but I don't have to tell her that."

Jack fought the urge to match her aggressive posture. Joining verbal battle with a lawyer could only infuriate him further. The sound softened and he said, relieved, "See, she's brought the volume down. Let's all go to bed and get ready to sail back in the morning." He wouldn't be seeking opportunities to extend the trip this time.

Grumbling, the mothers went below to their cabin. Marie said, "I may sleep on deck if the music stops."

Jack took a deep breath. Now that the passengers from hell were gone, he remembered how beautiful it was out there on the water. "It's a perfect night for it. Warm, light breeze, plenty of stars."

"The moon is full, too. When she's big, she gives me dreams."

Jack grinned at Marie. "I didn't know you were a moon-lover."

She shrugged. "Who isn't?"

"Wiccan?"

"Not really. I don't like groups, just the flow of the earth and sky."

"Fair enough." After the day he'd had, he didn't feel up to a discussion of the world and what forces governed it. He let the subject drop and they stood together at the rail in silence.

Then the sound came back and Jack lowered his head to the teak between his hands. Marie said, "I'll sleep in the forepeak." She left.

Buck stops here.

The mothers were back within a couple minutes, this time with the sound of screaming brats following them from the companionway. "Either you stop this or I will."

"I told you, we have no right—"

"My children are being tortured. I have every right."

"It can't go all night." But it could. Eve could be doing speed. She could be a night person with no desire to sleep before the small hours of the morning. She could even be fucking with them on purpose.

"You call yourself a captain, well, take charge. This weakness you're displaying makes me question your fitness to command a vessel of any size, let alone take responsibility for precious cargo like my family."

On purpose. As the idea soaked in, Jack became sure of it. He'd never noticed big piles of gear on her deck before. She hadn't come out to kick them off the beach.

Eve was trying to blast them out of the cove.

"You call yourself a man, but there's nothing but pussy in those pants. Just because you weren't born with balls doesn't mean you can't act like you have them."

Jack turned toward Lawyer. "Are you fucking kidding me? I can't believe you're going there."

"I can't believe you brought us to a place where we can't leave and set us up to be tortured. I can't believe you think your precious gender identity is more sacred that the well-being of my children."

Jack tried to inhale some calm. He wanted to argue, to present all the reasons why her words were not just inappropriate but harmful, and how she was teaching her children by example that they should get what they wanted by exploiting people's vulnerability. Getting it all out without letting rage garble the argument was only one challenge. The other was the wordless feeling that she would agree and argue that she didn't make the world, she just knew how to live in it.

He dove overboard. Cool water slicked across his hands and the force of the dive streaked bubbles across his face. The familiar turbulence at his ankles and feet spurred him to kick hard and stay underwater as long as possible. His lungs ached when he surfaced and twisted face up. He looked along his body, past his feet, at *Lysistrata* with fresh rage at having conceded the battleground—his own goddamn boat—to a real, actual enemy.

He didn't even know what he was going to do. All he knew was that he couldn't stand there and take the abuse.

Marie had come out of the forepeak through the hatch. She stood on the bow and waved as he turned and stroked across the cove, straight for Eve's deck. Water muffled the music, but it got louder as he approached. The rush of fluid in his ears gave it a carnival sound, stretching and contracting the notes eerily, modulating when he turned his head to the side to get a breath. He pulled hard through the water, transmuting rage and shame and insult into power.

When he reached sand and stood, the music rocked him back on his heels. It was as loud as he'd ever heard in a club, but without any echo. He could practically see the sound waves escape over the open water with only the tall palms to absorb them and nothing at all to reflect them.

He stumbled out of the water and past a lean-to made of driftwood to the deck steps, but the sounds changed, became music. What had driven him mad became intelligible and the driving beat maintained its flow.

As he caught sight of her, Eve took her hands from the console and started to sing.

For a moment, it had seemed that she'd completed the dense, complicated song. It sounded perfect until her voice picked out the missing pieces, provided the last bit of fullness, or sharpened the sound with a clashing note. That voice. He'd fucked to it, masturbated to it. He'd sung along during road trips and cheered drag queens who lip-synched to it.

Unreal.

Her hair was piled on top of her head again, but without the silver chain woven among the tumbled curls. The casual knot sagged to one side, and locks of hair traced her neck and collarbone, fell down her shoulder blades, and piled on her breasts. Her profile seemed more solid than everything around it. The strong line of her nose, the firm lips. Her throat expanded and moved with her voice, and her bosom rose and fell with her titanic breaths.

Bosom? Jack was sure he'd never used that word. It sounded a false note in his head, revealing the fantasy he'd fallen into.

His anger returned, turned on her. Still, he didn't know what to do. There was no stopping that song. He fought the allure, fisting his hands.

Eve reached for her headphones, did a little dip with them, then set them aside. She began to sway with the music, her hips leading the beat. She put a new record on and held one side of her headphones against her ear like she was deejaying in a club. When she stopped fiddling with the settings on the record player, she slid something across what he figured was her mixing board, and a new, seductive music slowly took over.

The siren's song towed him under as she turned toward him.

Multicolored lights limned her bare arm for a moment as she reached out to grab a wine glass from the deck's rail. She rolled toward him, thick thighs bare under a long shirt with the sleeves and neckline cut roughly away. Her breasts moved on their own, uncorraled behind the low, jagged neckline. The T-shirt said "CBGB & OMFUG," but it dropped from his awareness when she took a sip of dark red wine and licked her lips.

She advanced on him slowly and he quaked. She stopped, two steps away and above him.

"Would you like to come in?" She held out the wine glass.

Oh, boy.

❖

Jack loved her music.

Eve saw it in him when she turned from the mixing equipment. She had no false modesty when it came to her music. Six years at a competitive musical boarding school had given her a tough audience to cut her teeth on. The pumping energy exchange between a performer and a live audience mirrored the Escher-like waterfall of energy between her and a bottom in a scene. Give and take by everyone involved, with her at the controls. It wasn't just her need to be seen, to be valued for what she could make. It was the cellular-level sharing between human beings.

She sipped her wine and went to him. He stood, a study in potential energy.

Going with instinct, she handed him her glass. "Would you like to come in?"

Harmonie came through the open door with a tray before Jack could respond. His tension eased at the reprieve, and Eve could very well imagine the reason for his relief. He took the glass she'd continued to hold out toward him.

Eve gestured him to the table and he mounted the steps slowly. When he passed her, she fell in close behind to make him nervous. As they reached the deck, she met Harmonie's eyes. The amused resignation on Harmonie's face pulled a mischievous grin from Eve.

He stopped at the edge of the table, dripping saltwater on her deck. He stilled but did not turn when she came up beside him. Eve circled the table and stepped behind Harmonie. She took Harmonie's wrist in her hand, gripping the delicate bones firmly, and raised it to her opposite shoulder. Eve caught Harmonie's other wrist and dragged her hand across her belly, creating a two-person imitation of *The Birth of Venus*. Jack watched with his lips parted.

Eve looked down where the sheer fabric of Harmonie's white cotton shift molded against her bottom-heavy curves, and her own nipples hardened. With a deep breath of Harmonie's skin and hair, that familiar, stimulating combination of salt, lime, and coconut oil, she watched Jack flush and stiffen. His nipples had yet to soften.

Eve manipulated Harmonie's body like she did the sound from her speakers, the sounds from her body. She tucked her lips behind Harmonie's ear and spoke softly so that Jack wouldn't be able to hear. "Shall we fuck him?"

Harmonie tipped her head to the side and hummed thoughtfully. She leaned a little more of her weight on Eve and brushed her ass across the tops of Eve's thighs and the bottom of her belly. All that ass. Eve's sharp concentration blipped with the clench in her cunt, but she didn't miss Harmonie's nod.

Jack's eyes had twitched back and forth, watching them communicate, their bodies pressing and their hands moving together over Harmonie's body in something far more lascivious than a hug. He'd stopped looking like he wanted to bolt, but he couldn't be said to have relaxed. Their little show had been effective, no question about it.

She released Harmonie with a little bite on her shoulder, and Jack moved suddenly as though freed from an enchantment. He drank deep of the wine and coughed a little.

Down, girl. There's more to the plan than dominating this person.

Eve had cooked earlier, or at least had prepared the meal. Ceviche, gazpacho, and crackers filled the small tray. A bottle of tequila and its accompanying lime and salt sat out on the sidebar. She and Harmonie rarely bothered to eat out of separate bowls for meals like this, so there were no dishes, only cloth napkins. She dropped into a lounging chair, realizing only as she did so how long she'd been on her feet at the mixing console. Her feet hurt.

She tossed a leg over one cushioned arm and leaned against the other. She wasn't wearing underwear, but she didn't think the angle would give Jack his second peep show. They had business to attend to first.

She fiddled with the strings that tied the cushions to the teak. "Please sit, Jack. Would you like more wine, or will you join us for tequila?"

He chose the chair across from her. "I'll have tequila, if that's what the meal calls for." He looked between her and Harmonie. "Would you like me to pour?"

Harmonie's faint smile sharpened. Eve wasn't surprised. As often as Harmonie bottomed to her, she had a strong dominant side. Her eyes flicked toward Eve as she said, "Why, thank you, yes." Jack stood as soon as he had permission. "You must be Jack."

He jolted a little as he pulled the mushroom cork from the bottle. "Excuse me, yes. Jack Azevedo."

"Portuguese?" Harmonie asked with a wink for Eve as Jack focused on pouring. One of the benefits of flirting while poly. Partners could get info for one another.

"Yes, my family's from the Azores, but my grandfather was born in the US."

"*Você fala Portugues?*"

"No," he said, while bringing the shot glasses, salt, and lime to the table. "To my sorrow, I never learned to speak Portuguese. My family chose to speak only English with their American kids. It's on the list, though." He licked a drop of lime juice from the side of his finger, adorably eager in the moonlight.

Harmonie pursed her lips. Eve almost laughed at Harmonie's silent commentary.

I told you he was pretty.

His skin was darker than hers on his face and neck, but she imagined it was lighter under that top he always wore. He moved nervously, but not without a good deal of grace, as he served the drinks with their condiments. He took his shot like a champ, only blinking faster for a few seconds. She winked at Harmonie when he looked away.

Eve leaned forward to put down her glass. "You have a list?"

"I have lists for everything. Even the compartments on the boat have lists of contents. Which is super helpful until I forget to update a list after moving something or running out."

Harmonie took over the inquisition. "How long have you had *Lysistrata*?" As she drew out enough information for a fairly complete dossier on Jack, Eve ate ceviche with her fingers. The second shot put a little extra glow in the full moon and loosened Jack's tongue enough to talk about his day.

"I usually enjoy having passengers. This trip has been an exception." He was quite the storyteller. Harmonie's wonderful laugh spilled over his words several times, and he had to wait for her to control her hilarity. Eve took part in the conversation, but not much. The stories amused her, but the swelling of desire carried her along. Jack and Harmonie felt her vibe. They talked to each other but sat with their bodies oriented toward her. Eventually, her moment came.

"Harmonie, there's one chunk of prawn left." Eve spoke softly. They fell silent and looked at her, Jack with renewed nervousness.

Harmonie raised her eyebrows. Whatever she saw in Eve's face, she lifted her chin in acknowledgment. She cradled the blue-glazed bowl in one hand and nipped the dripping prawn from the lime juice with the fingernails on the other. She leaned toward Jack, against the cushion on the arm of her chair, and offered it to him. "The guest should get the last bite."

Jack's eyes flicked to Eve and back to Harmonie. Eve hadn't invited him to take more than two shots. She didn't want to worry about consent or deaden his nerves. The flush that darkened his neck was all hers. All theirs.

He scooted to the edge of his chair and leaned toward Harmonie. He started to reach out a hand but she shook her head. His swallow brought a surge to Eve's pulse and Harmonie's lips parted. Beautiful lips, dark and full. Eve flashed on images of pressing herself against them, biting them, but she waited.

Jack leaned toward Harmonie and his mouth fell open. His tongue looked soft and wide. It filled the bottom of his mouth and curled to cradle the flesh Harmonie placed inside. As she slowly pulled her fingers out, she drew her fingernail across his bottom lip. He left his mouth open, the prawn cupped by his tongue. Very well trained.

Harmonie curled her finger under his chin and pressed upward. Jack held her eyes and chewed the morsel. When his eyelids drooped, Eve approved of his enjoyment. He was more than a bit of a sensualist. The meal he'd fed her on the beach had clued her in, but this sealed it.

"Jack." His attention rocketed to her. "Harmonie and I are poly, and we'd like to fuck you. Co-top you."

He swallowed the tart mouthful.

Harmonie put a hand on the arm of his chair. "Are you interested in figuring out if we want to do any of the same things tonight?"

Jack tried to take a deep breath, but it stuttered in his nose. Eve saw his diaphragm flutter under his air-dried shirt. He tried again.

Harmonie didn't look, but Eve could feel her growing arousal. Harmonie's hand slid toward Eve and she picked it up, leaning forward in her chair. On the edges of their seats. Even if he had an exclusive relationship or just didn't want to be with them, they'd dine out on the influx of sexual tension for a week.

Eve tried to rein in her domineering vibe. Negotiation should be done with a clear head and without pressure. Eve couldn't contain a small smile. *Except those internal pressures that drive us all.*

"I'd love that, but I have to tell you. You two scare me to death."

Eve's cunt jumped, and Harmonie's nails bit into the cushion on Jack's chair. Skillful flattery and a turn-on as sure as a hand on a clit for predatory tops like her. He spoke their language.

Harmonie said dryly, "We don't want anyone to die tonight."

Eve couldn't help it. "Except *la petit mort*." Harmonie snorted, and Eve laughed out loud.

Jack looked surprised, then said, "Huh." Probably as close as he could come to a laugh while strung so tightly.

Eve waved away her little joke. "I'll start with this. Jack, I sleep with people of all genders, but I don't have straight sex. Your gender is your own business, but if you're too manly to be queer with us, you're in the wrong place."

CHAPTER EIGHT

E ve's bald statement took the haze off the evening. Suddenly, Jack could see the pattern of hibiscus flowers in the lounger cushions and the uneven glazing on the bowls. The scent of sea and candlewicks twined with tequila fumes and lime.

His thoughts cleared with his vision. Whatever was between Eve and Harmonie, they were using poly and kinky language. They couldn't have been any clearer about the basic shape of what they wanted from him.

He couldn't shake the fear that they were teasing him. That sense didn't come from anything they'd done or said, just from the feeling that he couldn't possibly get this lucky. He wouldn't get what he wanted unless he dove in, though the risk felt dangerous.

And what, exactly, did they want?

Jack looked at the tequila bottle, thinking he wouldn't mind easing some of his tension. Eve shook her head, a tiny motion that told him he'd already tuned in to her in a submissive way. He never would have caught such a subtle signal otherwise.

"Well." All or nothing. *Here's goes honesty.* "I'm queer as a three-hundred-dollar bill and kinky as an old hose."

Harmonie laughed and Eve's famous mouth did that thing. One side rose, then the other, then her teeth broke into view. He'd seen the series of motions a hundred times on television, but this time, he'd made it happen.

He went on, with a mental note that Eve's eyes always went to his throat when he swallowed. "I'm wound like an eight-day clock right now, deeply attracted to both of you. It's pretty overwhelming, but the specific nature of it is submissive, sexual, and service oriented."

"Wonderful," said Harmonie, her voice smoky and thick.

He looked between them. "Co-topping as equals, or are one of you also topping the other?" He left the direction open, though he was pretty sure he could see the dynamic.

Eve grinned. "I'm the top top. But it's nice to hear that you don't assume."

Jack figured he'd trot out the script. "I'm transmasculine and still feeling my way around what that means for me. The body I have gives me a lot of pleasure and creates some really uncomfortable moments at the same time. I've called yellow around dysphoria more than pain. No body parts are off-limits, though anything more than rubbing outside my asshole requires more in-the-moment checking in. My safer sex requirements are gloves or condoms for penetration, no blood spatter or sharing, and, well, I'll use dental dams if you want, but it's not important to me. I use red to mean stop the whole scene and yellow to ask for a change in direction." The comfortable rhythm of the quick negotiation eased some of his tension.

Eve nodded. "Anything you particularly want to or don't want to do? Can you list your hard noes?"

"Sure. Hard noes. Piss, shit, humiliation, feminization. For a first time, no face slapping. Pulling my hair pisses me off." He stopped at Eve's questioning look. "Not on the no list, just a warning so you can expect it." He wished for water. "I want to get my face in both your pussies if you'll allow it. I'll service you sexually however you want, though I'm not packing and"—he raised his hands and looked around—"I'm without all my tools. I don't especially want to take lonely pain tonight, facing away or without a lot of contact, though I love being caned."

Harmonie hummed. "Thank you for that. What a lovely breakdown of what you want and don't want." She scooted back in her chair and folded her legs under. "I'm soft femme and especially love being cupped and held in ways that emphasize my feminine shape. My asshole is off-limits and kissing usually puts me in subspace so we'll avoid that this time. When I'm receiving service, I like to give lots of orders, but not conflicting or impossible ones. I'm not into humiliating others, though I enjoy it sometimes from the other side. Our safer-sex rules match yours just fine, though we may have to get more specific about blood if we pull out the needles." She sent him a fleeting smile at his flinch. "I want to make you get me off, and I may want to spank you or hurt your nipples to motivate you. Your...what do you call your genitalia?"

"Um. I'm still working that out." When she waited for more, Jack sighed. This part was hard. "If it's hard and I'm thrusting it, it's usually my cock. If it's being rubbed, it's my clit. I usually prefer to hear about my hole and my asshole, if you know what I mean. That whole area, though. It's my crotch, I guess."

Harmonie reached out. Maybe someday he'd get to a point where the emotional charge disappeared, but until then, he found comfort in putting his hand in hers.

"Thanks, Jack. Guide us in the moment and we'll try not to use gendered language too much." Harmonie glanced at Eve and got an agreeable nod.

He tried to smile. "Thanks."

"Well, back to me." She squeezed and released his hand. "You said you like caning. How about other kinds of impact? Open-handed smacks, especially on and around your crotch?"

"Sometimes I love it; sometimes I take it for my top." Her grin made him tip his head warily. "Can't wait to find out what evil plans you're making behind that sweet face."

She winked. "I'm putting the harm in Harmonie."

Eve had watched their interaction silently, but now she laughed. "I'm not the only cheeseball at the party." Her face sobered slowly and silence settled before she spoke. Her dynamic fascinated him. He couldn't stop thinking that she was a performer, that she was used to controlling people thousands at a time. "If we agree to play, you will call me Evrim in scene." He started, recognizing her birth name. It came to him suddenly. Evrim Nesin. "That's not permission to be disrespectful. It's a requirement that you put as much obedience and submission into serving me as you would using generic terms like Mistress. I want you to serve me, not some picture of your dream domme. Can you do that?"

Jack's eyes widened. It was as though she'd read his mind. Of course, who would know better what it was to embody a fantasy? Who would have to work harder to be seen as a real person? Sympathy struggled with a mocking voice that thought, poor little rich girl. "Yes, Evrim, I can."

She half-smiled. "You know better, Jack. We're not in scene yet."

He shook his head, then nodded. Right. He needed to focus.

"I'll instruct you as to what I want and how I want you to handle me in the moment. Don't jump the gun and you won't cross any of my limits." Reasonable. "I want your service in both sexual and more mundane ways. Are you willing to do things like fetching blankets, pouring drinks, things like that?" She barely waited for his affirmation. "I can be voracious and may want to eat you up. Biting?"

He wrinkled his nose. "Big bites are great, but little ones can be hard to take."

"I'm not asking if you can take it. I'm asking if I have permission to give it."

Oops. "Yes."

"How much time do we have?"

Jack jolted. All he'd left behind on *Lysistrata* flashed in his mind, but going back was worse than unappealing. With the music's volume down, he hoped that everyone was asleep, including poor Marie. If they weren't?

He shouldn't have stayed.

Fuck. He couldn't want anything less than he wanted to limit their time together.

Eve watched him closely while he grappled with his wish to say he could stay all night. Her head moved back and forth to the sensuous music, hypnotizing him. An hour wouldn't hurt. Several hours, though? What if the mothers were still up, torturing Marie?

"An hour."

Eve nodded. "It seems so little." She grilled him quickly, running through a series of implements—floggers, canes, paddles, single tail whips, and far more, including different materials of construction—and absorbed his yes or no to each. She didn't take any notes, and he was fascinated by her recall when she summarized the list at the end.

Harmonie must have noticed his surprise. She said, "Eve can play a song back after hearing it once. She can even play multiple parts of a song on different instruments. She won't forget."

Eve hadn't taken her eyes off him. "Harmonie and I have long-standing agreements in place and you don't need to know all of them." Eve stood and looked down at Harmonie. "Do you agree to these conditions for play?"

"Yes, Eve."

"Are you ready to start?"

"Yes, Evrim."

Jack blinked. Nice. He imagined that they would mark the end of their scene with something similar, a mirror image where Evrim became Eve again.

"Jack." He looked up at her. "Do you agree to these conditions for play?"

He repeated what Harmonie had modeled for him. "Yes, Eve."

"Are you ready to start?" Eve's eyes narrowed, and the candlelight danced across their deep darkness.

He swallowed, just to see her eyes drop to his throat. A last act of control. "Yes, Evrim."

Harmonie pounced. He hadn't even seen her stand, but she had moved behind him. She pulled his arms straight over his head and Evrim dragged his shirt up his body to his captured wrists.

"Oh, lovely color," Harmonie said, when his back tattoo was revealed. "It's a compass rose," she told Evrim.

"Nice." Evrim pulled a lever, and Jack's chair back fell. He tensed abruptly, jerking in Harmonie's hands at the crack of wood hitting wood. She pulled him down flat on the lounger and held his arms over the edge.

Evrim said, "Don't open your mouth."

He had no time to signal his agreement. She hiked up her long sleeveless shirt and straddled his face. Her black hair was long, almost wispy, and trimmed on the edges. His quick attempt to memorize what he was seeing disappeared in the smell and feel of Evrim's cunt. Generous lips, long and complicated, dragged lightly over his nose, down his chin, up and over his forehead. In seconds, his entire face was covered in Evrim's cunt juice and he stole breaths when his nose was free. He pulled against Harmonie's hold as a distraction, fearing he'd forget and open his mouth with the sudden desperate desire to taste Evrim's cunt.

The hands on his wrists tightened brutally. Harmonie's strength surprised him, but she eased her hold when he stopped pulling. Evrim settled lower, not just wiping her labia on him but pressing down, spreading them against his nose and chin. She tipped her hips back, and the motion tucked his chin just inside her cunt. A hard breath escaped from his nose, but he managed to keep his lips together through the jolt.

Evrim stayed there and he opened his eyes against the stickiness in his eyelashes. She smelled tangy and rich, and he almost, almost licked his lips. Her shirt covered his face, and the candlelight barely silhouetted her belly and breasts. Her cunt and the shirt withdrew, and he saw her, arms above her head as she threw off the shirt. Thighs like pillars, black and pink cunt, soft belly, softer breasts, strong chin, hair falling everywhere. Click. What a picture. He hoped he'd have that image in his head for the rest of his life.

In the next instant, Harmonie twisted his hands and pulled them between her legs. "Curl them," she said. He cast his eyes over his head and watched Harmonie latch on to Evrim's nipple, soft in its wide areola. His fingers became his new focus as they were tucked between thick, crinkly hair and into fat lips. She pushed one of his hands back to her opening and released Evrim's nipple to say, "Give me two fingers." He pulled three fingers in and left two for her to thrust onto. Soft, so soft, lumpy and smooth in different parts. She wiggled her hips until his other fingers cupped her clit, between her cunt lips but over her hood. "Yes, like that. Pull a little at the end of my stroke."

When he complied, she groaned. Jack's world split between the awkward service he provided Harmonie and Evrim's cunt, just out of his reach. Evrim stroked Harmonie's hair and smirked at Jack. "You want this?" she asked.

He nodded and kept his mouth closed while he answered, "Mmm-hmm."

Her smirk turned wicked. "You are such a good boy. Imagine you remembering to keep your mouth closed when you're wrist deep in cunt and soaked to the eyebrows with my cream. I am impressed, Jack, and you get a treat." She lowered toward him and he pressed his lips together. He couldn't keep them still and she paused.

Harmonie slowly rubbed herself on his fingers, her clit growing in his hand and the walls of her cunt expanding. "Give me another finger, Jack."

He uncurled a finger, distracted from Evrim's hovering cunt, and added it to the two in Harmonie. Evrim's labia touched his nose and withdrew. She coaxed him with her voice and with her flesh. "Soften your lips. Keep your teeth together, but let me pull your lips open."

Soft hair, then satiny flesh, sang against his lips. Evrim's scent strengthened as her labia pulled his lower lip down, then pushed it back up. "Open your mouth and stick out your tongue. Just a little, yes, soft and flat. I imagined this when you ate the prawn from Harmonie's hand. Your tongue on my cunt lips, pushing my clit out into the open. Yes, you've got it."

Jack didn't try to lap at her or thrust. He firmed his neck to stay where she needed him and let go of all the tension from his forehead, his cheeks, his jaws, and tongue. He lost himself in the flood of sensation, hands surrounded by fat cunt, face smashed. As Evrim settled her ass on his collarbones and moved her cunt on his mouth, he caught glimpses of her pushing Harmonie's shift off her shoulders to be caught by her hips and her hands, which still held Jack's wrists in a changing grip that clued him in on the best angles for his fingers. While Jack drowned in cunt, he got flashbulb visions. Evrim twisting and pulling Harmonie's nipples. Harmonie nursing like a calf, butting her head into Evrim's huge, heavy breast.

Evrim's belly pushing out when she lowered her face to Harmonie's and took her mouth.

Evrim's hips took up a faster rhythm, and Jack firmed his tongue just enough to stay put under her hard thrusts. Harmonie crushed his fingers into her clit and rubbed so fast he couldn't help. For the first time since Evrim had brought her cunt back to his face, Jack became aware of the agonizing throb in his crotch. He pulled with his inside muscles and squeezed his legs together. Just a little come, please, just an echo from theirs.

Harmonie had been moaning since she stopped giving him directions, the only breaks coming when her mouth was full of some part of Evrim. Now her voice rose in pitch and volume, little yips taking over when Evrim pinched her nipples brutally hard. Harmonie seemed to fight her orgasm, pushing it back and bringing it forward again and again, until Evrim said with gravel in her voice, "Come."

Harmonie jerked and her cunt spasmed against Jack's fingers. She lightened the press of his fingers on her clit and flattened them to work it from side to side. She wailed and the walls of her cunt sucked at his fingers, then tried to push them out. He kept them stiff and let her cervix rub against his fingertips on each push.

Evrim hadn't stopped moving, but she had slowed, distracted, he assumed, by soaking up the wild waves of energy off her lover. As Harmonie slowed, inside and out, Evrim looked down at him. "How are you doing, Jack?" She didn't stop grinding so he hummed and blinked furiously. "Nod if you're okay." He jerked his head up and down.

Okay? Fuck. He couldn't be better. The dark hair of her cunt disappeared, then reappeared as lighter fuzz across the bottom of her belly. It pulled in when she stretched upward and pushed out when she leaned over to kiss Harmonie again. The broad crescents of her heavy breasts lay on her ribs.

Evrim wrapped her arms around Harmonie and heaved. Harmonie released Jack's wrists and rose in Evrim's arms. She straddled Jack's arms and face. Suddenly, he could see nothing but dark and darker bellies pressed together, wispy black hair with tightly coiled black hair just above, two cunt smells in his nostrils and heavy pressure on his chest. Harmonie's cunt touched his forehead and lifted with Evrim's ebb and flow. Her thighs tightened, and he realized he still couldn't move his arms. They were trapped against his ears by her legs, squeezed so tight he couldn't hear beyond the blood raging in his vessels.

Evrim's clit grew harder against his tongue and she dragged it in figure eights around his mouth. He was helpless to act, helpless to move, just there to serve Her need. He needed nothing else in that moment, just to be the instrument of Her pleasure. His own throbbing fell away from his awareness and Her pulsing, pushing, pressing cunt became his world.

Two bodies above him, writhing together, sliding and pushing into each other, a cunt in his mouth and one filling his vision. His sense of time fractured along with his attention to his own body. He breathed when he could and grew lightheaded, smothered in need and joy.

Evrim jerked, then jerked again and again. She switched from long motions to a short thrust between his tongue and his top teeth. He milked her clit with his tongue in tiny twitches as she thrust and he heard her answering cry, even through the flesh of Harmonie's thighs and his arms and the rampaging flood of his need.

She came on and on, stilling, only to push against him again. A hard press started her up again, twitching and yelling, and a soft swipe soothed her until the next press. He lost track of the dynamic, knew only an ecstatic state that never had to end.

Eventually, it did. Harmonie withdrew with a stroke of his arms. He'd closed his eyes at some point and when hands bracketed his face, he opened them to see Evrim holding him. She kept her hands on him as she unfolded her legs to either side of the lounger she'd been kneeling on, groaning at the stiffness. She slipped down his body and covered it with hers, cradling his head as she nuzzled his fattened lips. They felt ready to burst when she took one in her mouth and bit down, slowly, inexorably. She sucked and released it, then sniffed at his cheeks, his nose, his chin.

Evrim shifted to sit next to him, and Jack lay where he'd been put. He felt like he'd been through a dozen orgasms himself, but no one had touched his crotch the whole time. He blinked up at Harmonie, glowing in the candlelight as she stretched. Her naked body curved deeply at her lower back. Her breasts looked small, almost light compared to her ass and hips, and they were tipped by long, dark nipples.

"Isn't she beautiful?" Evrim leaned on Jack as she asked, stretching out across his chest.

"Gorgeous." He looked up at Evrim. She rested her head in her hand, elbow on his shoulder. Her breasts slid against each other and came to rest against his ribs.

She looked down at him. "You may lower your arms."

He grimaced. His arms were tight and stiff from being extended so long. Evrim didn't help, which probably would have hurt worse than doing it himself. When he got them below his shoulders, he didn't know what to do with the one on her side. Her lips bowed on one side and she put his hand on her breast.

She'd said not to do anything she didn't tell him to, so he didn't squeeze or run his fingers across her nipple, though he could almost feel it.

"Well," she said, "that took the edge off."

He started to grin, but his lips were too puffy and tight.

"Poor baby. Did I hurt you?"

He blinked and nodded, pouting a little. She smiled at his playfulness.

Harmonie appeared, pulling her shift back on. He couldn't remember her taking it all the way off, but he wasn't all that surprised. "Thirsty."

Jack jerked, but Evrim had him pinned. She said, "Don't worry about serving right now. I'm too lazy to move." She looked up at Harmonie. "I'll have lemonade, please."

"Jack?"

Jack tried to speak and had to clear his throat. Evrim and Harmonie both laughed, and he had to laugh along. Whoa. He'd been under. "Lemonade sounds lovely."

"Sure." Harmonie disappeared.

"How are you doing?"

Jack took the question seriously, as a check-in. "I'm floating and lightheaded, coming out of subspace pretty slowly." He hesitated, then asked the question that had started circling. "Are we done?"

Evrim stroked his collarbone. "We're surfacing. I know we talked about a lot more than we did, but we did a lot. That was intensely satisfying, Jack."

"For me too." Jack hesitated, shifted his head on the cushion. "I'd love to play with you again, when I don't have other responsibilities."

"Hold on a minute." Evrim sat up, but stayed next to him on the cushion. He realized that Harmonie had returned with their drinks. "Ready to sit up?"

Jack pushed himself up and blinked. "Whew."

Harmonie laughed again. "She's not gentle when she sits on your face."

Evrim lifted a hand. "Let's do this right. Harmonie, thank you for your service."

Harmonie nodded. "You're welcome, Eve. And, Jack, thank you for your service."

"You're welcome, Harmonie." Again, he caught their rhythm.

"Jack, thank you for your service."

He was reluctant to release her formally, but it was time. "You're welcome, Eve."

"Drink up." Eve followed her own order. "Or don't. We're not in scene anymore."

"Yeah, I caught that." Her smile warmed him.

Harmonie stretched and yawned. She looked between them and said, "I think you two have an invitation to discuss. I'm going to head to bed."

Eve reached upward and said, "Good night, Harmonie."

Harmonie leaned down for a kiss and a caress. "Snuggle you soon."

Jack downed the lemonade. He was thirstier than he'd realized. Harmonie walked into the house, and Eve drew her fingers down his arm.

"Your tattoos are gorgeous. Turn around and let me see the compass rose." He swung his legs obediently to the other side of the lounger and shivered when her fingers touched his back. "That's a wonderful version. It looks familiar somehow."

"It's from a portolan chart made by Jorge Aguilar in 1492. It's the oldest signed and dated Portuguese chart, but we've been the navigators and explorers since way before that even. These things were considered state secrets, they were so accurate."

"Where is this?"

He arched his back so she could see better. And so she'd stroke him again. "The Mediterranean and North Africa. The Straits of Gibraltar on my left shoulder and Sicily on my right."

Eve came around to his side. She stroked his forearms, tracing his anchors and then following the chain up his biceps to where they met across his shoulders. "And I've never seen such realistic anchors. They're usually cartoonish."

He turned again and brought his forearms together. "A CQR and a Herreshoff, the two types I've used most of my life."

"Lovely." She considered him with narrowed eyes. "About playing again. Let's talk tomorrow. We can check in by phone or email. Any talk of further dates can wait until then."

Jack almost frowned, but she was right. She hadn't tested his physical limits or his ability to take pain, but she'd put him way down into subspace. "Let's do it by phone."

She gave him her phone and he put his info in. He filled out all the spaces—why be coy with ways to contact him—and saved the contact. "I'll be sailing early in the day. Later would be better."

"I'll text first to be sure you're available."

Jack didn't know what else to say. He cast about for a way to get them talking, a subject he could use to prove he was a scintillating conversationalist, but his long day suddenly hit him.

"Come on, Jack." Eve chivvied him to his feet. "Let's get you home."

Eve handed him his shirt and he pulled it over his head. It smelled like ocean. "It's going to be a long swim."

"No, it's not." She pulled her T-shirt back on, still not bothering with underwear or pants. He followed, docile, as she walked out on her little pier. A wooden canoe drifted below, gleaming in the moonlight, and she climbed down the ladder to it. He followed again and didn't argue when she took the paddle and set off for *Lysistrata*.

At the side of his sailboat, he stood in the canoe and grasped *Lysistrata's* boarding ladder. Eve set down her paddle and stepped over the middle seat. She wrapped him in a firm hug. Jack wasn't too tired to feel her in this first full-body contact and stir at her soft, rounded heat. She kissed him and ran her fingers along his hairline.

"Sleep well."

"You too, Eve."

Jack climbed the steps and stumbled blindly to bed.

CHAPTER NINE

E ve stepped off the bottom rung of the ladder and turned to look over the buzzing, whirring servers in their neat ranks. Strangely sexy, their cool blue LED lights blinked or shone steady, reflecting softly off the matte black finish of the racks across each row. A blinking light represented someone accessing the information stored there, a human being reaching out for musical connection.

She gave them that connection. She and Harmonie made it possible for the music to find its own level, outside of the industry that couldn't care less about the artists. Her lip curled at the thought that *she* would be the one charged with a crime and accused of stealing from artists, when so few thrived inside the system.

She felt it begin and scrambled away from the old groove of hatred and bitterness, the undertow that sucked the energy out of her and left her useless. Hopeless.

Work would help. The workstation computers beeped as she started them up. She sat in the desk chair and swung it slowly back and forth. She'd slept deeply after playing with Harmonie and Jack the night before, but the energy she'd felt on awakening gave way to sadness.

If only she could think about Marc without the depression taking over. His friendship had added a personal dimension to her move from performance to production. She'd made the switch so she could advocate for artists like she had been at nineteen, promising but naive, and so easy to exploit. It had gone well enough at first, her first few releases garnering her awards and acclaim as a producer.

She'd found "High Wire" on SoundCloud and had known immediately that this band, Audion, could push pop music to new heights. The song needed her, though, just begged her to give it texture and tone. She emailed them directly—they had no manager, no booking agent, just a song recorded at their local pirate radio station studio and a dozen notebooks of material. She'd nurtured them until they had a solid album's worth of songs.

Marc Fern, the lead singer, had become a close friend. Their mutual musical respect formed the basis of the relationship, and he'd never importuned her sexually. He'd taken Harmonie's presence in her life as a no-go sign. She wasn't certain whether she regretted that, but she hadn't wanted to mix things up while producing their album. His need for support, for praise, drew him to her strength.

Even with a bitter battle and her previous successes, she couldn't get them the deal they deserved. The record label simply refused to give them more control, more freedom, or a bigger slice of the pie. She hated the final draft of the contract but gave in and encouraged them to sign it. If they didn't get the album recorded, the songs would get stale and the band would get sloppy. She made sure they played live regularly, to keep up their chops and stoke the fire that a live audience lit.

"High Wire" was the irresistible single she'd known it would be, and it went straight to the top of the charts. The hook drew from a decades-old song by one of rock's most powerful bands, and that sample ruined everything. When the old guys sued, the record label hung Audion out to dry. Eve had been protected through the specificities of the boilerplate producer's contract. When the judgment came through, the plaintiffs had been awarded a huge sum, to be taken out of any further earnings by Audion and, in case of the dissolution of the band, each individual band member. The moment Marc understood that everything he would ever create was in hock, he walked out on his balcony and jumped to his death on the rocks below.

Flying to Lajes das Flores, the southernmost town of the westernmost island of the Azores, had taken all her strength. Marc's family desperately needed to understand what had happened to the boy they'd known as Marcelo Fernandez. They made her welcome, begged her for stories of his successes, wept at the stories of his failures. They'd needed to feel that they weren't at fault for Marc's immigration to the US, and Eve had been able to convince them that he never could have stayed on Flores. He needed to play to larger audiences, needed to be heard by the world.

They promised her their friendship, no matter what, for her honesty and the valor she'd shown in bringing them the news herself. Lajes das Flores simmered in her imagination as a secret bolt-hole, a place she could go if her world fell apart. The Fernandez family would take care of her...a strangely comforting thought when strength and independence were bedrocks of her self-image.

Her attempt to change the record industry by putting herself between the moguls and the musicians had backfired. When she'd returned to the US, she had flailed for some way of turning her grief into rage so that she could take it out on the industry, on the lawyers, on the concept of copyright itself. Harmonie had provided a wailing wall, and it was in her arms that Eve had come up with the plan they were executing on Anne Bonny Isle.

The old charts called it Decker Island, but she knew it for what it was—the perfect location for a pirate. A previous owner had run cable across the sea floor, heavy-duty and fast. The servers chilling across the room connected to the Web, and she was the spider.

Even as she wrestled her thoughts around to the work, she recognized her coping mechanism for what it was—a way to turn the sorrow and rage into action, time after time. The guilt for releasing "High Wire" with the extra hundredth of a second that turned the sampled riff into a copyright violation? She drowned that guilt in righteous indignation. The shame of making it through unscathed and the horror of failing to predict Marc's jump faded with cleansing concentration.

She did the rounds, the regularity of the task smoothing her fingers' motion just like with all the other instruments she'd mastered through hard work and repetition. The record companies put pretty good security in place, but not world-class. She had paid dearly to learn how to access their systems and nothing they put up stood in her way for long. Her interest and aptitude had surprised Harmonie, a hobby hacker since high school, but Eve felt that it was only right she put her own hands on the keyboard. She couldn't leave the work to others, and her unexpected talent seemed to prove that she was on the right track.

She had to remove the pillars of the record industry with her own hands.

The main pillar was money, of course, but connections kept the money flowing away from independent artists and companies. The big dogs bragged that they could open doors, but their bigger power lay in closing them for the blacklisted.

Digital recording technology like ProTools helped independent producers. Studios with perfect sound were easier to build since music went digital, though without tons of cash, they would never be overrun with great sound engineers who'd show up whenever inspiration hit.

The goddamn tour buses. A band that had driven all over the country in a van, sleeping on floors, would sign almost any deal that would get them a fucking bus.

Eve heard a noise and jumped. Fuck. She'd gotten all wrapped up again. The trap door's seal released with a whomp and Harmonie's bare foot appeared. Eve shoved back from the computer and prepared to appreciate the view. Hell with the music industry. She had better things to think about.

Harmonie's shapely calf, for instance, her knees and thighs. Her toes curled on the chill metal rungs and her legs flashed with her hurry to get down. Swinging hips, then the long curve of her waist and back. Her locs twisted together and piled atop her head and rings flashed on her fingers.

By the time Harmonie's foot touched the cold concrete floor, pleasant tension had replaced Eve's ease. She crossed to Harmonie and trapped her against the ladder. A knee parted her legs, and Harmonie pressed her ass back. A long deep breath and a squeeze, and Eve released her.

Harmonie turned, wry smile in place. "Good afternoon to you too."

Eve touched the opal pendant resting just under Harmonie's collarbones. "What's up?"

"You've been down here for hours and I thought I'd see what you found."

Eve looked around as though the answer lay somewhere in the room. "Have I?" She flexed her shoulders. Perhaps she was a little stiff. She had no idea it had been so long. "Nothing new from the record labels. I trolled through the most recent emails from the A&R reps and most of them were blah blah."

"No new bands?"

"Not a one. They're all recycling recommendations from last year." Eve went back to her rolling chair and reclined in it.

Harmonie followed across the room and sat with her feet folded under her legs. "Anyway." She laced her fingers together. "About Jack."

A heavy pulse in her chest distracted Eve. "What about him?"

"What do you want to do about him?"

"I'm pretty sure he'll stay away if I ask him right." The thud came again, harder.

Harmonie searched her face. "And will you? Ask him to stay away?"

Eve forced herself to meet Harmonie's eyes. Would she? "He smells good, Harm."

Exasperation crossed Harmonie's expression, chased by resignation. "I had a feeling it was going to be like this."

Eve barely controlled the urge to ask, like what? She knew, and she wouldn't do Harmonie the disservice of pretending she didn't. "It's a fit. I don't know what to say." She rose and moved around the room restlessly. "He's mine somehow. We'll dance some more, but he's mine."

"What are you going to do with him? Bring him here? Leave him on the mainland? Can you keep him away from this?"

When Harmonie gestured at the server racks, Eve slammed her hands on the worktable. "I don't know! I don't have to know right now."

Harmonie's soothing tone scraped at Eve's pride. "You want him. I get that. But he might not be a good option for you. He's back and forth all the time. He couldn't be any better situated to bring unwanted attention to us here."

Eve forced a sardonic grin, stiff with irritation. "What about the old saying? Keep your friends close?"

"I don't think we want our enemies any closer."

The thick beat of her heart and the sharpness of her vision screamed danger, but maybe it wasn't having Jack that would hurt her. She turned away. The need was strong, harsh, and undeniable—she had to claim Jack. He was hers.

The acrylic CD-R cover hit the cinder-brick wall with a crash and rattle, but she craved the ring of breaking glass.

Jack sat at Justin's kitchen table, an Ethernet cable plugged into his laptop. Sometimes Wi-Fi just didn't cut it.

He texted Tigger "almost time" and got back a set of symbols he didn't bother figuring out. It was safe to assume she was excited for him.

When the charter from hell had ended—without tips—he'd gone directly to Tigger's house to spill the news. Most of it. He'd kept Eve's name out of it, again, though Tigger about burst with curiosity. He'd gotten Eve's text while he was there, so he took her call in Tigger's room for privacy. Much good that did, since he immediately told her everything that had happened, including Eve's request for a video chat date.

Justin had agreed to let him use his connection directly, so Jack had the dubious pleasure of staring down a cross-stitched turkey from sometime in the seventies. When Justin's parents had died, he'd been in his mid-twenties, living on his own. He'd inherited their house and moved in, but he hadn't moved anything out. Or cleaned much, from the looks of the floors and the stickiness in odd places.

Regardless, he had super-fast Internet, and Jack checked the weather while he waited for Eve's call.

When the video chat notice beeped, his pulse picked up speed and he glanced at the computer's clock. Right on time. He answered the call, a little window showing his goofy expression popping up inside the bigger one that resolved into the image of a megastar.

He held on to his smile, but shock stopped his breath. Eve La Sirena smirked from his computer screen and, for a moment, he couldn't grasp that she was looking back at him, communicating with him in real time. He'd seen concert footage, music videos, interviews, late-night TV performances—all with this face looking into a camera from some mythical location, never with the slightest possibility of reciprocity.

When she smiled wider, he struggled to remember that she was actually responding to him. She said, "Hello, Jack."

"Goddamn. This is beyond strange."

Her lips pursed and her eyebrows rose. "How so?" Her voice sounded agreeable, but her expression confirmed that he was about to put his foot in his mouth.

"Eve, hi. I'm sorry to be so rude. A famous person just addressed me directly from my computer screen, and it's pretty surreal."

Her mouth relaxed. "Not at all. I am very, completely real." She tipped her head to one side. "How do you feel about that?"

He thought he read mild curiosity from her. Maybe he'd be able to pass it off. "Pretty excited, to be honest. If I discovered I'd fantasized the night we played, I'd worry about my sanity."

"You've never fantasized about me before?"

The flush hit his face so fast that his skin felt tight. Even his eyes burned. Maybe he'd combust and avoid answering.

"Oh, you have!"

That rich voice, filled with delight, drew him back into the conversation. She beamed at him from the screen. "That isn't creepy to you?"

She waved a hand. "I'm not responsible for nor—usually— affected by other people's fantasies. So no, not creepy. Actually, I work hard to touch people. If I didn't stimulate people, I'd be a failure."

He managed a grin. "Anything but."

"Thank you." She tipped her head in gracious acknowledgment of his compliment, then shrugged. "Of course, it's much more pleasurable to hear about the fantasies when the attraction is mutual. As this one is."

The flush was warmer, more of a glow.

"So tell me."

"Tell you what?"

"Tell me a fantasy you've had about me. One from before we met."

Jack stared at the screen. Eve's eyes didn't meet his directly, so she was looking at his image and not the camera. "Seriously?" His pulse picked up again.

When her mouth did its three-stage blossom into a full smile, Jack wanted to do anything she said. When her eyes rose to stare directly from the screen at him, he could intellectualize all he wanted about her looking at the camera. What he couldn't do was resist.

"Imagine me lying on a hard, narrow bunk in the fo'c'sle of the schooner *Mary Elizabeth*. I'd just gotten back in bed after escorting the night's fling off the boat. I shared the fo'c'sle with five other crew members, but the others were still out at the bar. She and I had fucked on the ladder, my cock strapped on and her clothes all over the deck. I'd put on 'Rogue's Gallery' to set the mood."

"Oooh, *that* mood."

A rush gave him goose bumps. Of course she knew what that song did to people. To him. "When I got back to my bunk, the album had continued and 'Hard to Miss' came on." He studied her face. What was he about to reveal to her? What would she expose of herself in return?

"Different mood." Eve stroked her lower lip, pulling it between thumb and forefinger.

"Different mood altogether. I always feel such a conflict in that song. Brutal and tender, sad and exalted." He trembled on the edge of toning down the story, keeping the truth private, but she sighed at his explanation of the song and he knew that he could trust her. "I have a granite cock, no base, just smooth, hard rock with a twist chiseled into it. That thing has no mercy, just like the singer, just like your voice flowing over me inescapably. I heard a tenderness that made me believe you could be brutal, because that's what I needed. I fucked myself as hard as I could, pounding deep, imagining you doing it to me. Sad because you were just a fantasy. Exalted because the fantasy was so rich. So real."

Eve's mouth had fallen open as she listened with razor sharp attention. Her tongue ran across the edges of her top teeth and Jack could feel them sinking into his flesh. His breath shortened and he shivered.

She said, "I've known so many bottoms who can't find a top who trusts their hunger. I believe in that hunger. Mine is the perfect complement to it, the hunger to press so much sensation and emotion onto a bottom that they are full to bursting. I wrote it about not getting that, about missing the mental landscape that a great scene achieves. About finding it unexpectedly in a hookup and knowing that its unrepeatable nature is part of its strength. About the way that my strokes are pulled, magnetically, to the tenderest places on a vulnerable body. I wrote 'Hard to Miss' for you."

"I heard you." Jack could barely form the words. "You spoke to me."

"And to others." She nodded in acknowledgment of her own words. "We're not alone in these feelings."

He took a deep breath. Her spell wasn't broken, but she had put him back on his own two feet. "And thank whatever for that." The conversation's turn felt good and right. They'd gotten real deep, real fast, and he needed a breather.

"Do you play in public?"

"I do, some. I like Puss'n'Boots, the local BDSM club, a lot, but it's about more than having a place to get my rocks off. The community is important to me."

Eve's expression turned wistful. "I miss that. I used to go to clubs in costume—it's not hard to avoid being recognized if I really want that—but it's been a while."

Jack weighed his knee-jerk reaction, but not for long. "I'd love a play date at the club. Would you like to go with me?"

"That…is an intriguing invitation." Eve looked more torn than she sounded. "But I really need to stay on the down-low."

"Well…" Jack thought fast. "Maybe it would be better, even more fun, if we met there and pretended not to know each other. We could do a pick-up scene." Adrenaline pumped into him when Eve pointed a long finger at him. He resisted the instinct to pull back, though of course she couldn't reach him through the screen.

"You are brilliant. Yes." Her voice had sharpened. She sounded more like Evrim. "When's the next party?"

He thought about the club schedule. "There's a pangender party on Friday, then a women-and-trans party on Saturday."

"Which do you prefer?"

"The women-and-trans parties. Last time I went to a pangender party, a forced feminization scene really freaked me out."

"How so?"

Jack wondered if he'd gotten himself into deep water here. For all he knew, Eve—the infamous bisexual—loved ff. "I don't understand why it's humiliating to be decked out like a woman. I tried to hold back my judgmental energy—"

"Don't yuk my yum."

"Right. But I think forced feminization is an expression of sexism when it's done for humiliation. Where's the analogue? Forced masculinization isn't a thing. Ergo, sexism."

"Do all expressions of oppression in BDSM play have that effect on you?"

Jack's thoughts stopped. Do all…

"When you're seeing others play, or for yourself?"

He felt the flush again. Spending too much time around Eve was going to put him at risk for heart problems. "I…hadn't thought of it that way. I don't always respond like that. There's a lot of play that seems to replicate oppression and—" he had to be honest with her "—plenty of it seems hot to me. I guess I wasn't considering that forced fem play could be done in a self-aware manner."

"Do you know any men who might be doing ff that way?"

"To be honest, I'm starting to realize that I live in a strange reality where most cis men are faded and indistinct. I have one guy friend who's a captain, but the only other cis guy I spent real time with died almost a year ago. His boat is just sitting at the dock, but I do a little maintenance here and there to keep it from rotting away." Sidetracked, and Eve's patient look signaled she was waiting for him to come back to the point. He wasn't sure what the point really was, except that cis men were alien creatures. "I come from a long line of female chauvinists, and my preferring the company of women is at least partly, perhaps largely, about avoiding engagement with men's privilege. That's one aspect of my trans masculinity. I'm trying to be myself, to whatever extent that means expressing my masculinity, leaving out my least favorite aspects of male privilege."

"Well, I have known cis males who understand their own sexism *because* they've done forced fem or other highly gendered play." She shrugged. "Maybe there was a bad dynamic in the scene you saw. Maybe you just don't know enough to say."

"I'll think on it."

"And I'd like to know more about where you come from and how you experience your gender. Another time." Eve put a hand out like she was stroking him. "You're right, though. The charge in forced feminization lies in the undesirability of being female. I don't go there myself."

"Another way we're a good fit."

"I'd like to find out where else we fit. Let's go to the party Saturday. You show up just after Puss'n'Boots opens. I want you to put yourself out there, but refuse all offers. When I arrive, do not come to me. I'll come to you. Sound good?"

"Sounds great."

"Do you have additional limits when playing in public? Penetration or nudity limits, anything like that?"

"At this party, where my community is pretty solid, no. Outside of this space, yes."

"In that case," her face went sly, "bring the granite cock."

Gulp. "Sure." He had to change the subject or he'd be a gibbering mess. "I don't know much about your early life. I saw somewhere that you went to a music conservatory instead of a regular high school."

That did the trick, if erasing her sexy expression had been his goal. "Yes. That's right." Her expression approached frosty.

"I wish I could have replaced high school with something I loved doing."

She thawed a bit. "It's not really like that. We did all the standard classes, plus music day in and day out. I loved the music, for the most part. It was wildly competitive, though, so much worse than the pop world. The standards were high, and the dorms were brutal."

"You lived in dorms?"

"It was a boarding school. We went through puberty with less privacy than most litters of kittens."

"Brutal. Puberty? You started there young, I guess."

"Younger than most. The whole subject bores me."

Jack laughed at her Marlene Dietrich impersonation. "My family didn't leave much to the imagination, so privacy didn't figure much in my childhood either."

Before he could get out another question, Eve stole the momentum. "What does that mean?"

Without a plan or a frame of some sort, he wasn't sure where to start the story. "Well, there were four of us in the household. Grandma, Mom, my sister, and me. With three generations of feminists in one house, I got all the info I could possibly want about sex and bodies, usually long before I wanted it."

"Sounds like its own kind of hothouse environment. Were you all usually in accord?"

"Hell no." Eve burst out laughing. "The bookshelves in my childhood living room would have thrilled someone studying the 'waves' of feminism. It was a war zone."

"Ouch. And you didn't escape, I'm sure. Knowing you named your boat *Lysistrata*, you would seem to be old-fashioned about your feminism. Can a Greek play be called first wave?"

Jack stared at Eve. Sometimes he forgot how wacky his family was, but Eve was getting the survey. "Don't you know the most traditional way of naming a boat?"

Puzzlement wrinkled her forehead. "By deciding on a name you like?"

"No." He put an extra helping of condescension in his voice, as stuffy as an Oxford don. "One names one's boat for one's mother, wife, daughter, or some combination thereof."

"Your—" the math practically wrote itself across her eyeballs "—mom?"

"Yep. My grandmother gave birth to a healthy baby girl only a couple weeks after she lost her husband, my grandfather, in one of the twentieth century's undeclared wars. My mother's name is Lysistrata."

Eve stared from the screen, frozen, for a long moment, then breathed. "Wow. Big name. I was in a production of *Lysistrata* once."

He tried to imagine that. "Modernized?"

"Semi. Sixties flower children." She batted her eyelashes. "I was fabulous."

"Of course you were." His turn to be done with the subject. "Your ancestors are Turkish, right?"

The image swung around and settled back on Eve's face, but the background had changed. It looked like she'd changed seats. "Not just ancestors. My parents immigrated to New York after I was born."

"Neat. Did you get to visit when you were a kid? Do you still have family there?"

"No and yes. My parents didn't have the money to keep me in school and make big trips." Something changed in Eve's expression. She looked softer, more vulnerable. "I've been to Turkey a handful of times as an adult, but I haven't tracked down my family."

Sensitive subject. Jack waited, then turned the conversation yet again. "I'd love to track down my Portuguese family. They're really from the Azores. I've thought about flying over, but if I sailed there, I'd show up salty. Maybe they'd welcome me more as a sailor than as a tourist."

"I love the Azores. Some of the best people I've ever met were there."

"You've been? Tell me what it's like."

"Can't. You'll just have to experience it for yourself." She pushed her hair off her shoulders. "It's a great place to run to."

"When the coppers are after me?" His joke fell flat when she nodded.

"Exactly. It'll be our escape plan. Meet me in Lajes das Flores."

"Where's that?"

"Flores is the westernmost island in the Azores archipelago, and Lajes is the southernmost town. It's the best port on the island, and everything is either up one hill or down another one. I know some people there. You'd fit right in."

For a moment, Jack wanted to laugh, but she seemed strangely serious. He tried to get back to a lighter footing. "You'll have to order for me in the restaurants. The only Portuguese dish I know is soupish."

When Eve snorted, relief filled him. "That's not Portuguese."

"Maybe not, but the Portuguese people I grew up around made it. It's poor people food—traditionally made by boiling a bone, though we used some cheap piece of meat, and a sachet of herbs, then pouring the broth over stale bread." He kissed his fingertips. "Delicious."

"Not sure you're going to find that in a restaurant, but if you get a hankering, you can make it for me."

"When we run away to the Azores."

"To the Azores." She made a toast of it, raising a glass of what looked like tea. He raised his water and drank.

And wondered.

CHAPTER TEN

Eve waited in the short line to get past the front desk of Jack's favorite BDSM club, Puss'n'Boots, amused by her pride in the patience she showed by standing in line. It had been a long time since she'd been incognito, and even longer since she hadn't rated special treatment. Sweeping past lines of waiting people got to be a way of life. Even in a place like this, she only had to speak her name to get whisked inside and fawned over, but that would ruin the whole purpose of the disguise. Was it really patience when it served her purpose?

In front of her, a leather dyke sat straight in her wheelchair, arms cocked in an elaborately casual demonstration of her defined biceps. The black leather vest covered nothing but skin and snugged against her tits and ribs and waist. She had the badass demeanor that Eve was so susceptible to—all woman, fleshy and strong at the same time. Below the vest, more leather soaked up the entryway's lights like a black hole. Her boots gleamed, though, and the buckles shone.

There was no real holdup, just a good chat going on between the paying guest and the cashier. No one seemed particularly putout, and Eve didn't let her tapping toe hit the ground. Her sandals would set up an impatient sound, and she was going for under the radar. By demeanor, at least, though not in her costume, which both concealed and revealed.

When the leather dyke spun her chair in place, turning just far enough to look up easily, Eve sighed. Maybe she wouldn't manage the silent part.

"At least my feet aren't getting tired."

Her lips tipped without her permission. "Neither are mine. See how sensible I am?" She showed off her flat sandals and the woman laughed, a good, low sound with a slow roll to it. If she took that much time with every enjoyment...Eve reminded herself she already had a date.

"I'd call you fantastic, imposing, even outrageous. Never sensible."

"Shows how little you know me."

"I'm Jane."

"Hello, Jane. I'm Amphitrite." Eve flounced her queenly robes, all orangish-red and black as though she'd walked off an ancient Greek urn. Amphitrite, the goddess of the sea, was usually depicted with nets in her hair and crab pincers winging from her temples. Eve had gone one better and made a crab pincer mask that covered her face from forehead to nose to conceal her identity. The robes themselves were diaphanous, but the corset underneath cradled her torso and plumped her breasts.

"A goddess. I should have known. Are you meeting someone, Amphitrite?"

"Here's hoping. And you?"

"My girl."

"Is she a bootblack? I can't help but notice how glorious your leathers are."

Jane preened. "Good eye. She's the bootblack at a lot of these parties, tonight included, but it doesn't look like you'll be waiting in line for her services." She took the excuse to give Eve a slow up and down look.

"Not this time, no. Besides, your services might be more to my taste." So bad. She couldn't help herself, though.

"Really?" Jane shook her head. "Because I'm not sensing a lot of bend in you."

Eve leaned at the hips, her waist held straight by the corset, to show off her cleavage. She tuned her voice low and let it throb. "There's not. But wouldn't it be fun to try?"

The intrigued cast to Jane's face shifted when the cashier said, "Hey, Jane, you're good to go in. Tigger paid for you both."

"Thanks," Jane said. She turned back to Eve and pulled a card from her vest pocket. "Get in touch if you ever want that battle. I think you're right. It would be epic."

Eve took the card with a slight bend of her head and watched Jane roll away. When she turned back to the cashier, the woman was grinning. "I'd say welcome to the club, but it looks like Jane took care of the formalities."

Eve gave a noncommittal answer and did the small bit of paperwork. She was used to private clubs that kept on the right side of the law by making everyone who wanted entry a member. It was not unusual in a world that was still frightened by consensual kink almost as much as it was fascinated by it. A fake ID maintained her privacy.

In the foyer, separated from the play space by heavy drapes, she bypassed the plain wooden rack of cubbies like the spaces for a kindergartner's lunch, since she hadn't brought a bag. A well-stocked BDSM club should have safer sex supplies, and the rest of her plans were low-tech. She drew a deep breath and pictured the thread pulling up from the crown of her head, then pulled aside the heavy brocade fabric and swept through.

Her pulse made her fingers tingle, but she didn't let her gaze dart about. The room was dim enough that peripheral vision picked up quite a lot of detail. She didn't immediately see Jack, so she stalked a long circuit around the room. First-rate equipment flowed by like trees on the banks of a river, and she noted a sling and spanking horse side-by-side in a corner.

As she turned to circle the large structures for rope play in the middle of the room, she found him.

Jack stood with his feet spread like a sailor, arms crossed over a black chest harness that came together in the middle of his back at a shiny ring, probably stainless steel. His compass rose tattoo covered the bulk of his skin, with the light scribing of chart details radiating along his shoulders and sides, disappearing into his dark blue jeans. He was in three-quarter profile, and she could see the tattooed chain loop around his arm and cross his shoulders, but not the anchors on his forearms. His tousled hair caught the light over the scene he watched, giving him a nimbus that contrasted with the dirty-boy tone of his presentation.

Eve maintained her pace without a slip, though the swelling of her flesh inside the corset ratcheted up the thrill of knowing she would have that boy. A woman, bound in what looked like miles of thin, cutting ropes, tried to scream around her gag and danced at the end of the ropes holding her upright. Wrap after wrap stretched from her wrists to her elbows, pulling them together behind her back, while more rope wraps held her knees together. The top tickled her sides in fast bursts, pinching and prodding other body parts that came within reach. She laughed at the bound woman's struggles and made some comment to Jack that Eve couldn't hear.

Jack shook his head and Eve saw his smile. Relaxed, amused, and maybe even a little smug. The couple must be friends of his. The charge built in Eve's arms and legs, making her hair stand on end. He was nowhere near subspace. She'd bring him down, and the fall was better when it started higher.

She must have come into his range of vision, because he started and turned toward her. His arms dropped away from his chest, covered only with the leather straps and a buckle so that she could see his nipples harden. She'd planned to start aloof and make him work for her attention, but she couldn't contain her sly smile. No reason to stick to a plan when an opportunity stared one straight in the face.

She wanted to walk right to him and grab him by the neck. She wanted to see his eyes widen and feel his breath catch, but, yes, a DM wandered close by. She'd have to give the impression of negotiating.

Eve stared into Jack's eyes as she approached, daring him to look away. She stopped so close his short breaths warmed her neck. The couple of inches she had on him gave her the high ground and she took it. "I want to beat you with my hands, open and fisted, and fuck you with your granite cock. Do you agree to that and the conditions for play that we set out both the night at my house and in our video chat conversation?"

"Yes, Eve." He didn't hesitate.

"Are you ready to start?"

"Yes, Evrim."

The joy burst through her. To be heard and understood, for him to remember and value her ways. What a gift.

Not that it softened her. Anything but.

"Get the cock and take care of any side trips you need to make. Meet me in that corner," she pointed, "with two bottles of water and your cock as soon as you're done. Don't change anything you're wearing." She dropped her eyes to the lump in his pants, either a packing cock or stuffing. She'd find out later.

"Yes, Evrim."

Evrim watched him walk away, nearly laughing out loud at the skip in his step. No second thoughts from this one. She turned and saw the rope top eying her. The mask hid most of Evrim's expression, but the top responded to her wink with a nod and quick smile and went back to her own play.

The DM wandered by, and Evrim pitched her voice high and light. "I'm going to play with the spanking horse and sling in that corner. Would you put a word in the ear of any watchers that I'd like quite a bit of room?"

"Using something with tails?"

The downside of community. Impertinent questions. "No, but once we move to fucking I want to be able to focus."

"Fair enough. I'll ask people to keep back." She pursed her lips. "We do have a room with a bed and a door."

"Thank you for that information." Evrim maintained her civility, but she was out of practice in having her instructions questioned. "I do prefer the sling."

"Your choice, of course." The DM's resurgent cheer grated and Evrim turned away.

Yes, she had seen what she'd expected. Chux—absorbent pads used in hospitals and for messy sex—sat in neat stacks on the shelves beside the sling, along with a huge bottle of water-based lube and a box of gloves. Eve draped the sling with a pad and put another on the spanking horse for good measure. She turned to find Jack at her side and struck as swiftly as a rattlesnake.

A groan tore through her throat at the feeling of Jack's throat under her hard hand. She squeezed the muscles on either side of his trachea and his wide eyes flickered. "Give me the cock."

He handed it over and she put it on the table without looking away from him. He kept his hands down and stood still, waiting for her to do what she would.

Evrim drew out the moment. He flushed slowly, though she wasn't cutting off his blood flow. She stared at him from inches away until his throat jerked hard against her palm and his eyelids fell to half-mast. That was the signal she'd been waiting for.

A hard, thudding blow to his chest with the side of her fist. He shuffled his feet to lean into the blows he correctly expected, and she tenderized him, beating him slowly, heavily, between his collarbone and his nipples. She switched sides, releasing his throat to do so, then used both hands, simultaneously and in a rhythm that drew the first sounds from him. Grunts, groans, signs that it was starting to hurt, that his reddening, swelling flesh was signaling its danger to his brain.

She kept going, finding the edge where he groaned without screwing up his eyes, then going over it. Her hands glowed, receiving just as much of a beating as they were providing, and Evrim gave herself a break by switching it up.

With her palms flat on his tenderized chest, she shoved hard enough that he swayed, then brought himself back with a flex of his stomach muscles. Fucking hot. She made him do it again, for the sheer pleasure of watching his body jerk, then dug her fingertips into the area she'd beaten. He flinched, his shoulders curving in as though to shield himself from the pain, but his hands remained by his sides.

"You may put your hands on my waist."

His eyes darted to hers, his surprise clear. "Thank you, Evrim."

Hmm. Telling, that. He wasn't used to having permission to touch his top. What kind of services had he performed in the past?

"But keep your shoulders back. If you need me to slow down or wait, tell me."

"Yes, Evrim."

When his hands touched her corseted waist, she could barely feel him. Not at all what she was after. She put a finger out and pressed it lightly against the end of his nipple. He stiffened as though electrocuted and his hands tightened on her. Better.

Evrim stroked both his nipples, squeezed them, gathered them in her hands, and pulled. Everything she did brought him to a higher level of tension until he was strung far too tight to maintain it. She punched him hard with the sides of both fists, three times in a row, and he shouted.

At that sound of release, Evrim unleashed her craving. She beat and pulled and twisted and squeezed, moving too fast for Jack to process one sensation before another crashed over him. She overwhelmed him, and his cries became nonstop repetitions of two words that flew into her like thunderous rain.

"Please yes please yes…"

His unfocused eyes drifted with the rain of blows, then flashed their shock when she reached around to grab what she could of his short hair and pull his head back. She pinched his nipple hard at the same time she pulled him into her body. She bit the strong muscle of his shoulder, and the combination made him hold on to her as though he would fall otherwise. She pulled him in and squeezed hard.

Breath sobbed from his open mouth against her neck, hot and damp. His body shook and twitched in her arms, and she held them solid for him. When his arms went slack, she nudged him with her hip, got him moving backward, and bypassed the spanking horse for the sling. She'd beat his ass and thighs another day. He was primed for a deep, hard fucking.

The lump in his pants was too firm to be a soft packer or a sock. He'd packed hard though he knew he was going to get fucked. A new bit of insight into his gender, though she wouldn't place bets on what exactly it meant.

When they reached the sling, she gentled her touch and ran her hand down his belly from the harness to his buttoned fly. With two quick flicks, she opened his jeans enough to push her fingers inside, the back of her hand against his skin. Jack's breathing slowed, and Evrim put her other hand on his jaw, thumb in the softness just behind his chin.

He met her eyes. "Wow."

"What a lovely release. I hope you're not done, though."

"No." He shook his head as though mesmerized. "I don't know if I'll ever have enough."

Of what? Her or the things she did?

Damn. Her body recognized his already. Physically, she'd bonded with him harder than she wanted to admit. It was a kind of love, this yearning and cherishing feeling. His youthful spirit evoked both her tenderness and brutality. Even more, though, she wanted him to need her.

She nudged his cock with her hip, but pushed her hand inside his underwear. His belly clenched as when she'd shoved him and she muttered, "Nice." The cock was held by his underwear, though, rather than a harness as she'd imagined. She tugged his pubic hair with her fingertips. He hummed and spread his legs.

"Pull your jeans down." He complied with alacrity, leaving them at his ankles. "You're so well trained. You do what I tell you and no more. I like it."

"Thank you, Evrim."

"No, thank you." She wanted to continue dominating him, but she needed more feedback for the next part. "Tell me what you liked about my fingers on your nipples."

"Well, um, pretty much all of it."

"Boots off. Step out of your jeans and take your underwear all the way off." When he immediately bent over to unlace the black boots, she scraped her nails down his back. "What isn't covered by 'pretty much all'?"

He darted a glance over his shoulder at her. "Light touches are frustrating. But it's kind of like how I said hair pulling pisses me off. You did that just right where it sent me over the edge. You have great instincts."

"Thanks, my sweet. You're pretty communicative, physically."

"Doesn't always seem to do the trick, though. I'm pretty noisy in general, but not everyone catches the signals." He got his second boot off and slipped his jeans off.

While he picked them up and folded them, Evrim pulled on nitrile gloves. "Tell me about your chest. You seem pretty comfortable with it." She plucked at the revealing harness.

"I'm lucky puberty didn't hit me with huge breasts." He straightened after setting his jeans on his boots and put his thumbs in the waistband of his underwear. "I wasn't the trans kid who knew and told their parents and got the puberty delaying hormones. I was scared my fiercely feminist mother would hate me for wanting to be a boy, so there was nothing to do about it."

Evrim listened closely, one gloved hand against the center of Jack's chest. He didn't sound torn up about it or like he was looking for sympathy. She matched his matter-of-fact tone. "And now?"

"Taking testosterone might shrink my chest. I might give it a try, eventually, but I'm not sure about HRT. I don't know if I'll ever be ready." He put air quotes around ready.

"Meaning you're not convinced you need HRT?"

"Meaning my uncertainty about changing my body comes from a lot of directions, but…"

"Worried about not being trans enough?" She'd wondered. It seemed like a Catch-22—folks feeling either not trans enough or too attached to the binary.

He grimaced. "Now and then. I try to focus on being me enough."

"You are quite wonderful, just as you are. And however you grow and change, you'll still be amazing."

Jack looked at her for a long moment with a flat expression. "Harder to hear than to say."

"Sure. I get that." Gender talk could be sexy, but this was not pumping the eroticism of the moment. Evrim glanced down at his hands. His thumbs were still hooked in the waistband of his underwear. "Are you going to take those off or do you want me to cut them off?"

Jack's wry smile plucked at Evrim's heart. "Since it's my favorite pair…" He pushed down slowly.

"I'm bluffing. I don't even have scissors."

He looked up grinning and she attacked. With his legs hobbled by the underwear, he fell gracelessly into the sling and she followed him fast. She grabbed his crotch, the whole thing in one hand, and squeezed. His eyes screwed shut, but his feet kicked to be free of the underwear. She pulled and squeezed harder while he situated himself in the sling, legs up and spread in the ankle straps, ass barely on the edge. Once he was settled, she leaned over to the table and slicked the cock with a pump from the lube bottle.

"Can you take the whole thing right off the bat?"

"Right now, yes. I'm throbbing like crazy down there."

Evrim moved back just enough to see his crotch and spread him open with the slick granite head. She pushed it inside him, just an inch, then grabbed him with her other hand and squeezed his flesh around the rock. "Feel it. Tighten around it. Make me work to get it in."

"Yes, Evrim." His hands made fists on the chains holding the sling up, and his inner muscles pushed against the cock. She shoved roughly in shallow surges, the ridges in the stone making for an easy grip. When she got it halfway in, he flinched.

"Take it, Jack. Open up." His clit thumped against her knuckles as she moved his softness back and forth over it.

He did open up and she got more inside, but he flinched again. It was too hard a cock to be the first thing she wielded inside him. She growled, but she didn't want to give up the fantasy. "Grab this cock and fuck yourself with it." When he took the end from her, she moved to his side. Now she had full access to his torso and his crotch, except where his arms made straight lines down his sides. She tortured his nipples and kept up the indirect stimulation on his clit while he thrust the cock in over and over and over. He built fast, his chest reddening and his lips open. She slipped her fingers into his softness and his hard clit pushed out at her. She brought her face close to his and bit his lips, sucked and kissed them until his tremors became a fast vibration.

"Come for me. Come now." He pushed the cock in deep and worked it in shallow thrusts until his belly hardened under her arm and his clit disappeared. His orgasm stopped his breath, and she put her mouth on his, waiting for the moment when it came back. In a hard rush, he undulated, breathing with each wave, sending the energy deep into her.

Evrim swelled to bursting with it, with Jack's come and his ecstasy. She drew her hands down his torso over and over, conducting the music he danced to, until he barely moved with each wave of pleasure.

She took the cock from his hands and put it aside, then moved between his raised legs to get close. She leaned over him, folded her arms on his chest, and took a deep breath. He breathed with her and they stared at each other.

"Not bad, eh?" Her question sounded smug. She hid the part of her that needed to know she'd done well. Hadn't left him wanting or scared him by being too much.

"So good." She searched his face, the last of her tension leaving with the openness of his pleasure. "Thank you."

"You're welcome."

"I'd love some water."

She handed him the bottle and he drank deep. "Jack." She waited until he looked at her. "Thank you for your service."

Eyes heavy and muscles lax, Jack gave her the answer she sought. "You're welcome, Eve."

CHAPTER ELEVEN

Jack closed up *Reliant* after airing it out all day. Much as he and the harbormaster were at loggerheads over anchoring in the harbor, the guy didn't give him any shit for keeping the boat afloat.

Steve had died of a heart attack, what—a year before? He'd build *Reliant* himself out of aluminum, a custom job using mail-order plans. The Colvin-designed junk rig had caught Jack's eye, and he'd introduced himself to Steve. The guy was out of his depth with sailing, but not with construction. He'd been a union welder all his life, and *Reliant* was gorgeous, strong, and well-appointed. Jack had gone sailing with him, helped him work out the details of the sails and rigging, then provided a sounding board and cheering section while he'd stuffed the boat with every great piece of technology he could make for himself or buy on the cheap. In return, he'd made Jack some very valuable pieces of equipment for the cost of materials.

After Steve died, the boat just sat. Jack had taken it upon himself to go aboard and shut down the systems. He'd pickled the watermaker, turned off the battery switches, and closed all the open hatches and portholes except the one that was under the awning. Without any air circulating, the boat would start molding pretty quickly.

He still went aboard now and then to be sure the bilge was dry and nothing was rotting. No one cared about the boat, not Steve's kids and not the marina management, but Jack hated to let a great boat die at the dock. Steve deserved for his work to be respected.

Jack's passengers left almost an hour ago, but *Lysistrata* was still snugged up to the loading zone on the main pier. It made his skin itch, being on the harbormaster's territory. Ever since the guy had stopped and searched him over and over...

Filmy lines drifted all around the next pier down, fishers lining the railing or sitting in folding chairs, their coolers behind them. They always hoped to empty them of beer and fill them with fish, but only reliably managed the first. Just beyond, the harbormaster's office tried to blend into the waterfront, but the government building looked like the authoritarian intrusion it was. That pissant fucker was probably sitting at his desk, lazily ruining people's days.

He strode up the marina's gangway and headed for *Lysistrata*. Familiarity battled alienation whenever he was on the pier, like an adult going back to a childhood home that held mixed emotions. He rolled his shoulders. Now he was being dramatic.

Heightened emotion characterized his recent state of being, ever since getting tangled up with Eve La Sirena. Evrim Nesin. Amphitrite. No matter what her identity of the moment, she dragged emotion from him with every word, every look. He would have imagined the rock goddess to be overwhelming, too much to handle. He would have imagined feeling suffocated by all that...glory.

Instead, he craved her. As much as she communicated— verbally, non-verbally...fuck, it felt like emotional telepathy sometimes—she soaked up even more. Far from being the selfish, demanding lover he'd have expected, she turned her energy into a spur for his own and kept it flowing between them, richer and stronger as it circulated.

How the fuck was he supposed to fight her pull? Damn it. He had shit to do and all he could think of was her.

A couple of strange boats floated in the anchorage among the long-term boats. The liveaboard friends Jack had abandoned continued to fight for their right to anchor in the harbor. Jack could hardly meet their eyes when he saw them, though they gave him hearty welcomes and insisted that he'd done the right thing moving from the anchorage. He was trying to run a business, after all.

Heat and humidity thickened the air on land, though a slight sea breeze fooled the tourists into thinking they were in heaven. Jack looked around at the vibrant crowds, the T-shirt shops alternating with ice cream and shaved ice, and the boats racked up in the marina like eggs in a carton. If they only knew how much better it was even a quarter-mile offshore, he and Charlie Rhodes wouldn't have to hustle so hard for passengers.

And if he could stop rushing into love with Eve, he could keep the passengers he'd booked.

He stepped aboard *Lysistrata* and shook hands with the other captain, who'd been shooting the shit with Marie.

"So, you need a favor?" Charlie sipped beer from a glass bottle.

Jack leaned on *Lysistrata's* railing and crossed his arms over his chest. He wanted to get a good brood on, but Charlie was the only man he was at all close to since Steve's death. He didn't deserve Jack's piss-poor attitude.

"Can you take my Thursday sail?"

"On *Lysistrata* or on *Gypsy*?" Charlie sounded agreeable.

"*Gypsy*. I double booked." Jack couldn't control the quick glance at Marie, who looked predictably horrified.

Marie wasn't kinky, so she hadn't been at Puss'n'Boots the previous night for his scene with Evrim. During their day sail, he'd thought he was remarkably clearheaded and emotionally balanced considering how deeply he'd gone into subspace for Eve. They'd made out like bandits on the tips. His pecs ached and two deep bruises delineated the muscles, but he wasn't striped with welts or feeling shaky.

It wasn't until he heard her voice on the phone for their check-in that the shudder moved through him. His breath shortened, and all he could think of was setting a date to see her again. He invited her sailing on *Lysistrata* and she'd agreed, but she'd put him off until later in the week. He'd agreed, thoughtlessly, and now he was paying the price for letting his cock do the thinking.

He narrowed his eyes at Marie and turned back to the other captain. "Look, Charlie, can you do it or not? This bridal party has been emailing me twice a week for months. They're so excited about this trip that I can't cancel on them."

"A'course you can't cancel. Make us all look bad. I was fixin' to fly *Gypsy*'s pennant and lure daytrippers at the pier, but I always prefer a sure thing."

"It's only five people and you usually take more. I can't raise the rate on them at this late date."

Charlie looked affronted. "Get the fuck out of here." Since they were on *Lysistrata*, Jack figured he meant it as a figure of speech. "I got this."

"Thanks. And, um. Marie?"

Charlie's confusion made his words superfluous. "What about her?"

"Can you take her too?"

"Sure, come on over, Marie. *Gypsy*'s a great boat. We'll show them the time of their lives." Charlie seemed pretty laissez-faire about taking on a crew member he'd never sailed with.

Marie crossed her arms. Uh-oh. "You double booked but you don't need any crew?"

Jack held Marie's gaze a moment, but he couldn't hide the truth. "It's personal. It's, you know, the woman from the island."

Charlie slapped Jack on the shoulder. His muscles, bulky and knotted from decades of hauling huge sails and sweating lines to cat anchors, gave the blow serious force, and Jack resettled himself on the railing. "You mean you're giving up a booking for a date? I've got to hear more about this woman."

Marie sat on the cabin house and pulled her knees up. She looked young and shiny, fresh from the shower with her hair pulled back, and the lost look that came and went on her face tripped Jack's guilt. She wrapped her arms around her knees loosely and said, "You've never wanted the whole boat to yourself for a hookup before. It's not like I've never heard you fuck."

Jack felt himself heat and hoped the flush was lost in the deep tan he'd built since coming south. The words came out before he could analyze them. "This is different."

His quick defense drew stares from both his friends.

Charlie settled himself on the railing. "How so?"

If he had mocked, it would have been easy to shut the conversation down. Instead, it was just an invitation to talk it out. Jack blew a breath. "Well, I like her."

Marie tipped her head to the side. "You're a friendly person. You like almost everyone."

"I mean, I really like her."

Charlie raised an eyebrow. "How long have you been out of junior high?"

Jack stared at Charlie a moment, but he couldn't muster any outrage. "Feels like I'm right back there. My heart is racing right now, thinking about her. When she texted me the first time and asked if she could call, I saved her in my contacts, then assigned her a picture and a ringtone and tested it a dozen times. When she called, I almost dropped my phone."

"Sounds like you're all aflutter, kid."

"What ringtone?" Marie enjoyed poking at Eve's identity far too much.

But he had to admit. "'Hard to Miss.'"

Marie controlled a laugh. "You're a goner."

Just what he didn't want to hear. "I was getting wrapped up in her before, but it was the challenge. The battle between sailor and landowner."

"Wait, this is the woman who tried to kick you out of her cove?" Charlie blinked.

"It's not hers," Jack muttered, automatically. He stopped himself. Charlie had heard the rant plenty of times. "Yeah. That's her. I don't even know if I've won or lost. Is she okay with us anchoring there, or is she just a master plotter?"

Marie said, uncertainly, "You think she's running a scam on you? Getting you off balance so you'll agree to anything she says?"

Since she knew Eve's identity, she knew what was at stake. She also knew how dynamic Eve was.

"I hope not. No. I don't think so. I can't imagine her doing anything with me she didn't want to do. Why would she waste her power on that? She isn't trying to run me off anymore, but I can hardly think straight. I left you alone on the boat the other day, Marie. What if someone had a stroke or the anchor caught some coral and dragged? Could you captain the boat in an emergency?"

"I'm pretty sure I could keep the boat safe long enough for you to get back."

Great. Now he'd insulted Marie. Again.

Charlie looked puzzled. "Her power? The scope of her life? Who is this woman?"

Marie's pique gave way to a smothered smile. "It's a secret and it's absolutely delicious."

"Is she famous?" Charlie's heavy eyebrows rose.

"Yep. And gorgeous. And Jack's dream woman." Marie's singsong delivery was a gentle tease, but was she giving too much away?

Did he stand out as an Eve La Sirena fan? It wasn't like he had fan gear, hats and shirts or old ticket stubs lying around. And Charlie was old enough that he may not know much about her.

"Dream woman or not, the moment I heard her voice on the phone, I was like an automaton. 'Yes, yes, anything you say.' I never even thought about prior commitments. I just said yes."

Charlie's earlier amusement held a worried tinge. "Sounds like complete infatuation. And you're doing BDSM with her?" Jack had to smile at Charlie's careful use of the acronym Jack had taught him. "Could this be dangerous?"

"Not physically. I think she and I have a lot of the same boundaries. Not necessarily about what specific acts we'll allow, but about how a scene should go. How much clarity should be required for consent and all that. I don't think she'll use my...infatuation against me."

Marie stared at him and put her feet on the deck. "You almost said love." He grimaced, automatic denial struggling with his habit of talking things over with her. "Seriously? You go from engaging her in battle to being submissive to her and now you're thinking in terms of love?"

He sighed. What the hell. "I know it's not necessarily the love of my life. It could be the intoxication of having a new top who's really, really fucking good." He shrugged. "Scene love or love all the way around. Who the fuck knows?"

Charlie shook his head. "She sounds like a witch."

Jack suddenly remembered Eve's cover of "I Put a Spell on You." "Not a bad description. Without the pact with the devil. I think."

"I still don't understand how you can give away your power, only temporarily."

Jack pondered. Having friends outside the kinky community was useful sometimes, making him think things out and spell them out. Talking to his family about it wasn't an option. They absolutely didn't want to know the details, just that he was safe and not getting himself into truly dangerous situations.

He spoke slowly. "It's tricky and, as you can see from today, not foolproof. BDSM is, in part, about making explicit something that hovers in lots of relationships. Who makes what kinds of decisions, what the partners are agreeing to do or not do." He paused and started over. "I didn't come out as trans until well into my twenties, and power was one of the reasons. Women are so powerful, so compelling and deeply in touch with what really matters in most situations."

Marie sneered. "Not all women. Remember the nightmare family."

"Sure. Of course. But being a man seemed to trade all that for a bunch of shitty, unearned power that, as a feminist, I would have to train myself not to wield."

Charlie twitched. "The problem with feminism is that it makes it sound like women need to be in charge of everything. I wish we could just all be humanists."

Marie shook her head. "The problem with the world is that there are too many structural imbalances to pretend we can all be taken plainly, for who we are, and have our strengths and weaknesses valued fairly. We'll need some form of feminism and intersectional social justice movement until the kyriarchy is dismantled."

Jack smiled at her. They'd met at a group for white people working toward racial justice. He already knew where she stood. "Anyway, to bring it back to power exchange, I have to feel powerful, in that I can agree or not agree to the scene itself as well as all the aspects of it, in order for D's to work. I can feel frightened or excited or nervous at the same time, but the bottom line is that, without the power to refuse or withdraw consent, it's not kink. It's abuse."

Charlie nodded. "I get that."

"So in the scene, the power exchange is in the constantly renewed yielding of the bottom to the top. The top is the...the permanent magnet in a generator—" to use terms Charlie would grasp right away, "—and each thing the top does or requires the bottom to do spins it. When the bottom takes it or does what the top says, they're the copper coil, cycling the charge over and over."

"So," Charlie seemed to be listening hard and thinking about it, "you're saying there's not a magic moment when you give up your power and then you're powerless until the end of the scene. That's how I thought it went."

"No. There's sometimes a magic moment when the players agree to try to start and they both put themselves in the mental or emotional or physical position to begin building on and trading the power between them." He hesitated to bring it into the personal realm, but Charlie was honestly trying. "For me, submitting is where the excitement is. Sometimes that means fighting the top, sometimes it means the opposite. Sometimes, I submit over and over so thoroughly that it melds into a seamless state of being. People call that subspace. Even there, though, I'm present and continuing to submit. Without that constant handing-over motion, I wouldn't be doing my part to create the energy between us."

Marie hummed. "Sounds kind of like the flow in some of my really good sex. I mean the times when we get really deep into each other at the same time as the physical stuff is going on."

"Emotionally, or mentally, or spiritually deep. Yeah, exactly. Submission is one way to find that generator." Jack flashed a grin at Charlie, who looked illuminated. "Some find it through giving and receiving pain. Others through giving and receiving pleasure. Plenty of people stumble onto it accidentally in an especially great hug or hunt it down by doing rituals together."

Charlie's mouth dropped open. "The birth of religion."

"Perhaps." Jack followed that line of thought a moment. Fascinating. "The getting together to pray part. Yeah, probably. You hear about religious retreats where the members spend days in ecstatic states, dropping out and rejoining the body of the group as their energy allows."

Marie wrinkled her nose. "And it all devolves into rules and laws and you must and thou-shalt-not."

Jack laughed. "Just like BDSM can." He sobered quickly. "And poly. Did I mention she's already got a live-in lover?"

Charlie's eyebrows rose. "No, you skipped that part."

"A gorgeous bombshell femme who bottoms to her."

Marie whistled. "Complications everywhere."

Jack tried to laugh. "Thinking about it dispassionately, this is no different than any number of relationships I've enjoyed. All of a sudden, though, I'm scared shitless. I want to be more than the lover on the side."

Marie shook her head. "There are no guarantees in love."

Charlie slapped his hands on his thighs. "Sounds like a toast to me. Got a bottle?"

Jack's mood soared. "Of course I do. Against all my expectations, the family from hell came through with a check for the damage they did, so I have some good stuff."

"Jack even tipped me out from the payoff." Marie sent Jack an appreciative look. The evidence of her good opinion of him buoyed his mood further.

Charlie stuck to the important part. "Rum?"

Jack put on a wounded look. "Am I a sailor or aren't I?"

"You'll never finish that bottle, left to your own devices. I know what this situation calls for. Let's text everyone we know and tell them to bring something."

Jack glanced at the harbormaster's office like a whipped dog, but a jolt of outrage followed. "Hell yeah. Party on *Lysistrata*."

❖

Eve and Harmonie stood, hip to hip, arms slung around each other's waists. Eve rubbed the deep curve and watched Jack row toward them silently. The small boat cleaved the water, and the reflections that had been so crystal clear undulated behind him.

Thoughts of him had interrupted her more than once, but she'd worked through the distraction and earned a full day off.

They stood on her little pier, picnic basket at their feet. She'd texted Jack, asking how she should prepare, and he'd told her to wear soft-soled, non-marking shoes, suggested a hat, and informed her that the guest was responsible for food. Finger food, something easy to eat between tacks or while steering. She'd spent the previous day making tiny spanakopita and baklava, using an entire package of phyllo dough. That morning, she'd fried little falafel balls and made tzatziki, spicy Harissa, and a mint sauce.

Harmonie had packed it all while she'd gotten dressed. It took her two hours to fuss over her hair—was there an attractive 'do that wouldn't get ripped to pieces in the wind? She went with a complex herringbone braid and built her outfit from the shoes up.

She didn't want to wear athletic shoes. Yoga pants and a light shirt might be practical, but she felt like retaining at least some of her punch. She'd gone with ballet shoes, loose pants that banded close around her ankles, and a cap-sleeved bodice that hugged her curves. The perfect bra let her lean over and work without falling out of her shirt. She'd danced in less.

A little nervous excitement tingled in her belly. It felt good, unfamiliar. Almost forgotten. She felt more like she was about to step out on stage in front of eighty thousand screaming fans than like she was going on a date.

Of course, she hadn't dated in a while. Even when she had, too many evenings had been wrapped up in furthering her career instead of furthering an interesting acquaintance.

She smiled at the idea of calling Jack an acquaintance at that point. The excitement came from the opposite direction. She liked him, a lot, and she was wound up at the idea of spending more time with him. In and out of scene. She savored her nervousness, rolled it around like fine wine in her mouth, then swallowed.

The excitement held reverberations from a surprising yearning for a regular life. Well, as regular as Jack's. Community, a club he enjoyed, friendships on the docks. She'd skew it if she tried to be part of his world, but it attracted her nonetheless.

Eve caught the rope Jack threw her and handed it to Harmonie. She wrapped her arms around her and pulled her close. Harmonie snuggled up, their tits pressing. Eve lowered her lips to Harmonie's neck and breathed her in. Familiarity, love.

Harmonie said, chin on Eve's neck, "Be good."

Eve nipped the soft skin of her neck. "Be bad."

Harmonie would be spending her day hacking into Eve's record label's backup files. They needed to know whether the label planned on suing Eve for breach of contract, and emails were included in those backups. She owed them one more act. She was supposed to identify the next big thing, hook them and reel them in, then produce a lucrative album without giving a penny more than necessary to the artists.

She would never do that again.

The tide was high and she only had to use one step of the ladder before dropping into his little boat. He'd said there wasn't enough depth for *Lysistrata* at the dock. She wondered how he knew.

"Hello, handsome." He stood, steadying the boat against the pier, and she leaned into him. She dropped her lips open a touch and pressed them to his, a slow, sensual greeting. She wanted to feel it all, every step of the way. He took a deep breath through his nose, slowly, as though savoring her smell, and she was glad she'd put a little oil of cedar and sandalwood in her bath. Only a mere hint would remain. She pulled away.

"Hello, Eve." Her name resonated in the light voice that intensified the impression that he was a very young man. "Harmonie, how are you?"

Harmonie grinned down at them. "Looking forward to a little peace and quiet."

"Happy to get her out of your hair for a while." Eve pretended to glower. "Will you be around when we get back? Maybe we can take a turn around the island, all three of us."

"I have a lot of work to do. We'll see."

"Sure." Jack shrugged, easygoing as usual.

"Here you go." Harmonie lowered the basket to him, biceps tight with the weight. God, she was hot. Strong, solid. She looked exactly how she was.

Jack took the basket with an oomph. "This is provisions for one meal?"

Harmonie leaned an elbow on the piling. "There might be a little more than that. I included a few bottles of wine."

Eve shrugged when Jack glanced at her. He said, "Thanks. I won't be drinking much, but maybe I'll bring this one back sozzled."

"Whatever works." Harmonie tossed the bow line back to Jack and blew kisses at them. "Bon voyage."

Eve touched two fingers to her lips and waved them at Harmonie. She faced front and said, "Tell me what to do. I want to help with everything."

Jack shot her an amused look. "If you say so."

"I do." She put on an extra regal expression to make a joke of the intensity of her demand. It wouldn't do to come on too strong, but the idea of sailing away—running away under sail—had circled her thoughts for days. They could be themselves out on the water, without her fame complicating things. She'd have to become an expert, though, if she decided to do any such thing. She'd never put herself in a position of such weakness as to need a captain or crew.

Jack pushed away from the pier and sat at the oars. His long-muscled arms bunched and shifted as he rowed, and his neck stretched when he craned his head around to see where he was going. He nosed the little boat up to the big boat's side and steadied it once again while she climbed the wooden ladder. It hung from two hooks on the side of the boat and had padding to protect the boat's paint. Once on deck, she looked around *Lysistrata* for the very first time—barring the spying she'd done through binoculars—and it struck her how purposeful it all was.

Clever little hooks for the ladder, lines and pulleys and rings she couldn't guess the purpose of. She'd need more than a basic orientation before jumping on and sailing into the sunset...or sunrise, since the sun set over land. She pondered that phrase. More Eurocentrism?

Jack, still standing in the little boat, pulled himself around to the back.

She followed him to the back of the boat and looked down at him over the railing. "What's first?"

"We'll haul the yawl boat, then I'll give you a tour."

"Perfect." So much specialty language. Eve took a deep breath and made a mental note to get a beginner's book on sailing. "How can I help?"

"Uncleat the falls—the line attached to this"—he shook a hook that hung just above his head—"and leave it slack so I can pull this down."

She put her hand on the line she thought he was talking about and got his nod before trying to untie it from the cleat. Awkwardness brought defensiveness and she glanced at Jack. He watched silently, letting her puzzle it out, and her self-consciousness faded. "Okay, it's loose."

"Don't let it all the way out of your hand and don't let it slide through your fingers. You can get rope burn like that. Just feed the line toward me while I pull down." He drew the hook down and she kept the line from getting tight. The yawl boat—she could learn this language—had rings in the sides and he connected the hook to one side. "Pull the slack out and wrap the line around the cleat. Don't worry about getting it exactly like it was before."

She wound it around, as much like the line on the other side as she could get, then they repeated the process. Jack climbed a little ladder and swung himself up on the high deck. Muscles flexed in his arms and, she imagined, under his shirt. His agility gave her a frisson.

"Now for a tour." Her demand was met by a shake of his head.

"We're not done here. Let's see how strong you are."

With that challenge as impetus, Eve put all her strength behind pulling the line he handed her. The yawl boat rose on her end. Whoa. Heavy. He laughed, grabbed the other line, and pulled until they were even.

"These ropes are called the falls?" She stopped pulling a moment to ask the question and realized that holding the weight was as hard as pulling it. Heave ho.

"Yep. But there's only one rope on this boat: the bell rope. All the others are called lines."

"Okay, then." They kept pulling. Bit by bit, the yawl boat rose out of the water and against the… "What are these called?" She waved at the metal bars arching behind the boat. The falls went through a pulley at the end.

"Davits."

She'd kept up with him. Satisfaction had her eying Jack, until he grinned back and whipped his "line" around its cleat so fast that she didn't see what he'd done.

"Come on, Jack."

"You don't want to hold that weight while I teach you to cleat a line."

His knowledgeable tone, added to the stretch in her shoulders, banished the suspicion he was fucking with her. Showing off, probably, but not trying to be mean.

He taught her how to cleat a line, while holding the weight of the yawl boat with one hand. She cleated and uncleated it several times before they were both satisfied that she had it down.

"Now for a tour," he said. "Since we're at the stern, we'll start here."

Eve lost track of the number of new words she heard within a few minutes. She memorized them as they came and tried to attach them to the items or concepts he explained. She prided herself on being a quick study, but once again, she realized how much there was to learn.

At the side rail, near the place she'd climbed aboard, she said, "What kind of wood is this?" She stroked the satiny railing, then turned and ran her thumb over the grain of the...right, the halyard block.

He sat on the deck house next to the halyard block. "*Lysistrata* is made of cedar planking on oak frames. Most of the topsides wood was originally teak because it weathers well and was cheap and plentiful for years, but it's expensive now. Too much was logged. I've been replacing it with ipe and iroko whenever I have to scarf in a repair."

Eve blinked at Jack, who rubbed his hand over a section that looked extra bright. "Okay."

Jack looked up and took in her expression. "Have you reached saturation?"

Much as she didn't want it to be true... "Maybe. Just until I've used some of these words a few times. Seems like you'd have to be a monomaniac to know as much as you do."

"I have to be way into it all. It's my home and my livelihood." His tone revealed a guardedness she hadn't expected.

A swelling in her chest took her by surprise, but she put her hand on his. "It's brilliant. I like a person who dives in deep when they're into something. I wish people brought so much passion to every part of their lives."

She held his gaze until his expression changed from guarded to relieved. Damn, he was endearing. Jack's demeanor invited more from her, more than she was certain she wanted to give, until she leaned over and captured his mouth with hers. She rode the onrushing passion, pressing him into the deck house roof with her hands on his thighs, tempted to straddle him then and there.

She did want to go sailing, though. They hadn't even left the cove and she was in danger of tossing the plan for a quick fuck. Breathing carefully, she pulled away and studied Jack. His beseeching expression could have meant anything, but she knew that any words out of his mouth would sound a lot like *don't stop*.

Injecting a firmness into her voice that she wasn't feeling, she said, "Finish the tour."

Command voice worked on him and they went below, where she oohed and aahed over the smart systems in the galley and the composting toilet in the head.

"Did *Lysistrata* come with the electric engine?"

"Actually, no. When I first saw her, the big downside of this boat was a forty-year-old leaky sieve of a diesel engine. Eight horsepower—"

"Eight or eighty?"

"Eight." Eve's look of disbelief amused Jack. "Eighty is more common in a boat this size. I researched getting it replaced, but anything stronger was too big for the engine compartment. A crewmate on the schooner *Intrepid* handed me the answer one evening in the fo'c'sle. An electric motor took up a fraction of a diesel's space and would give me clean, quiet power."

"Smart."

Jack bowed from the waist. "Independence-wise, renewable power and composting heads are must-haves. I did a ton of reading on both before settling for the systems I have. The electric motor, though…it's still a specialty thing. I mean, so is a composting head, but most people don't even think of electric motors as an option. For me, it completes the environmentally-conscious picture and saves me a ton of money on fuel."

"Too bad you can't grow your own food. You'd be really independent then."

"Can't is the right word, though. Between the way salt affects most plants and my complete black thumb, I focus on other means." He seemed a bit embarrassed to admit to a weakness. "The boat already had four sizable solar panels when I bought her. I added a wind generator, a towable hydro generator, and a much improved charge controlling system. Four banks of batteries—two for the motor and watermaker, two for the house loads like lights and navigation gear—alternate, one of each charging while the other discharges during use. Check this out."

His explanation of the electrical system went over her head, but the neat and tidy runs of cable, well marked, gave her a deeper respect for his grasp of the subject.

Of so many subjects! "You really are a Jack-of-all-trades." She acknowledged his eye roll at the weak joke. "Okay. I'm officially overwhelmed. Can we go sailing now?"

"Love to. You still want to help?"

"Definitely."

By the time the anchor and the sails had been raised, Eve wondered if she shouldn't have gone with athletic wear. Her woodsy scent had long given way to the smell of fresh sweat, and her herringbone braid felt loose. Perhaps weekends in the Hamptons drinking champagne and tipping the crew weren't sufficient preparation for this kind of sailing. She'd never seen anyone on those boats work as hard as she had. Physical exertion other than dancing was rare for her, but the combination of salt breeze and rolling waves made it all worthwhile.

Her island lay flat on the horizon as they put a couple of miles between the cove and the boat. The wind felt strong when they sailed out, but Jack turned them somewhat away from it. The sails were full—all three of them—and the air caressed her neck and cheek.

She stood in the cockpit with Jack, highly pleased with herself. He held the wheel lightly, seeming to let the boat have its head. "Can I steer?"

"Sure." He gave her a short lesson on the theory and practice of steering, as he had done every step of the way. He was a natural teacher, clear and concise, showing her what to do and then letting her try. She couldn't help distracting him with the occasional touch, just to connect with him and feel him respond, but focused on grasping the tasks at hand.

She took the helm, and the boat came into the wind enough to lose speed. She turned the wheel and the bow swung away, filling the sails. Okay. Then the steering got stiff and she found herself pulling hard just to keep the wheel from moving.

"There's a perfect spot, right about...here. As you feel the pressure against the rudder grow and fade, feel for this spot, this amount of pressure. If the sails seem full but the pressure grows too strong, it's the signal to steer up or sheet out the sails."

This was more like it. The brute labor to that point faded into insignificance compared to the complex sensory input of steering. The wheel felt like a new instrument, something she could use to play the boat. Each wooden pin sticking out of the central circle gave her feedback. She tried loosening her grip, steering with her skin and muscle rather than her bones. The lighter she held the wheel, the more information she got from it, until a point where her control wasn't strong enough and she had to hold a little tighter. Another sweet spot.

And they were sailing. As she shifted her focus from the precise action of her hands on the wheel—another thing she knew as a musician, the switch from playing the instrument to playing the music—she looked out and realized that they were flying along.

"How fast are we going?" she asked over the whistling wind.

"About four knots," Jack replied after a look at the chartplotter. She saw the number he'd referenced. It rose and fell, hovering around four but often above or below.

"What's that in miles per hour?"

He tipped his head to the side like he was calculating. "About three and a half."

"Miles per hour?" She was stunned. "That's an easy walk."

Jack grinned at her. The sun was high and the shadows sharp-edged. His eyes, as far from icy as blue could get, glowed in the light. He looked exhilarated, and she realized she was grinning back at him like a fool.

He pointed at the chartplotter. "See this anchor symbol here?"

"Yes." She lost her wind a little and brought her focus back to sailing.

"That's where I anchor when I come to Lysistrata Cove."

"Lysistrata Cove, is it?" Her arch tone didn't dent his ease.

"See how there's no island there?"

Ah. "Yes."

"Do you have any idea how dangerous it is, having land spring out of nowhere?"

"But it says there are rocks, right?"

He narrowed his eyes at her. "Why do you know that?"

"Won't boaters avoid coming near the rocks?"

"Eve, rocks are little. Plenty of people will barely cut around them."

"Hmm. Perhaps I can do something about that."

"Write to the chart companies? Look, the island is on the paper charts, just not the electronic ones. I even checked on a different brand. Still not there."

She put on an overdone mysterious look. "I have vast powers, beyond your wildest dreams."

He stared, then laughed. "My dreams are pretty wild."

She dropped the pretense of cool and laughed with him.

CHAPTER TWELVE

Jack set up the self-steering gear to give Eve a break at the helm. She'd taken to driving the boat like a born mariner—was there anything she couldn't control with ease?—but the wind and waves were too consistent to keep it interesting once she had the rhythm of it down.

He'd let her laugh off his questions about the chart, but it bugged him. She'd known, though she didn't know anything at all about sailing or navigating. She'd known that her island wouldn't be on the chart. How would she know that? He guessed it could be part of the process of buying an island. He certainly didn't know anything about how a person went about that. But her reference to powers stuck in his mind. He just *knew* that she'd made the island disappear.

She rummaged around below while he fiddled with the settings and came back with a feast. Her natural flair asserted itself when she gave him the rundown on the dishes, and he said, "You'd make bank as a server."

"Better believe it. Well, the part of the job that's about showmanship and making assholes think we're best friends. I don't know how I'd handle the running around."

He poked at one of the triangle pastries. "I've never been into spinach."

"Popeye jokes aside, you should try it."

She was right. The spanakopita were stunningly good, and the falafel was almost too good to cover with the sauces. Once he tried them, though, he groaned. "I could drink this mint sauce."

"I'll make you a mint tea you'll never get over. Next time you're at the house." She sipped her wine but waved him off when he tried to refill it for her.

"You cooked this?"

She studied him over the edge of her wineglass. "Your incredulity is not flattering."

For the first time in what had been an easygoing day, he felt his face flush. "I didn't mean to imply you couldn't." Her eyebrow rose. "Or wouldn't. I just love it all. Is it all Turkish?"

She eased back against the settee and took a falafel ball. "Turkish, Middle Eastern, Mediterranean. The spices and ingredients traveled throughout the region, but yes, my recipes lean toward the Turkish variations."

"Did you get much of this at school?"

Her expression flattened, as it had when he'd brought up her childhood in their video chat conversation. She didn't like the subject much. Family and childhood were hard subjects for a lot of folks, queer and trans especially, and he'd never pressed for information before. With Eve, he wanted in so badly that he was overstepping and shame prickled at his neck.

"I'm sorry, I don't mean to pry."

"Yes, you do. It's okay." She shook herself and dipped the falafel in the spicy Harissa. He hadn't had much of that one. "I don't love talking about my childhood, but mostly because of the way people have covered it in the media. Sent away to boarding school. Why? Didn't your parents love you?" Her mouth twisted and he wanted to beg her to stop. "They couldn't handle me. I was stubborn and demanding. My tantrums were like forces of nature. I got into the academy because the only thing I loved doing was singing. They put me in front of strangers who asked me to sing, and those people thought I was just wonderful. They found out the truth before long. I was wonderful as long as I was making music. Otherwise, I was a nightmare."

"How old were you?"

"Seven." That ripped a groan from him and she shook her head. "Anyway, you asked if I ate like this at school. Bottom line, no. School cafeteria food all the way. Boston was right down the road, though, and it's big enough to have a little of everything. When I was old enough to take the bus on my own, I went to Turkish restaurants and grocery stores. I thought I was sneaking the heritage my parents had stolen from me by leaving me at school, but really, I was stirring memories from before we moved to the US." She fell silent.

Jack couldn't pursue his questions. Did they spend holidays together? Was she in touch with her parents, or were the walls too high? He drank from his water bottle and settled back against the cockpit cushions. He couldn't have demolished the sexual tension any more thoroughly.

Clouds bunched on the horizon, darker than they'd been all day. Eve's story had taken his attention away from the weather system and it was growing fast. He switched the VHF radio to the weather band. The electronically synthesized voice called Perfect Paul droned on with the current observations in the area as Jack scanned the cloud bank headed at them. Though black where it was thickest, no curtain of rain hung below it. The observation for the nearest island that direction described a wind change, though, and heavy gusts.

He set the radar to transmit and watched the returns form, overlaid onto his electronic chart. It wasn't a large system, just a storm cell moving quickly, so he decided to batten down and sail through it. He swept a last look around the area with his binoculars.

"Eve, it may get pretty windy for a little while, but it'll pass. I'm going to close everything in case of rain. Keep a lookout, will you?"

Eve sat up straight and said, "Sure. What am I looking for?"

"Hard things. Like other boats or floating debris. Did you see that movie about the guy who hit a submerged container in the Indian Ocean?"

Her forehead creased. "Are we worrying about that?"

He shook his head. "No, but whoever's on deck needs to keep their eyes moving, looking around, just in case."

"Okay. I can do this."

"I know you can." He waited until he was belowdecks to smile.

She had packed all the food containers back into her picnic basket. "Thanks for cleaning the galley," he yelled. She was a boating natural. He moved through the boat, closing portholes and dogging hatches. He thought about getting his foul weather gear out, but it wouldn't take that long for the storm to pass. On the other hand, he never went into a tense situation without emptying his bladder.

He entered the small head next to the companionway ladder. Eve yelled down to him, "Where are the binoculars?"

Shit. He yelled through the hatch. "I carried them below with me. They're on the settee. I'll get them in a minute."

"I'll get them."

The boat would be fine, though it always made him feel itchy when there was no one on deck. The steps creaked under her feet and Jack thought about the first time he'd noticed her feet, on the blanket, feeding her conch. Her toenails had been blood red and the bells around her ankles had chimed softly when she tapped her feet. She was always moving a little, as though there was a constant soundtrack in her head.

He heard a thunk and a cry, then a thump at the bottom of the companionway ladder. "Eve? Eve?" He wiped fast and pulled his pants up. When he pushed the hatch to open it, it came to an abrupt stop with only a one-inch gap.

"Eve!" Her braid lay on the cabin sole just beyond the door, and he could see the top of her head, just beyond. He pushed harder, shifting her, making her moan. He reached through the slim opening and shook her shoulder. Her black hair looked wet, but he didn't recognize what soaked it until he saw his fingers.

Blood.

His split-second of agonizing over the best course of action ended with a slow, steady push on the door that shoved her across the cabin sole. "Eve. Come on, Eve. Answer me."

Her head lolled behind her body, her neck taking on an awkward angle. What if she'd hurt her neck? What if she had a fracture? The first thing they say about such things is to immobilize the wounded person's neck.

He couldn't immobilize shit from inside the head. He slipped out as soon as he had a big enough gap and caught his breath at the blood splattered on the sole, the steps, and...oh, hell. He'd opened the companionway doors but he hadn't latched them. He could picture what happened. She came below for the binoculars, went back to the companionway, and the boat lurched over a wave, swinging the door right into her face.

As the images flashed in his head, he grabbed kitchen towels and knelt beside her. He pressed a towel to her bloody forehead, not even trying to figure out where exactly it was cut through the pulsing, pouring blood. Head wounds bled a lot, he'd heard. It wasn't necessarily all that bad.

She raised a weak hand toward her head, eyes closed, and he murmured, "No, let me."

The door didn't have enough weight to crack her skull, just enough to pop the skin. He didn't think it could have broken her neck. She must have dropped straight back like a felled tree.

Her hair was drenched with blood, her eyes pooled with it. He mopped it out of the orbits of her eye sockets gently with the edge of the towel he kept pressed to her forehead.

Jack looked around desperately. Why did he leave Marie behind? Just to up his chances of getting laid? A captain had to be more clear-headed than that. Marie could have reefed the boat while he took care of Eve. Now he had horribly competing priorities, both urgent.

Eve wasn't going to bleed to death. "Can you hold the towel in place?" His stomach dipped when she didn't respond right away, then settled when she moaned. She shook her head and her breath caught with a wince of pain. "That's okay. You're going to be fine." He willed himself to believe it.

The weather, though...that was coming no matter what. Meeting a storm with full sails endangered them both, and the boat.

He could blow out sail panels, broach and knock down the boat, even lose a mast that way. He could sink them, saving nothing and no one by staying attached to her side.

Jack clenched his jaw. *Love may be a drug, but I'm not that high.*

He stooped over Eve and got his hands under her shoulders. "We gotta get you on the settee. Up you go." He pushed until he had her by the armpits, then dragged her down the single step between the galley and the saloon. He winced when her ass, then her heels, bumped on the way down.

Jack sat on the settee, hugging her to his knees. How was he going to get her up? She weighed a good forty pounds more than he did. "If you can push with your legs, do it now." He dragged her onto his lap with a grunt, tipped her to the side and squirmed out from under, then put her legs up. Blood welled in the center of her forehead, more slowly now, darker, and her braid left a sticky trail on the cushion. Good, good. The wound was clotting.

"Eve. Can you hear me?" He knelt beside her, arranged her arms and her neck so that they looked more comfortable.

"Jack…"

"That's right. You're going to be fine. I'll be back as soon as I can." He wanted to stay, to wipe the blood away and bring her back to full consciousness, but he couldn't.

It was more important to keep them both alive than it was to take care of her right that moment.

Jack pulled the lee cloth from below the cushion and fastened it on the handrail that ran the length of the cabin. It would keep her from rolling off the settee, which seemed more and more likely as the wind built outside and the boat started to heel. The steering system would keep them on the same course, relative to the wind, until he changed it. Unfortunately, it wouldn't allow for the increased intensity of the wind. That was his job.

He jumped for the companionway ladder and slipped in Eve's blood on the way up. The boat lurched at the same time that he caught himself on the handhold above, and something in his shoulder wrenched out of place. The lightning strike of pain didn't loosen his grip, but he cursed the fall. Bad, bad, bad.

On deck, the sky was black above, but ringed with blue. The storm center rushed at him, visible in the swirling thunderheads. Wind-whipped waves crashed against the stern, and the battens in the sails creaked ominously. He went straight for the halyards and pulled three sail panels down, favoring his throbbing shoulder.

Had to injure his dominant arm. Damn.

Lysistrata came upright and took the jagged waves more gracefully. The wind built to a shriek as he returned to the cockpit and sheeted in the sails just enough to maintain control.

When the wind died, fast, with the black clouds centered on *Lysistrata*, Jack bolted for the windvane. The storm circled around an eye, and when the wind came back, it was from the other side altogether. The sails crashed around in a wild jibe before he could take control, and the windvane was blown flat. It tried to compensate by bringing the boat onto the opposite heading, but Jack disengaged it before it could turn him back toward the center of the storm.

Holy shit. Would a boat on a windvane keep steering back and forth, crossing the eye of the storm forever? No, the storm was moving faster than the boat. *Lysistrata* couldn't get lost in the storm, though she could have ended up chasing it.

He took the wheel and battled the boat's tendency to turn into the wind. He settled into the new tack and reengaged the windvane, groaning at the relief to his strained shoulder. His focus was broken only by thoughts of Eve. How was she doing below? Was she bleeding again or was she safe enough for the moment?

Sailing was said to be long stretches of monotony punctuated by moments of sheer terror. Was love the same? He'd been more upset by Eve's weak responses than by the sky-spanning storm cell. Their relationship, whatever he wanted to call it, hadn't even hinted at monotony, but it would take a thousand quiet, calm days to balance these long, heart-stopping minutes. Would he ever share a soft rainy day with Eve, reading across from one another on the settees or sharing popcorn while watching something on his laptop?

He wanted to. He wanted whatever being with her would bring.

As the wind eased and the sky above him turned back to faded blue, Jack prepared to jibe again, this time with a little control. Within moments, the wind proved him right when, no longer being spun by the storm system, it backed around to its original heading. More work with the sheets and the windvane got them back on course in light winds.

Ordinarily, he would have raised the sails again, put back up the panels he'd lowered when the winds were gathering force. Slow sailing sounded fine right at that moment, though, with a bleeding woman on his settee and a swelling, painful shoulder.

He surveyed the boat quickly to make sure nothing had broken loose or come undone in the wild jibe. When he was satisfied that he could leave *Lysistrata* to her own devices for a little while, he patted her wheel and went below.

The blood on the ladder was sticky rather than slick this time. He had a lot of cleaning ahead of him, but that was the least of his worries.

Eve. She lay against the lee cloth, her eyes open, her eyelashes crusted with blood. She turned her head toward him and one side of her mouth rose, then the other. When her teeth peeked at him, Jack almost dropped to the floor with weak relief. That famous slow smile.

"I guess I was the damsel in distress."

When Jack left the cabin to deal with the storm, Eve pressed against the hammock or whatever it was Jack had wrapped her in after he boosted her onto the settee. She rolled away from the hammock and managed to put her back on the tipped cushion.

She'd come below for the binoculars. The haziness in her mind worried her, but the throb eased and localized to her forehead. She tried to open her eyes, but her eyelashes stuck together.

"Ugh."

She raised her hand to her head and found the towel sticking to it. Trying to pull it away brought her stomach floating up her throat, so she dropped her hand back to her side.

The cabin tipped to the side, so the boat was running hard in the storm. Out of control? What was Jack doing?

She heard steps on the deck, followed by unidentifiable sounds. With a couple great surges, the boat came nearly upright and the wind's noise modulated to a less frightening tone. The boat's motion eased as well, and she relaxed in the strange cradle.

The wind died and she struggled to sit up, but a crash rang through the boat and she felt, in her ears or her core somewhere, the boat twist through the water, though nothing in the cabin appeared to move.

Jack would have to make it right, whatever the problem was. She lay back down and contemplated the strange ease she felt at that thought. She trusted him. Good thing, too. She'd be worse than useless if there was an emergency.

Closing her eyes, she hoped for the best and tried to relax. The skewing sensation came back and the boat settled into sailing. An eternity later, the wind died until she couldn't even hear it, and the sound was replaced with footsteps on the ladder.

Jack appeared over the edge of the cloth she'd been half lying on. She turned her head to look at him straight on and the strangest thing happened. Her throat thickened, her breath almost stopped, and her pulse went slow and heavy.

She'd imagined him heroically battling the storm, and his expression fit that warrior mold...until he met her eyes. His face went slack and relief poured from him. She must have scared him pretty badly. His eyes glittered, but with tears, not rage. His passion had no tinge of self-interest, no hint that he was afraid of the consequences of mishandling a star.

She didn't even know that mattered to her. She'd forgotten it was possible.

She smiled at him. "I guess I was the damsel in distress."

He smiled, insouciance blanketing his concern. He did something at the railing above her, and the hammock fell away. "Does that make me the hero for saving the day or the villain for bringing you out here?" He put his hand to the towel on her forehead.

"Oh, the hero, definitely." She swung her legs down and tried to sit. Dizzy. Whoa. She could play lighthearted too. "Did you try to rouse me with a magic kiss?"

"I wouldn't...you weren't even conscious...I'd never do that." His distress got her blood stirring again. Who knew she'd fall for earnest? "Don't sit up yet. I need to get you cleaned up and it'll be easier if you'll just lie there."

What kind of mess was she? Her whole face was stiff and sticky. When she put a hand to her hair, it felt soaked in egg white. A sudden understanding of how much she'd bled made her stomach try to sneak out of her belly again. She swallowed dryly and let Jack cluck around her while she took deep breaths to control the nausea.

"I'm going to lift your head a little. There you go. I'm going to get some supplies, but I'll be right back. Just stay put."

Where would she go? Time for a little swim?

Might be the easiest way to clean her hair, but that much blood meant a good-sized cut. Speaking of...

"How bad is it?"

"I haven't gotten a good look yet."

"The door swung closed. It hit me like a baseball bat."

"I figured. Your skin didn't get sliced; it got busted open."

She groaned, but kept her eyes closed. "What a mess. How far are we from a hospital or clinic of some kind?"

"Well, hours in *Lysistrata*. Maybe forty-five minutes for a tow boat to get here and another forty-five minutes to get back. Plus the ride from the waterfront. I doubt the Coast Guard would dispatch a helicopter." His voice neared and she opened her eyes to look at him. He set an armful of things on the floor. "The bleeding has slowed considerably. I'll try to get the towel unstuck without ripping it open. Then some butterfly bandages, gauze, and tape will keep your brains from spilling out."

He didn't carry off the careless tone at the end there, but she was distracted by the pull and pain of him wetting the towel and easing it away from her skin. She tried not to frown, since that hurt worse than what he was doing. "Am I going to scar?"

He froze. His eyes darted to hers with a touch of the panic she'd expected to see earlier. "Shit, Eve, I didn't even think. Your face. I am so sorry." He finished removing the towel with trembling hands and started washing her face.

She let the idea settle. She'd always been so careful of her face and voice and hands. A French film about a pianist stumbling her way into masochism had a line that had become a joke between her and Harmonie. "Not the face; not the hands!"

"No," she said thoughtfully. "It's okay."

"I feel like I've broken your prized vase."

It felt good to laugh. "That's the most romantic thing anyone has ever said to me." Jack's mouth tightened, and he scrubbed at her cheek with his cloth. "No, really. My face...my looks have gotten me a lot of attention, though never as much as what I earned with my music. Too dark, too fat, too..." She shook her head under his hands, letting go, again. "Even those who loved me thought my looks were a crucial part of me." She caught one of his hands in hers. "I like that you see the package as something I use and enjoy, but not as the sum total of what I am."

Jack smiled, but his brow wrinkled. He brought her hand to his lips and kissed her fingers, then went back to his ministrations. He gave her no words, but she didn't mind. She'd had a lot more time than he to think about the side effects of fame.

His fingers and eyes were gentle, but it hurt. Her head ached, with a particular pain along the centerline of her forehead. He finished cleaning her—or gave up, she thought, remembering that her hair was drenched—and spread antibiotic up like a Hindu blessing. He stood and went to the companionway, looked all around the boat, and came back.

My captain.

"Okay," he said, all business. "You need to relax as much as possible. I'll pull the edges of your skin together and tape it closed as well as I can. I'm pretty sure that's what they'd do at the hospital. Just bring the two sides as close as possible without puckering."

"Sounds about right to me." She had no idea if he was right, but his nerves didn't need questions just then.

She appreciated scars on other people. The life and stories they implied brought a richness to faces, arms…wherever. She could rock a scar.

Her vanity hoped that it would be flattering.

He did as he'd said, the concentration narrowing his eyes and tightening his lips. She watched them move, those lips, taking on a determined line as he pulled her skin, tightening on one side when he so obviously needed another hand to hold her skin and pull the backing off the bandages, and finally easing, falling open in a deep sigh after he let go and everything stayed where he'd put it.

Damn. She hadn't planned to fall in love with him. A little infatuation had sounded like fun, but this…he was part of her now.

When he got the gauze and tape on, she wrinkled her nose and moved her eyebrows in little, testing jerks. Nope, she'd have to remain calm, or at least maintain a semblance of calm.

Holding his hand, she sat up and let the world settle into place around her. The cabin moved only a tiny bit in the aftermath of the storm and she realized that they weren't going anywhere, or not much. She turned her eyes to Jack, who pulled a stray piece of sticky hair from her cheek and smooth it into her braid.

"Are we still sailing?"

"The wind died after the storm. I think it'll come back a bit later, but we can motor back to the island if you just want to get home."

"No, I want to be here with you." She fought a desire to lie down and nap. "Let's go sit in the cockpit. I could use some air."

Jack looked concerned but didn't say anything. She grabbed his shoulder to use as a crutch, but he shied and grunted.

"What happened? Did you hurt yourself?" She hadn't noticed anything and remorse flooded her. "You've been taking care of me. What do you need?"

He pulled away, shaking his head. "No, I'm fine. I just pulled my shoulder a little."

"What happened?"

A self-effacing grin crossed his face. "I slipped in your blood going up the ladder."

"What?" She looked across the saloon and through the galley. "Damn. It looks like a slasher film in here."

That got a laugh from him. "I know, right? Plenty of proof that, goddess or not, you're a red-blooded woman."

The laugh that burst from her was edged with retroactive fear. "Is this the type of excitement you show all your passengers?"

"Oh, no. You're special."

She rolled her eyes. "Great. Well, you'll have to be gentle with that shoulder and I don't know if I'm up to scrambling around on deck. How are we going to get *Lysistrata* back home?"

"No problem. She's easy to sail and it's not as hard to let the sails and anchor down as it is to raise them."

"Okay, then, hero. Let's get out of this stinking cabin."

Jack's expression turned wry. "I'm not looking forward to cleaning it, but it's not going to get any easier if I let it soak in and dry."

"Oh, no. No, no, no." She made her voice as firm as it could be. Firm enough to dominate presidents of record labels and stop heads of state from getting handsy. "I'm going to hire someone to do the cleaning and replace the upholstery. This is my mess, my clumsiness, and I'm not going to see you scrubbing for the next week with a bad shoulder."

He bit his lip uncertainly. She turned up the glare a little, but he just knelt there by the settee and looked at her feet. Exasperated, she lifted his chin in her hand. "What?"

"It's my fault. I didn't latch the door open. It never should have swung into you."

She waved his guilt away. "Inconsequential. I will get my way in this, so your options are to let me climb that ladder by myself and stumble around the cockpit, unsteady as I am, or help me up and sit with me awhile."

His lips twisted in a grudging smile, but lines showed around his eyes. She used his other shoulder when she tried standing again. So far, so good. No nausea or additional pain, and her exhaustion had receded. Jack helped her to the ladder and stood below as she negotiated the steps slowly. She went directly to a cockpit cushion and sat.

It occurred to her that she might be spreading more blood around. She checked, but her pants had only the smallest spatters on them. Her shirt was wet around the neckline and where her hair had touched it, but she must have fallen so fast that most of the blood went directly into the wood in Jack's floor. No, sole. It was a sole on a boat.

Her mind was clearing, though an enormous headache hovered. When Jack joined her in the cockpit with a couple of pills and some water, she gave him a soft look. She didn't bother to ask what they were. She had no allergies.

He froze, looking over her shoulder, and she twisted in her seat to see what had arrested his attention. She grimaced as she found the bruises on her ass—from the fall, she assumed—but awareness of her body disappeared when she saw what he was looking at.

A waterspout twisted a few miles away, the snout of a giant invisible elephant in the sky. "Is that our storm?" Awe vibrated in her voice.

Jack put a hand on her shoulder and said, "I do believe it is. I thought it was building, but I didn't expect this." His voice was soft, amazed. He stepped close against her and squeezed her shoulder as though to assure himself that she was safe.

She watched the storm rage away, her shoulders against his thighs, her head on his belly, his hand stroking her neck and shoulder, until the waterspout dissipated and disappeared.

CHAPTER THIRTEEN

Once the waterspout disappeared, Jack felt steadier. Eve would be okay. She was sitting in the cockpit, looking alert, if strained, and he turned his attention to getting her home.

"I'm going to raise the sails." He talked over her initial exclamation. "My shoulder's fine and I'll be careful."

The first part was an exaggeration, but he wasn't about to let her move around the boat. If she fell overboard...well, it just couldn't happen. He started with the lighter sails forward and aft, using the winches to take the bulk of the strain. At the main mast, he sighed and looked for an angle that would let him use his back and lower arm while babying his shoulder. All that arm needed to do was maintain the pressure on the cleat while he turned the winch with the other.

Using his non-dominant arm to winch up the sail took longer than usual, but the whole effort proved doable. He returned to the cockpit with relief. They'd be back in Lysistrata Cove soon.

Eve opened her eyes when he approached and followed him to the helm. He sheeted in the sails, and *Lysistrata* picked up speed as each sail reached its optimum angle. With all the work done and Lysistrata Cove at the edge of the chartplotter screen, he sat with a sigh.

"I'm thirsty."

He'd never heard such a soft tone from her. Worried, he handed her his aluminum water bottle. "I should check my book on marine medicine. Isn't there some kind of injury where you're not supposed to have anything to eat or drink?"

"It's about what kind of medicines they might have to give you." Eve sounded sure. "I'm fine. I don't even think I have a concussion. The pain is pretty crisp, right where the skin is broken."

"Okay. Sounds reasonable." He shifted in his seat. "I'm sorry, Eve. I wanted a romantic sailing day and got us both hurt. The only thing I managed to save was the boat."

"*Lysistrata's* okay? I didn't want to ask, in case the answer was no."

Her wry look brought him out of his funk. "Boat's good. Nothing broke. I got the sails reefed in time." He studied her without the haze of guilt. "You look pretty good."

Only Eve could manage to look imperious with a great swatch of white bandage on her forehead. "I look what?"

Jack slid to his knees in front of her. "You look amazing. You are amazing. All day, you've thrown yourself into learning to sail and now, even injured, you're trying to make me feel better instead of berating me."

She sighed. "I don't want to be the person you seem to think I am. Overbearing, entitled, satisfied with ignorance."

"No!" Jack cupped her hands in his. "I'm saying the exact opposite. I never thought I knew you just because I'd watched you being interviewed or read some gossip about how you treated your hairdresser. Your persona fascinates and attracts me, but you're a person, behind and beyond that, who I admire." He struggled with the thought of saying it all, that he loved her. Insecurity won and he left it at that.

She raised his hand to her lips. "I don't even know how to take a compliment like that. I'm used to being praised for what I can do. My skills get plenty of attention. It's not often that someone wants anything but the rock star."

"I do."

Jack sat beside her, where he could keep an eye on the sails and the chartplotter. When they approached Lysistrata Cove, he turned on the electric motor and dropped the sails. Eve didn't offer to help, and he couldn't stop studying her face for signs that she was hurting. He found some, but only as much as she'd already admitted to.

The wind was light in the cove, and he set the anchor without incident, backing down extra hard since he wouldn't be diving to check it visually. He needed to know with certainty that *Lysistrata* would be okay while he got Eve to her house.

Launching the yawl boat alone would be more than he could manage, so he put Eve on one of the falls, much as he would have preferred to let her keep resting. It didn't take but a few seconds for the boat to hit the water and for him to take her line back. He climbed down and let the pain of using that shoulder wash over him. Useful skill he'd learned in BDSM scenes.

He unhooked the falls and pulled himself and the yawl boat to *Lysistrata's* side. Eve met him with the boarding ladder, which he'd forgotten to put in place. "Thanks."

"Sure."

Their looks were more communicative than their words. Each checking on the other, both slowing when their gazes met. Jack saw Eve getting tired and groggy, and he figured she saw the ache in his shoulder build. He stood in the yawl boat and waved her into his arms.

She turned her back and descended the ladder. He held it with both arms so that she lowered herself into the cage of them. No chance she could get dizzy and fall in the water.

Moments later, he tied up at her little pier. She pulled herself up and stood swaying, several feet above him.

"Come in. Please."

He couldn't possibly leave her alone and Harmonie didn't appear. *Lysistrata* was safe enough. "Of course."

He followed her to the deck and into the quiet house, through the dim living room and back to a room he'd never seen, though he recognized it. A playroom.

Across the room, a double bed nearly spanned one wall. Between the door and the bed, a dresser stretched on each side of a glass-fronted wardrobe, inside of which hung crops and floggers and canes. A spanking bench and St. Andrew's cross took up the rest of the room.

Eve stripped her shirt over her head as she crossed the room and Jack said, "Let me help." She nodded and he unhooked her bra. Livid lines showed where it had wrapped under her arms, and he smoothed her skin while slipping the bra off. His only thought was to ease her, but she moaned and stretched under his hands. When he wrapped his arms around her and palmed her breasts, her areolae tightened.

She unsnapped the waistband of her pants and let them fall to her hips. He slid his hands over her belly and pushed them off with her underwear. She toed her shoes off and lowered herself to the bed. She looked at him, the bandage the only bright spot other than her eyes. "Will you lay with me?"

"Of course."

That was his answer for everything she wanted from him, and she must have grasped that. "I want you naked."

He pulled his shirt off his good arm, then over his head, so he wouldn't hurt his shoulder raising his arm. Everything else came off in one movement and he crawled into bed next to her, under the arm she raised for him. He cuddled close, his head on her shoulder and his mouth only inches from her soft breast. A yearning so strong it felt like mourning swelled in him. He wanted to love her freely, without pain or question, but their lives were so different that something would have to give if they were to weave them together. There would be problems, so many specifics to negotiate.

If he wasn't alone in falling in love. If she could love him back.

He draped his bad arm across her belly and kissed the soft skin of her shoulder. He nestled his crotch closer against her thigh, trying not to give the impression he was humping her, though tension invaded his body along with desire. His nipples raked across her side and he strove to still himself so she could rest.

"I don't want to sleep."

Whether or not she'd read his mind, she'd said exactly what he wanted to hear. He raised his head. "Are you sure?"

"I want you to love me. Make me feel good."

Her soft words made him shiver, exposed in the hot light of her knowledge. "I do love you, Eve, and I want you to feel good. You're not a hundred percent, though. Do you like it gentle?"

"I like you. Anything you do will make me feel good. I don't know about coming without getting more energetic than either of us is up to, but let's just enjoy each other."

Jack thrust aside the pain of her returning liking for love and the gaping fear of being so vulnerable to her. He focused on what she wanted, what she'd asked for.

Inch by inch, he kissed and caressed her. Second by second, he melted her, softened her every muscle. He took her nipple between his teeth without biting and hoped she was yearning for more.

He wanted her to yearn.

When her legs lolled open on the linen, he palmed her cunt. She didn't move, but her breathing stuttered, and he knew she was with him. He opened her and used long, slow strokes to wake her nerves, but his shoulder complained and he stiffened.

Her hands drifted into view and cupped his face. She raised his head. "Use your mouth."

He salivated like one of Pavlov's dogs at the memory of her cunt cruising over his face before crushing down on him. He knew what to do.

Slipping to the end of the bed, he found just enough room to kneel on the floor beyond. Eve followed and braced her feet on the wall behind him. Open and gleaming in the dim light of the room, her cunt lay exposed and he took what she'd given him.

He buried his face in her cunt and barely moved. His cheeks and lips wet, his nose and chin and tongue all nudged and pressed and swiped against her. He wanted to eat her up, to put her in his mouth and swallow, but she was more than he could encompass. He could only delve deeper with his tongue stuck out, up and down with it flat and soft. Eve's moan, more air than sound, reached him from far away, but her hand on his hair connected them.

Her pulse throbbed, strong and slow, in the hollow of her thigh and he strove to keep it from speeding even while intensifying his attentions. No penetration. That would make her want to thrust. He needed to keep her relaxed, but he might be able to make her come even so.

Without any concept of time or duration, he surged slowly against her, turning his face into her cunt lips in figure eights and never, never putting pinpoint pressure on her clit. When her whole cunt pulled in and then relaxed against his chin, he focused and sped up, just a little, just enough to spur more waves of clench and release. Her hand fell from his head and she moaned in long, rolling waves with the contractions. When her breathing broke and a shudder ran through her body, he replaced his mouth with his hand and climbed on top of her. His fingers on her cunt and his forearm against his clit, he ground himself to a slow orgasm of his own, her clenching of his fingers setting up a feedback loop that tumbled him over the edge.

They slept.

When Jack woke, he opened his eyes to see a dark line of shoulder. The wall chilled his back and Eve heated his front, spooned against him with her hand holding his wrist at her belly. A light beyond her caught his attention and he raised his head slightly. Harmonie stood in the doorway a moment and disappeared.

As he wrapped his muzzy brain around the direction and quality of the light, he disentangled himself from Eve. He slid to the bottom of the bed—flashed on doing the same thing earlier—and stood.

His shoulder ached. Even in sleep, Eve's mouth was tight with pain. Such good care he'd taken of her. He hadn't even insisted that they take anti-inflammatories. Self-disgust battled the memory of her firm orders. She hadn't given him time, but she was the one with a head wound. She had an excuse for not thinking clearly.

He stumbled on their clothing and reached for his pants and shirt. The house was dark, except for one light coming from the living room. He froze as he realized what he'd done.

Maybe it wasn't that late.

The hallway stretched oddly, his head still not clear after such deep sleep. Harmonie stood in the living room and watched him enter.

"Can I get some ibuprofen?"

She gestured at the low table where water and a pill bottle awaited. "That was for Eve, but we have plenty."

He wasn't sorry to put off thinking a moment longer. He didn't know what to say to her, since he didn't know enough about Eve and Harmonie's relationship to know if they'd broken an agreement by using the playroom bed. Before they got into all that, he had another burning question.

"What time is it?"

Harmonie kept her voice as low as his. "Nearly midnight."

A groan tore through him. "Fuck."

"What's wrong?" She waved his answer off. "Hold on. I'm going to close the play room door."

Jack sat among the cushions and took three ibuprofens. When Harmonie returned, he said, "I need to borrow your phone."

"Where's yours?"

Her question set his teeth on edge. "On the boat."

She stared for a long moment. "What happened?"

"I need to make a phone call. Please."

Harmonie stood, radiating irritation. She came back shortly with a cordless phone.

Jack stared at the keypad. Holy shit. He didn't even know Marie's number.

He let his head fall back and emotion flowed through him. When he gained a little control, he looked at Harmonie. She'd curled up nearby, her legs under her and a steaming cup in her hand. The smell of mint followed the sight of the cup. He was clicking back into reality.

"We were having a great time, when a storm cell came up on us. It was a real tropical storm, twisted, with high winds. The door swung closed, right in Eve's face, and it broke the skin. I wrenched my shoulder trying to take care of everything. We got back here fine, but it was seriously exhausting. She led me into that room and we... went to sleep." He didn't see any reason to be more explicit.

"I wondered, when I saw the bandage, how bad it was. Did she bleed a lot?"

Relief. She was focusing on Eve's injury. "Yeah, but the door isn't heavy. I don't think she has a concussion. A bit of a bump maybe. I closed it with butterfly bandages and covered it with gauze."

Harmonie sipped her tea. After a moment, she asked, "Didn't you need to call someone?"

Guilt and disgust flowed back into him. "Marie. She was expecting me back hours ago."

"Don't know her number?"

"No."

"Is it online somewhere? Do your contacts sync with your email?"

He shook his head.

"Who is she with?"

"She spent the day crewing on another boat, with passengers that booked their trip with me. Fuck." He fisted his hands. "I can't believe I did that."

"What?"

"Any of it!" Harmonie's gentle questioning drew it all out. "I canceled a booking to take Eve sailing and kicked Marie off the boat. She lives aboard with me!"

Harmonie blinked. "That sucks."

"I basically stole her home and haven't brought it back." He tried to stretch his shoulder and groaned at the pain. "I don't think I'm up to single-handing all the way back by myself. Not in the middle of the night."

"Damn."

"I have to tell her, at least." He dropped his head back on the cushion. He marshaled his thoughts. "I can get Charlie's number from his website. If she's still on the Gypsy, he can put her up for the night."

Harmonie rose again and came back with a laptop. Jack got what he needed and made the call. "Charlie? Is Marie with you?"

"She is indeed, my lovely boy. We're corrupting your crew with drink and low company. Marie! It's Jack!"

Charlie's bellow hit Jack's ear hard and he winced. The background noise proved his words. Sounded like a bar in full swing. Marie's voice joined the cacophony and then she came on the phone. "Jack! Come on down, we're having a great time!"

"Marie, are you sober enough to listen?"

"Duh."

Jack sighed. "I'm still at Eve's island, Marie. Eve hurt her head and I hurt my shoulder and I won't be able to make it back tonight."

"But...where will I sleep?"

"I'm sure you can bunk on the Gypsy."

"I don't have any clothes."

"I'll be back tomorrow."

Her voice got smaller. "I thought..."

"*Lysistrata* is your home, Marie." His vehemence hid the spark of hope that he'd be planning his life more around Eve, somehow. Guilt punched him hard. "I'm so sorry, Marie."

"I have to go." She sounded nearly sober. "Since I'm homeless and all, I better make arrangements for a place to sleep."

The click hurt, though he'd expected it. He glowered at the phone until Harmonie took it from him.

"Don't beat yourself up about it, Jack. Sounds like a bizarre set of circumstances. She'll understand when she sees you tomorrow morning."

"Is this what love means?" He looked at Harmonie. He'd soft-pedaled the story earlier, skipping the part where they'd had sex, but who could understand his quandary better than Harmonie? "It's like a drug. I don't think clearly. Bringing boatload after boatload here, just so I could see her again. Sending Marie away for the privacy. Then, once Eve was on the floor bleeding, I couldn't think of anything but her."

Harmonie's face communicated little at first. Finally, she leaned forward. "Jack. Love is the best drug in the world. Eventually, you get used to the feeling and get some sense back. I'm not saying it loses its power. Just that things will get clearer over time. Good loves get you high but let you move past the stupid mistakes phase into solid partnership."

He stared at her. Feature by feature, he studied her. "I don't get the impression you're warning me off, but it feels like that's the subtext."

Surprise moved across her face and she leaned back. "No." She snorted. "Just the opposite. Me and Eve...we're solid partners, but whatever drug effect there was is long gone. The more we disagree about how to handle the music industry, the less our partnership works for us both."

What to say to that? Jack turned the water glass in his hands.

"I'm glad you two met. I think you stimulate her more than anything I've seen since she stopped performing regularly." She stood. "I'm going to bed. If you're going to have a tough sail tomorrow, you might want to sleep some more too."

She walked out of the room, straight-backed and strong. Jack followed her advice and slipped into bed with Eve, who sighed and pressed back against him. He didn't sleep, though, not for quite some time. Too many thoughts flew through his head.

Chapter Fourteen

Eve looked up from the staff paper when Harmonie cleared her throat, but she left her elbow on the key cover of the piano. Notes traded places in her head and she tried the new run on the piano. The pencil bobbed and danced between her racing fingers. Better. Her head was clear after a few days of doing nothing but healing. Harmonie had kept her supplied with a headache-soothing tea made from the root bark of the Jamaican Dogwoods that shaded the house. The tea also helped with insomnia, so she'd gotten plenty of rest.

She noted the change on the bass staff and stuck the pencil into her hair. With a flourish, she played the extended phrase, a full sixteen measures to pop music's usual four measure phrasing. Mmm. Much better.

This would be her answer to "Goofy's Concern" by the Butthole Surfers, the rudest love song ever written.

Harmonie nodded when she checked in with her. "That's getting richer and richer by the minute."

"I like it. The lyrics are a struggle. There's no topping the original."

"I'm sure you'll manage. If you can't out-crass them, maybe you'll have to out-raunch them."

Eve stared at her staff paper, the penciled-in quarter and eighth notes dancing as the idea soaked in. She got a hint of how it would go and nodded. "Brilliant." She flashed Harmonie a smile. "Go with my strengths."

Harmonie's answering smile lacked in the sincerity department. "Even the paparazzi recognized that you strode right past crass and planted your flag in the sexual territory beyond."

Eve focused on Harmonie, realizing that as hard as she tried to joke, something had disturbed her. "What's up, honey?"

Harmonie joined her on the piano bench and started the second movement of Schubert's *Fantasia* for four hands, taking the secondo part. Eve took the primo part and helped her play away some of her tension. After they reached the bold ending, Harmonie tipped her head against Eve's, hands in her lap.

Eve put an arm around Harmonie's waist. They'd built their relationship on these quiet moments when they could feel like students of music together. Their musical tastes dovetailed nicely. They enjoyed many of the same sounds, but had different enough ears that they continued to turn each other on to new acts. They played together as naturally as blinking, and improved each other's work by taking improvisational play in unexpected directions. Eve knew that her music would have a slightly different flavor when Harmonie wasn't around to add her spice.

Eve wasn't fussing about some vague future anymore. She could feel Harmonie releasing her, turning to different aims and goals, getting ready to set off on her own quest to change the music industry. Harmonie's quiet relief about Jack had tipped her hand. It chafed that Harmonie had waited to leave until Eve wasn't alone, but she'd always known that, top or bottom, Harmonie was the real caregiver of the relationship.

Harmonie had gotten her through the deep depression after Marc's suicide. She'd provided the form Eve could shape her overwhelming emotions around. She was the only person on the planet who knew what Eve had tried to do, who could appreciate her intentions, even though she'd failed with Audion.

Pride, though. That was the nasty side of Eve's feelings. Her pride was taking a hit. The hole would heal, but she was losing some of what kept her afloat in the public world of music. It took a lot of confidence to face the inevitable attacks and adoration at each and every public appearance. Eve would never let Harmonie know that she'd left a vulnerability in Eve's armor.

Suddenly, she was glad Harmonie had waited until Jack. God, was she really so dependent on others for her sense of strength and pride?

Eve thrust the thoughts aside. "Did you need me?"

A faint smile crossed Harmonie's lips. "Always." That struck a sour note against Eve's thoughts, and she was glad when Harmonie went on. "But I got a very strange email. It's packed full of trigger phrases, references to places that don't exist and shows you never played. It was either a deranged fan or a code, and the deranged fans almost never contact me."

Eve turned on the bench. "And?"

Harmonie gripped the piano cover with both hands. "I'm pretty sure it's a coded message from Stephanie Watersley, your judge in Massachusetts."

Eve's eyebrows twitched at the name, but the bandage covering her forehead aborted her frown. "What would Stephanie have to say that she couldn't send directly?"

"I don't know, because it's not in the email. All it says, really, is to call a certain number at a certain time."

"She wouldn't go to all this trouble for something small. She's pretty normal for being pretty much obsessed with me."

Harmonie rolled her eyes. She didn't have to say it. Eve knew she was hard on the people who treasured her music the most. "Regardless, she's also the kind of judge who approves or denies warrants. I'm thinking they're on to us."

"Fuck." Eve laced her fingers together so she wouldn't bite her fingernails. "They must want to search the Boston house. When does she want me to call?"

"In about an hour." Harmonie handed her a scrap of paper. "At this number."

"Okay." Her thoughts couldn't get any traction. "What do we need to do?"

"Nothing until we know the story. Maybe it won't affect us here, since the island is in my name."

"There's nothing in the Boston house that can lead the FBI to us. Probably."

An hour later, Eve watched the morning sun glisten over the cove while she listened to Stephanie's concise precis on the situation. She perched on the side of the lounger she'd fucked Jack on, wondering what she'd do about him if her safe haven disappeared.

"They're not just after search warrants anymore. They wanted an arrest warrant, and got it. They went to your house and you weren't there, of course, so they've put the US Marshals on finding and arresting you."

"How did they get the arrest warrant? What proof do they have?" Eve's awareness that Stephanie was already breaking the law made it easy to push for more information.

"It's always the money. Your brightest idea really fucked you over. You're right that people should be able to pay for music they've downloaded if they decide they like it enough. But it made a whole web of financial connections when you moved the money for them. They took the money-laundering aspect to the aggregators and one of them rolled on you. You're the most famous person they've ever hunted in this program. Every other person running pirate servers is a nobody. You're the big coup for whoever brings you down."

"I still don't know how it comes back to me. I thought I'd covered myself." Eve shook her head. "Regardless, what's their next move?"

Stephanie sighed heavily. "I haven't even given you the bad news yet. They know where you are."

"What?" Eve sat very straight in the lounger. "How did they find me?"

"A lawyer here in Boston heard rumors of the case against you. They've been casting a wide net, and it's common knowledge that you're a prize. She's with the biggest firm in town and well up on the gossip. This woman says she saw you while she was on vacation with her wife and kids, some kind of sailing trip down south." When Eve began to speak, Stephanie talked over her. "Don't tell me anything. I don't want to know where you are or what you're doing there. Her researchers found some kind of corroborating evidence, and she turned it all over to the FBI."

"Motherfucker." Eve stared through the open sliding door to where Harmonie was listening on another phone. "What should I expect?"

"It'll probably be a mixed team that shows up. Marshals, FBI. If you're offshore, probably Coast Guard, maybe local sheriffs or harbormasters. I don't know. But you'd better get the hell out of there before they show up and I'd suggest wiping everything you can't take with you. Once they get to you, they're indicting you for racketeering, money laundering, and copyright infringement. We're talking about fifty years in prison if you can't get rid of the bulk of the evidence."

"Thanks, Stephanie." Eve finished the conversation in a daze. She put the phone on the deck's railing.

Harmonie stalked toward her. Anger sparked from her and she bit her words off. "Well, at least we planned for this." She slammed a fist on the railing. "I didn't want it to end this way."

Eve hardly heard her. "Fucking Jack." She pushed off the railing and swept a caged circle on the deck. Her heart pounded.

Harmonie's surprise passed fast. "Holy shit. The lawyer was his passenger."

"I told him. I fucking told him that his visits put us in danger. He led them straight to us." Eve fisted her hands on a lounger cushion and pulled, but the heavy fabric resisted her need to tear into something.

Harmonie shook her head hard and bit her cheek.

"What?" Eve's challenge grated in her throat. She didn't want to fight with Harmonie while their lives fell apart, but she couldn't control the need to make a stand. Some kind of stand.

Harmonie strode over to stand just across the lounger. She pointed a long finger in Eve's face and Eve's snarl didn't make her back down. "You're the one who had to go flaunt yourself for his passengers. Three times, Eve, three times you let people see you. You're not immune from sense, damn it. Why are we in the middle of the goddamn ocean if not to keep people from seeing you?"

Eve sputtered, unable to grab an individual idea among Harmonie's rant to demolish. Finally, she ground out, "Flaunted myself?"

Harmonie put her hands on her hips. "Hell yeah. I could have handled these people. If you were so desperate for adulation, I could have set up a show."

Eve had never heard disgust in Harmonie's voice before. Not aimed at her. It tore at her control and threatened to release her rage. "That bitch didn't turn me in because I went aboard and started signing autographs. She worked damn hard to figure out who I was."

Harmonie put her hands on the back of the lounger and leaned in. "Your music was a damn fine clue. Add a set of binoculars and the resources of a law firm's entire research division and here it is. We're now on the run." She turned and gripped the deck's railing.

Eve stared over Harmonie's shoulder where the sun angled across the cove. She made a grab for calm and missed. "Your precious plan gone awry, has it? She didn't say anything about you being named in the warrant. You're free to go whenever you want, and I know that you've been itching for the right moment to leave."

Harmonie turned and leaned against the railing. Her strapless, brightly patterned dress and dark skin glowed in the bright tropical sun. Her locs framed her stiff face and her arms spread to either side, hands gripping the satiny wood of the railing. Eve froze with an overwhelming rush of love and fear, her anger stripped from her in the deluge.

"Don't speak," Eve begged. She rushed over and put her hand on Harmonie's jaw, but the muscles tightened against her. "We don't have to do that right now, okay? Let's do what needs to be done. Get what we can off the island and erase the servers. You are in danger too; I know it. This is the only way I can protect you." Harmonie stood like a statue, only her fingertips moving restlessly. "Please. Let's clean this place and get the hell out of here."

Harmonie nodded stiffly. "One thing, first. I love you, Eve. I'm glad you know that we've been heading for a split. I figured you did. This isn't how I wanted it to happen, but we knew we might be leaving here in a hurry." She hesitated. "I've got plans and ideas of my own. Your way is ending. Think about whether or not you want to be part of mine."

Eve let Harmonie turn and leave the deck without breaking down. When she heard Harmonie's steps descend to the server room, she put her face in her hands and let the tears come.

She didn't have time to indulge in a real bout. As she pulled herself together, her anger crystallized. She'd played a part in destroying this idyllic sojourn, but finding other focuses for her rage was easy. That lawyer was going to pay. Somehow, Eve would bring her down for this.

And Jack. Something twisted in her. Her secret, tender love showed its opposite side, and she wondered if she would hate him for this forever.

❖

Jack tried to focus on anchoring and settling the boat, but he couldn't help his repeated glances at Eve's deck. She was nowhere to be seen.

Private embarrassment flowered with his realization that he'd expected her to be there, skirts blowing in the wind, watching out to sea for him. She had softened to him and given him hope that they were building a relationship. That there was a chance his love was returned. Even though he'd left early the morning after their disastrous sail, she'd woken enough to take some painkillers and assure him that she wasn't mad. She'd kissed him tenderly, as tenderly as he'd made her come, and held his hand until he'd pulled free despite the agony of separating himself from her.

When the cleaning crew had taken over the boat to get rid of the blood, he'd spent the downtime listening to Eve's Kitten Caboodle releases. Sexy songs. He'd been driven to christen his new settee cushion by jacking off there as soon as the workers had left.

He had to find a way to love her without losing himself in her.

The passengers on this trip were locals, four women who met regularly and yet never made it past the beach. They'd decided it was time to get out on the water instead of sitting in the sun and paddling around in the shallows, so they'd asked around about tour boats. Jack was gratified to learn that his reputation was solid with the locals. He didn't market his trips as tours, per se, because he refused to set specific itineraries, but the ladies had been intrigued by his salty explanation of how the weather shaped one part of the boating experience and the flexibility of the boat's plans shaped another. The organizer, Jenny, had noted that he specialized in queer cruises and made sure he was okay with taking out a bunch of obnoxious straight ladies.

The surprise of the trip was Chauniqua. She was the quietest of them but flirted with him subtly, and he wouldn't have felt like a gentleman if he hadn't reciprocated. He met too many strangers not to have made his gender identity part of the welcome-aboard chatter. He'd gotten it down to a couple of short sentences between the main orientation to the boat and the safety briefing, and most people tried to remember. He hadn't caught any whiff of the freak show in her attention and she'd gotten his pronouns right from the beginning, so he was disposed to like her.

This group was half married, half single, and Chauniqua had been explicit about being one of the single ladies. If he hadn't hoped to see Eve that night, he might have put himself out a little farther to see if she was really interested or just enjoyed a light flirtation.

He looked at the deck again. Still empty.

Marie nudged him. "You look like a puppy dog waiting for your person to come home."

"That's revolting." He glared at her. As smitten as he was, he knew it wasn't that bad.

Her eyebrows rose. "Slow your roll, there, stud. I was just teasing."

He stopped turning away and looked back at her. When had he become so sensitive? "I'm sorry, Marie. I don't know why I've been such a jackass lately."

"Coming out of your cocoon, perhaps?" Her tone was joking, but her lips barely moved.

He sneered. "That's right. I'm a punk rock butterfly, damn it."

That got her to grin. "Whatever. Do you want me to check the anchor? You're usually in the water by now."

He jolted and tried to hide it. "Yes, please. Do you know what the ladies are leaning toward? Picnic on the beach or on the boat?"

"Boat. Jenny talked everyone into avoiding sand in their coochies—her words, not mine—and letting us take care of them."

He wanted to go ashore and leave her with the ladies, but he was still making up for leaving her homeless for a night. "I'll get dinner started, then. You can take some time off, if you like. Hang out or hide out in the forepeak."

Suspicion creased her forehead, but she knew better than to question time off in the middle of a cruise. "Maybe I'll go swimming."

"Sounds great. I'll set up the boarding ladder." Jack didn't feel guilty at all for banking some free time for himself later. He'd entertain the ladies a while, then pass the reins to Marie for cleanup and let them know they'd be on their own that evening.

He'd hardly started grilling the red snapper he'd gotten on the pier when the smell of the marinade brought the ladies to the cockpit. The next hour went quickly, trading stories and eating generous portions of fish, corn on the cob, and biscuits with whipped butter and jam. These weren't fancy people, but they appreciated a good piece of fresh snapper. None of them kept butter around the house, so the biscuits were a huge hit.

His ribs took a beating from Jenny's elbows. She'd caught him looking at Eve's deck one too many times and had chivvied the admission from him that he was "sort of dating" the woman who lived there. Chauniqua looked disappointed, so she had held an interest in him. Did he have the energy—emotional or physical—to start dating another woman right then? He wouldn't mind trying a sort-of-straight relationship, though it had never sounded attractive before. Maybe it was just that Chauniqua seemed so straightforward, even predictable, compared to Eve.

When he bowed out and left the ladies to their own devices, he tapped Marie on the shoulder and tipped his head toward the bow. She followed him up the side deck and sat on the cabin top with him.

"What's up?" she said, without the insinuating overlay of before.

"I'm going to head to Eve's and see if she's into hanging out. I'll be back within a couple hours." Marie looked away and he bumped her shoulder with his. "I promise. I'm going to be more thoughtful about you from here on out. I fucked you over the other night, and I'm sorry. I like having you aboard, but I'd forgotten that this is your home too."

"For a while," she said noncommittally.

"Yeah. I'm also sorry I brought the temporary aspect of that to the front of your mind. I hope you crew with me for as long as you enjoy it."

She sighed. "I had forgotten that this isn't my home, that it's your boat. I still think you did a shitty thing, staying away without any notice. But it's gotten me thinking about where I'm going. I never planned to sail with you forever, and you've given me one hell of an education. I just need to decide what I want to do with it. Keep crewing, for you or someone else, or go back to school for my master's, or make some new plans altogether."

"You'll figure it out and there's no hurry. As long as I'm doing charters here, you have a job as crew."

Marie bumped his shoulder back. "Thanks. It's nice to know I'm wanted." They sat in silence a moment, back in accord. "Go on, visit your Garden of Eden."

He sighed as he stood. "Right now, it sounds more like heaven itself."

Marie made a rude noise and followed him back to the yawl boat. His shoulder twanged a little as he and Marie lowered it, but that was a great improvement over the way he'd felt when pulling it up on the davits—by himself—the day after he'd hurt his shoulder. He jumped aboard and zoomed away from *Lysistrata*, cheers and graphic well-wishes from the tipsy women following him.

The roar of what he'd started calling an "infernal combustion engine" would have better matched his powerful drive to see Eve, but his oars spun glowing luminescent creatures off the blades without the stink of fuel. Stars popped out fast as the hectic flush of day settled away. It occurred to him that he should have texted to see if she was in the middle of anything—or anyone—but it seemed disingenuous to bob on the water just off her pier while rectifying that mistake.

Poly 101, via Andre 3000.

Humming "I'll Call Before I Come," he made fast to the wooden piling and climbed the ladder. Low tide, so he had a fabulous view of *Lysistrata* in the cove from atop the pier. She shone with lanterns and citronella candles and rang with laughter. Marie had covered the sails. He'd have to remember to thank her for taking up the slack while he'd mooned over the empty deck. He could admit, now that the moment was past, that he'd reacted so strongly to the puppy dog comment because she'd accurately pinpointed his feelings.

He'd take the chance that Eve was busy composing or putting Harmonie in her place. The image made him smile. He'd love to see them play. The possibility that he would be invited to join put an extra spring in his step as he climbed to the deck.

He knocked, since he couldn't find a bell or buzzer. The mosquito netting moved sinuously in the light breeze, but no signs of life appeared.

If they were playing, they were too wrapped up for him to be banging on walls.

He pulled his phone from his pocket and thumbed out a quick text. *I'm on the deck. You busy?*

His phone gave him nothing back for long minutes, and his expectations lost their cheery tone. Shit. He fidgeted, scraping the scattered sand against the deck's wooden surface with the toe of his shoe, turning in circles to look at *Lysistrata* and then back into the darkened house.

A shadow moved inside and resolved itself into Eve's curvy body. He clenched inside, and his instant wetness would have made him blush if anyone could have known.

Eve stopped on the other side of the netting, arms akimbo, one foot forward. He waited for her to speak. Something was wrong.

"You have some fucking nerve bringing more people to this cove."

CHAPTER FIFTEEN

He reared back as though dodging a blow. There was no standing firm against the vitriol in her voice.

"What do you mean, Eve? I…" He didn't know what to say. He didn't think she'd mind? She'd never said he couldn't. He hadn't been back with passengers since the nightmare family, just for that one sail with her. She had been omnipresent in his mind, and he'd spent the entire time feeling as though he'd been with her, literally, when they hadn't actually seen each other since he'd sailed away with her kiss on his lips.

Lye burned in her voice. "Your money-making joyrides have cost me everything, Jack. That bitch of a lawyer you brought here? Well, she identified me and ratted me out. Harmonie and I have to get the hell out of here before the shit hits the fan."

Horror stopped his breath when she brought up the lawyer. He couldn't even claim to be surprised. If anyone had been a problem in the making, it was her. He should have known she'd had something worse up her sleeve when she'd paid his repair bill without a quibble.

His second reaction, though, had an irritated edge. "How on earth does this mean you have to leave? The paparazzi don't jump every place you're reported to be." He tried not to show that he thought she was blowing it out of proportion. If her ego was big enough to be that sensitive, she would shred him for questioning her importance.

"You selfish ass." Her growl couldn't shock him like her words. "You have no idea what's at stake here. I'm looking at decades in

prison and you think I'm hiding from cameras?" Her last words rose
to rival the shriek of the storm they'd weathered together. "Harmonie
is busting her ass to clean our mess. Either you get the hell off my
island or get your doubting ass down there and help."

He heard her words, but they wouldn't compute. "Prison?"
Maybe she'd been running drugs after all.

She'd offered two choices. His innate caution wouldn't let him
take either path. He knew without being told that he would never
see her again if he left now. The love he'd been bathing in, the hope
and joy that had suffused his every moment, they urged him to fight
for her.

At the same time, her words, her tone, her very being shouted
that she had no love for him. She was royally pissed, and if prison
was a real possibility, he could understand why. If he stayed, what
would he be getting himself into?

Eve's voice was an instrument and he played back his memory
of her words. She'd called him vile names, but she'd also been
insulted, perhaps even hurt, by his minimizing of her danger. She'd
said straight out that she and Harmonie would be leaving together,
but also opened the door to him if he was willing to help. Even
more, the way her voice had quavered the tiniest bit when she'd shot
the word doubting at him...

He trusted her, but that didn't mean she wouldn't get him in
trouble.

"Let me in and tell me what I can do."

Eve let out breath like a steam train getting ready to move, but
she slid the mosquito netting aside. "Come on."

He followed her through the darkened den and down the spiral
stairs to the music room, aglow with equipment LEDs. She surprised
him by heading across the room to what he'd assumed was a closet
and opening the door. The coats and shoe boxes that would have
confirmed his impression were shoved aside and a trapdoor yawned
from the floor. A plain steel ladder led down into bright light.

A secret basement. He tried to fan his curiosity and suppress his
fear, but they were neck and neck when she disappeared and he put
his foot on the first rung.

He kept his eyes on the wall behind the ladder until the blazing lights were well above him. His foot touched the floor and he turned. A gasp tore from him, followed by, "Wha…"

Eve stood a couple feet away, her hands on her hips and her face set. Harmonie sent him a harried glance over her shoulder. He heard a muttered, "Are you fucking kidding me?"

Eve looked at Harmonie and back at Jack. He couldn't take his eyes off the racks and racks of servers, filling the footprint of the house. Every high-tech modern spy film had a scene in a room like this. Cool blue LEDs blinked all down the line of matte black housings. The quiet surprised him. He would have expected more fans.

He spoke slowly. "What do a couple of musicians need with a server farm?"

Harmonie stacked small external hard drives in miniature towers, USB cable spaghetti connecting them to inset ports. Her side of the room looked like a workshop, with a workbench at a convenient height for her, tools pinned to pegboard above, and an articulated arm with a clamp at the end, the kind used while soldering. Plain tables with utilitarian tops lined the wall. The only empty floor space was between the ladders and Harmonie's workbench, and Jack could picture them loading servers into racks in the space before rolling them into position with their kin.

Eve asked Harmonie, "How long until we start wiping?"

"Half hour, probably."

"What can we do in the meantime?"

"Wait."

Eve took the stool at Harmonie's workbench and stared across the gulf at Jack. He hadn't yet released the ladder, as though he could still choose to climb out of the basement and leave. He waited for an explanation.

Finally, Eve spoke. "You're the captain, but I'm the pirate."

His eyes flicked to the servers and understanding dawned. Disappointment batted at his thoughts. All this to download stolen movies? And music, he assumed.

Her jaw clenched at whatever she saw in his face. "Copyright is one of the evils of our time. It fucking *ruins* people—and art—all in the name of American individuality. The idea that my songs belong to me after I play them to others…it's simply madness. If my songs don't exist independent of me, what do I achieve by writing them? I give *birth* to those songs. Parenting means protecting a creation long enough that it can thrive on its own. Anything else is slavery."

Jack released the ladder and turned to look straight at Eve. Harmonie still hadn't met his gaze and hurt prickled at the idea that they blamed him for whatever was happening here. "This is all very high-flown theoretical talk, and I can see your point on a philosophical level, but what does that have to do with stealing movies?"

Even in three-quarter profile, he could see Harmonie's sneer. Eve leaned against the workbench and put her hands on the surface behind her. Jack couldn't stop the glance he slipped down her body, but she was as focused as he'd ever seen her.

Her tone went professorish. "Stealing presupposes ownership, which I don't grant the copyright holders of the material on these servers. If I've stolen anything by loading music here and trafficked in stolen goods by inviting people to download it, it's the money that would have been paid by some small fraction of those people in buying the music. First, most of these people wouldn't have paid to buy the overpriced albums. Second, what do you think would have happened to the money that would have left that tiny percentage of pockets? It would have been sliced by all the entities taking their cut. RIAA, BMI, the record label, the lawyers. The actual labor put into an album—physical or digital—would have been paid something between comfortable money and starvation wages. The factory workers who make discs, the computer operator who loads the music, the programmer who tags the tracks. The marketing intern who does cover mockups, the person who plastic-wraps the final product.

"Then there is the original creative laborer. Touring is the only way artists make money, and more people go to shows if they already love the music. My first record contract was so favorable to the record company that I nearly went into bankruptcy while I had a string of number one hits on the radio. I struggled out of that hole by performing four, five, six nights per week until I fell apart physically and had to get sober long enough to heal. Without the training I got in school, I probably would have done what so many others do and burned out my voice, the instrument I needed most. I did better later, but not much."

"You still get paid, right? For record sales and radio play?"

"Me? Yes. Unlike some poor musicians, I never resorted to the devil's bargain. The last step, the last desperate option for a musician who's lost in the whirlpool, is to sell their copyright. At that point, there's no natural tie whatsoever between the person who created the music and the copyright holders who laugh all the way to the bank. It's just a product!"

Jack couldn't argue with Eve. He didn't know enough about the music industry, certainly not a fraction of what she knew from firsthand experience. Her ragged breathing worried him, though, and he crossed the room. Approaching her, he didn't know if he should offer a shoulder or a hand.

Harmonie cradled a hard drive, one that must have finished loading whatever she'd sent it. She jerked when Eve picked up her argument and set the drive aside.

"Then there are those who run afoul of the law. Sampling is a technological way to do what musicians have always done. Adopt and adapt the sounds that wedge their way into our heads. Copyright law slows the spread of new sounds. One second too long and a life might be forfeited." Eve put her hands over her face and drew her shoulders in.

Jack was lost, though her pain was clear enough. "Eve. I don't know what you're talking about. What do you mean?"

Eve's withdrawal wasn't that easy to pierce, but Harmonie turned, finally. She pressed her lips together tightly, then said, "Production seemed to be where the power was, so Eve changed direction. She kept writing but fed the songs to young, promising acts. She started producing albums, and her most brilliant find was a group of young men who called themselves Audion."

A certain numbness took over Jack's face. He knew the story, though he hadn't heard, or hadn't remembered, that Eve was their producer. Harmonie fell silent. She must have seen that the rest of the story was already running through his mind. Audion had been sued for using a bit from a classic rock song. They'd lost everything.

The lead singer had killed himself.

For the second time that night, horror swept through Jack's body with a hard chill. "Eve, Harmonie. I'm so sorry." Useless, useless. There was nothing he could say to take the stark assumption of guilt from their faces.

Eve turned away and lowered her hands to the computer terminal. She clicked through transfer windows and removed the hard drives that were completely loaded. "The FBI or the Marshals or both will be on their way here soon. We could have days, but there's no counting on it. We'll get out with what we want to keep and wipe the rest with magnets."

It dawned on him that arresting Eve La Sirena and charging her with online piracy—whatever the actual charges would be, that would be the headline—could make an agent's career. She was more than a tasty little morsel to the people trying to close down the Internet downloading sites. "I'll help."

Harmonie shoved hard drives into a duffel bag. They must have had a plan the whole time. They didn't act like people making this up as they went along. Jack's respect for them rose as he processed why they were doing this and how well-prepared they were.

Whatever escape plans they'd made, they probably didn't include him. "What comes next?"

Harmonie said, "We get these off the island and into a safe place. There's leverage in there, in case it gets really bad, as well as information about our contacts around the world. Stuff we don't want to erase but can't leave for the authorities to find. I'd rather that happened sooner rather than later."

"I can help with that. I'll take them to the mainland while you two finish closing things up here. My passengers are locals, so I'll refund their money and leave them behind when I come back for you. They can just go home. Marie, though." Jack wished he could sit down. He was going to fuck her over again. He had to find her somewhere to go for more than just a night or two. If he was going to help them escape—and "if" wasn't really the word—*Lysistrata* might become too hot of a home for the innocent.

Eve stirred at Marie's name. Her voice creaked, then firmed, as she said, "I have cash you can give Marie. She should be able to get a room for tonight. I'll give you enough to keep a roof over her head for a month or so." She reached into another duffel while Harmonie continued to transfer hard drives. Her fists came out filled with strapped bundles of twenties, thousands of dollars. After all Eve's talk about where the money went in the music industry, he was shocked to see her overestimate a month's worth of living expenses for someone like Marie. His expression brought a faint smile to her face, the first he'd seen that day. "Don't count it and don't worry. Being on the record label's side as a producer is remarkably lucrative." The smile twisted and disappeared.

"I'll make sure she gets it."

He took the money and she added one more bundle. "That one's for refunding your passengers."

Harmonie spoke over her shoulder. "All done here." She tucked the last of the hard drives into the duffel and Jack added the money on top.

He hesitated. "I guess I'll see you soon." He tried to do some quick figuring in his head. The wind often laid down overnight, so he might have to motor or motorsail partway. "I'm looking at a six or seven hour round trip. I'll clear out the guest cabins for your things. Pile anything you want to bring along on the pier. We can load and leave within a couple hours of sunrise."

Harmonie manufactured a smile for him. "Sounds good. We'll be ready."

"How were you going to get off the island without me?" Curiosity prompted the thought, but a wedge of jealousy found a crack in his composure.

Eve spread her hands. "I have fans everywhere, including Cuba."

"Is that where we'll be heading after I get back? I should update my charts, if so."

"No," she said, stomping on his last words. "Don't do anything that could give them hints about where we're going. If you don't have Cuban charts, we can go somewhere else."

"The Azores?" Jack mustered a wry smile.

"For starters, sure. Lajes das Flores is a safe place for a short time, but Portugal would extradite me in a minute if they found out I was there. Harmonie will take the lift off the island, but she's not going on the run. There's nothing tying her to this except her relationship with me, and she knows how to handle that."

He stared. "You make it sound like we'll be leaving forever."

"That's what on the run means." Eve zipped the duffel closed and left her hands resting on top of it. Finally, she looked up. "I'm going to be indicted for racketeering, copyright infringement, and money laundering."

"Money laundering? I thought you were a pirate?" Jack's couldn't think straight. On the run with Eve La Sirena.

"My site funneled money to the musicians when someone downloaded something and loved it enough to come back and pay. We also handle fundraising for production costs, basically getting paid based on the potential that people think you have." She jerked. "Oh, shit. We have to get the money dispersed right away. Damn it! They may have already frozen the account."

Harmonie rushed across the room. "On it." She climbed the ladder so fast she seemed to fly.

Jack's overloaded synapses fired and he gasped. "You're talking about Integrated Music. That's you?"

For the first time since he'd arrived, Eve looked genuinely glad. "It's good, right?"

"It's great, from what I hear. I really thought Integrated Music was going to change everything."

She collapsed into a chair and took several unsteady breaths. Finally, she choked out. "Me too."

"Eve." Jack knelt in front of her. "Maybe you can start it back up. Other downloading sites have gone down and come back. Some do it regularly! Use other people's servers in other countries or…or buy more of your own and make them mobile."

"Install them on a boat, right?" She touched his neck, slid her hand around to the back, and held on. "Can't serve this much music by Wi-Fi. There's got to be a big pipe connecting me to the rest of the world, or it's just a little vanity project."

"Get help, then." He grabbed her knees. "You don't have to run away. Just stay off the radar for a while, let it die down. We'll take a vacation—sail the islands. If you get other people to run the site, you don't have to leave forever."

Her lips twisted and she stroked his cheek. He leaned into her hand, desperate to pump his own heat into her chilled fingers. The cold came from farther inside her than he could reach, though. "You aren't going to be able to solve, in a couple of minutes, what we couldn't figure out in the years we've been here. Integrated Music will come back, if all the contingency plans work as they should. But I can't."

Jack pushed back and stood. He rubbed his arms, the cool room getting to him too as the heat of passion receded. "When I sail you away from here, what's next? Drop Harmonie off on an island somewhere and then what?"

Eve spread her hands. "My plans were for planes, trains, and automobiles, not sailboats. I have ID and paperwork stashed here and there around the world. If we sail off together, we'll need to get several sets of registration for *Lysistrata*." Her words came fast, but she was obviously making it up as she went along. She'd never planned him into her life. She stood and started pacing. "We'll have to change the name."

"I don't know."

She stopped and looked at him closely. "You don't know what." Her expression closed up, just like she'd closed up on interviewers who stepped past the lines of her privacy.

Jack stared at her again. This person was both real and a fantasy. She had no idea what it would do to him to pick up and leave his life. "I don't know if I can leave it all behind. Go on the lam and never see my friends or family again."

"You'd have me. And the world." She swept her arm out as though offering him everything he'd ever wanted.

"I want to travel, sure. But there are people here I love."

She stepped close to him and took his face in her hands. "Maybe someday you could see them again. But not soon, and not for certain."

A shaft of pain pierced him. "At least you're not lying." He took her hands in his and kissed them. He needed more. "Eve, I'll always be on your side. I love you."

Her soft expression crumbled at his words, but she didn't reply immediately, and her face expressed more pain than joy. His vision tunneled in the elongated silence. Had he misread her? Was he the patsy here, having his love exploited by someone who didn't feel the same? Embarrassment and shame welled before she grabbed him close and whispered, "I love you too."

He hugged her back and hid his full eyes in her hair. "Don't leave me behind, okay? I'll go where you go." He just wouldn't think about what he was leaving behind. She'd fill him so that he wouldn't need anything or anyone else.

Eve's voice was thick and rich. "I wouldn't have it any other way."

After a long moment, she released him and stepped back. He let her go, almost secure in the knowledge that she wanted him. She loved him.

Eve loved him.

He climbed the ladder and she hefted the duffel bag of evidence and money up to him. He couldn't have dreamed that morning as he and Marie cleaned the boat that he'd be going on the run that night. Everything was about to change.

A quiver of excitement fought with a chill of dread.

CHAPTER SIXTEEN

E ve took the heavy magnet from Harmonie and hefted it like a dumbbell. "We'll get a workout tonight."

"Just what we need. We've been getting lazy here on the island."

Harmonie slipped between the wall and the first row of racks. She ran her magnet over the back of the rack slowly and Eve waited. When Harmonie moved to the next rack, Eve went over the front of the rack Harmonie had already finished. They were hoping to scramble all the data, right down to the ones and zeros, so badly that there would be no evidence left. They had no way of transporting the servers out in a hurry, so their plan was to leave nothing but metaphorical scorched earth.

Eve hummed under her breath in the absolute silence of the basement. The hum of electricity, of hundreds of servers, of the water rushing through the sea-cooled heat exchanger system had disappeared when Harmonie had cut power to everything but the lights. Years of work had become a tidy junkyard.

Eventually, Harmonie broke the silence. "We made our escape plans more in fun than in earnest. I hope they'll stand up under such dire circumstances."

"We expected search warrants, not an arrest warrant." Eve shrugged. Her arms were getting tired already and they weren't a quarter of the way through. "I think we did a good job, though.

The plan is flexible and robust, just like the program. They couldn't break into our system. Hopefully they won't be able to predict our next moves."

"It's harder to come out strong against the industry from hiding."

Eve could only catch glimpses of Harmonie through the air slots in the server racks. If only she could see her face. Their earlier blowup hadn't been settled, only put aside.

However they snapped at each other, they were on the same side. Eve hoped Harmonie knew that.

"I said this all wrong before, but you're not named in the arrest warrant. I think Stephanie would have told us if you had been. Once we get away, you should be free to come and go as you please." Harmonie made no answer and they continued to work, almost face-to-face, but veiled from each other's sight. Eve finally faced facts. "I'm going on the run. I'll spend the rest of my life in non-extradition countries or under fake names with fake passports. I don't know how long I can carry off being someone else, so it'll probably be Belize or Argentina for me."

Harmonie's tone carried a laugh in it. "You've perfected being Eve La Sirena and you may be right that you couldn't live for long as someone else." Eve heard her sigh. "I've always loved Evrim Nesin, though. Maybe you could be her full-time."

The idea sparked both yearning and rejection in Eve, as did every mention of her life before boarding school. She'd loved her parents dearly, and she'd thought they loved her too. She yearned for them for years before she'd rejected them completely, feeling that they'd spurned her and grasping for any tiny bit of control of her circumscribed life. Eve La Sirena didn't belong to them.

"Perhaps," was the best she could give Harmonie. She'd never forced herself to contemplate why she used Evrim instead of Eve or Ma'am or Mistress when topping. Superficially, she had some idea, but she shied from the deeper reasons.

"We've gotten off topic. I want to talk about you." She gave Harmonie a second to reply then jumped back into the silence. "I had my chance and it didn't last long enough to cripple the industry like I'd hoped it would. I know when I'm done, and I won't be setting up a new server farm. That doesn't mean I won't support others doing this, but it's too slow. It'll take a long, long time to end copyright this way. Maybe forever. We're no Prohibition-style mobsters, racketeering charges notwithstanding, but…anyway, I'm done."

Harmonie's shoes scuffed along the floor, then she came around the end of the row of server racks cradling the magnet like a baby. "I'm sorry, Eve. I know you were hoping for more."

This was why she loved Harmonie. As much as Eve had frustrated her, insulted and attacked her, Harmonie recognized Eve's best intentions, her most glorious possibilities, and wanted to be part of realizing them. "And you didn't have much hope. So it's your turn. I've signed my property over to you. I did it a while back, so it should be safe from any asset forfeiture proceedings. All the real estate in the US—the house in Boston and the land in Montana—and the musical instruments on loan to the Met." Harmonie's surprise and pleasure reassured Eve that she'd done the right thing. They'd lived together long enough that Harmonie knew what the money meant and how to hire the right people to take care of it. She'd be comfortable for the rest of her life, if she wanted to settle for that. "There's a trust with enough money to keep it all insured and maintained. You'll be in control of the trust, so you're free to squander the money elsewhere if you like. It would make one hell of a trip to Atlantic City."

"Or I could sell it all and put the cash into starting my own co-op record label." Harmonie studied Eve, clearly looking for her reaction to the idea. Selling her antique musical instruments alone would keep something like that afloat through the startup period.

Eve put the heavy magnet down so she could focus. "It's yours, no strings except the preexisting trust that protects the land in Montana from development. You can sell any or all of it, but you don't have to. I'll invest, publicly, as one of your first…let's say five acts to join. Fewer and it would look like my pet project. I'll help you get enough star power and hard cash to get this going, and I'll promise you now that you will be the only company I'll do business with. Can't promise I won't give my music away free, but…"

Harmonie put her magnet down, freeing her hands to make wide sweeps through the air as she spoke. "You still don't get it! In my concept, you won't be doing business with me as a company. We'll *be* the business, together with the other musicians who join. We'll own the means of production as a group and pool the returns. We'll have free use guidelines along the lines of the Creative Commons set. It'll open us up to each other's music and let us stop defending our copyrights."

"I love the sound of it. Maybe a pocket of freedom like this can bring about more freedom in general. Maybe it'll get huge. Maybe there will end up being a ton of small versions." Eve took Harmonie's hand. "Regardless, I'm behind you."

"As much as you can be, from Belize or wherever." Harmonie pulled her in and hugged her. Eve breathed deep, fixing Harmonie's smell in her memory. Harmonie squeezed, then released her. "Meanwhile, we have a lot of cleaning to do here."

Eve picked up her magnet. "Let's get to it." Harmonie disappeared again, but this time the silence was broken by her voice, soaring in Fleetwood Mac's "Go Your Own Way." Eve took up the harmony line, softer, more wistfully than Harmonie's angelic attack.

They sang from their shared repertoire of the best harmonies in music as they worked and Eve thought about Jack. She'd put him at risk, letting him help. If he were caught with the hard drives, no one would believe that he wasn't involved. His boat and his business were at risk as well. The Marshals weren't shy about seizing assets, and it was notoriously difficult to get anything back from them.

Why had she told him she loved him? Flat out like that, without qualifying statements or defining her terms. She wasn't surprised to hear it from him. Well, a little surprised to hear it, but not that he felt it. In just over a month, they'd gone deep together. She'd exposed herself more than she had in a long, long time, and the gamble had paid off. If Jack loved her, he loved the real her, the person behind the persona, the soft, vulnerable core of her as well as the sometimes abrasive, prickly exterior.

And he did. Jack loved her.

Eve hefted the magnet and ran it over another server rack.

She was going to be playing chess with the government, racing pawns and bishops all over the board to hide the sudden, slippery motion of the queen. Her lawyer was already on a plane to Mexico, where she had no intention of going. Her physical trainer from Boston was headed to the Philippines and her booking agent would board a plane to Iceland within the hour. Jack could only distract her from the decisions that would have to be made suddenly, moment by moment. She could get them both caught.

Or she could accept his help as far as a nearby island, then send him away, suitably chastened for expecting a place in her life. That thought made her heart ache worse than the idea of Jack following her around the world while she lost her pursuers and her identity. His entire adult life had revolved around sailing. An ever-changing, horribly repetitive round of hotels, flights, hired cars, disguises, and untrustworthy accomplices would wear him out.

She almost smiled. Sounded like life on tour with more wigs and fewer screaming fans. A shiver overtook her, though the room had begun to warm without the cooling system working.

She didn't have to decide right away, but her decision had to be made before they got to their first stop after the island. She had no idea which direction she'd take. Invite Jack into a life on the run or send him away for his own good.

Harmonie switched to girl-group doo-wop and Eve followed gladly. A little touch of innocence in the commission of crime.

❖

Eve looked over the server room from the bottom of the ladder, one hand on the strangely warm rung. It was done.

All the music she'd stolen—liberated—over the years existed only in other people's hands. The tunes that hadn't satisfied her in their studio versions, the extra effort to find and copy the track data so she could show the hit-mill what it should have sounded like. Most of those had been adopted by the bands themselves, rereleased and played on the radio with her arrangement and mixing. The music couldn't disappear.

"Harmonie!"

"What?"

"I think we should stash the magnets so they don't know the servers are blank."

After a moment of silence, Harmonie continued their shouted conversation. "Bring them on up."

Under her breath, Eve said, "I wanted to hand them up to you, silly. They're mad heavy." Still grumbling, she went halfway up the ladder and boosted one to the floor above, groaning at the stretch and ache in her shoulders. Really, building stronger muscles wouldn't be traitorous to the fat pride movement.

She'd likely get heavier before she had time for anything of the sort. Travel food and sitting around, waiting for transportation. What would she do? Read, of course, but she'd need some small instrument.

As she climbed out of the server room for the last time, it came to her. A harmonica. The instrument of tramps and hobos. It would do no good to linger over the piano, the cello. All the pieces too big to load onto *Lysistrata*. She grabbed a Hohner chromatic harmonica as she rushed through the music room. She forced herself not to dwell there, to keep moving up the stairs and into the main floor hallway. She'd cry if she spent too much time saying good-bye to her instruments.

Harmonie passed, dragging wheeled luggage with both hands.

"How much are you packing?" Eve followed her down the hallway, noting that she'd closed up the house like a storm was coming. There'd be at least one before anyone came back.

"I figure I'll just keep packing until we're out of luggage or Jack arrives." She bumped the bags onto the deck.

Eve took one and pulled it down the steps toward the dark pier. Heavy. On the way back to the house, she stopped in the driftwood folly and rested her hand on Buddha's head.

The abrupt end of her time on Anne Bonny Isle cut her up. With her feet in the sand and her fingers stretched to touch both wood and jade, she fixed the place in her memory as best she could. She struggled against the familiar sensation of being cut off from who she was, who she had been, and forced into an ahistorical new life that would find her so alone. Her last look at her parents as they drove away from the boarding school. Signing the contract that took her out of school at sixteen and put her on the track to superstardom. The horrible sight of Marc's body on the rocks.

Not this time. She wouldn't close off her past, reject the person she'd been in this place. She wanted to carry this time more honestly than she carried those others—though she was actually leaving honesty behind, for who knew how long. The prospect of fake names and disguises threatened to puncture the bubble of energy she needed for getting through the last hours on her island. Perhaps she'd be able to sleep once they were away on *Lysistrata*.

She left philosophy behind and went to her bedroom. Her dresser top was nearly bare. A glance in the wardrobe showed her favorite clothes gone. "I don't know how much I should bring. I'll be on the move for a long time." She threw on a light robe to fight the internal chill.

Harmonie appeared in the doorway, a surprise, since they often conversed at the top of their voices from anywhere in the house. A benefit of being singers.

Eve stopped stirring through her things when Harmonie didn't speak. Her ashen face and shaking hands startled Eve into rushing across the room. She grabbed Harmonie's face in both hands. "What is it?"

"They're here. It's too late to run."

"Fuck." Eve put her forehead on Harmonie's shoulder and jolted at the contact with her healing wound. Finally, she understood the whine coming through the closed walls of her home.

Mighty engines on fast boats.

❖

Jack steered back by hand to eke every last fraction of a knot from the wind in his sails. The satiny wood of the old wheel comforted him with its familiarity. Alone, in the dark, all the sounds and lights out on the water merged unless he maintained a preternatural attention. He followed the buoys out to sea by their lights or by finding their reflective tape, one by one, with his handheld spotlight. He marked each in pencil on the waterproof chart as he passed, maintaining a dead-reckoning plot, though his electronic chartplotter showed the little boat icon moving safely along the channel.

He had no intention of relying overmuch on any single navigation tool while alone, exhausted, and frightened. He passed a boat, most likely fishing, and was passed by two others.

Jack's shoulder ached enough that he hadn't doused the sails at the pier. He'd been able to tie up long enough to offload the passengers, and an overwhelmed, confused Marie, while the sails shook slack in the gentle onshore breeze, sheets flapping.

Marie had looked tiny and tired among the spare bedding and other supplies he'd left behind in the yellow halide light on the pier. Her wounded expression, and Jack's guilt, had almost disappeared when he'd given her the bundles of cash. She hadn't questioned its provenance, probably assuming it was from Eve though he'd refused to explain. For her own safety.

The duffel bag itself, stuffed with information that might as well have been dynamite, had fit into his locker in the boaters' shower room. With a little shoving. He wondered what kind of leverage they'd loaded on the drives. Embarrassing? Explosive?

His biggest fear was that Eve had sent him off with the hard drives to get him out of the way. A speedboat could have arrived and taken her into hiding while he made the slow round trip under sail. He replayed the memory of her declaration of love and wished he'd made her promise to wait for him.

If she had left, would he feel at all as though he'd been let off the hook? Could he go on with his life as though he'd never met her while she wandered the planet alone?

For a footloose sailor, he sure was feeling the pull of the people he'd leave behind for her. Friendships of unprecedented closeness, enough friends and friendly acquaintances to feel like he was part of a community. The charter business and his increasingly glowing reputation.

Still, his chest seized up at the idea of her having left while he was gone. If she didn't love him after all, nothing in that whole cherished community would fix the wound.

Her island made a vague lump on the backlit horizon, and his anchor mark appeared at the edge of the chartplotter's screen. The wind wouldn't cooperate, varying from slight to weak and back again, but he left his electric motor off. If they got into a tight spot later with currents or with some sort of authorities, he wanted to have a full battery's worth of maneuvering time.

The approaching sunrise would be an anti-climax after the dramatic changes in the pre-dawn sky. Even without direct light, he could see clearly now, and he turned off his running lights. The solar panels would start charging his batteries soon.

He came abreast of Eve's island and the cove opened ahead.

His muscles jerked. Even before he could see directly into the cove, the tops of stainless steel towers gleamed in the brittle morning light. There were boats in Lysistrata Cove. The sun powered over the horizon and lit the scene as Jack realized what he was looking at.

Agents in FBI jackets swarmed the house. Some other kind of officials pulled things from the luggage on the pier. The two boats tied to the pier were fast, powerful.

Jack didn't want to believe what he was seeing, but there was no mistaking the circling Coast Guard Defender-class response boat with a machine gun mounted on the bow.

Suddenly, he hoped that Eve and Harmonie had left without him. He wished with all his might that they were zooming across the open water in a drug-runner's cigarette boat.

The officers and agents didn't act like they'd lost their quarry. The mood seemed exuberant, and Jack's empty belly curdled.

He sailed on past the island.

By the time he'd reached the next reef, Jack had decided. He dropped his sails and let the boat drift with the slight current. He set up every fishing pole on the boat for cover, and pulled out his binoculars.

He watched for hours as they broke down and carted off Eve's gear. He was too far away to see in detail, but boats came and went. Perhaps Eve had sabotaged the power for the house somehow and they didn't know that the servers were blank. Or maybe Eve and Harmonie hadn't succeeded in clearing them all of data.

He didn't see Eve or Harmonie, so either they'd been taken away before his return or they were out there somewhere still. He didn't hold much hope for their freedom. He wasn't sure he held much hope for his own.

How could he run without Eve's connections? Did he need to? The FBI might recognize that something had been removed from the house, but would they be able to track down who'd taken it? Would they be able to find evidence that *Lysistrata* had been there, and left, just before the raid?

Jack fished and watched all day and even caught a couple yellowtail snapper that he released after carefully pulling the hooks out. The last of the boats left the cove and he waited an impatient hour before he raised sail and returned to Lysistrata Cove. The wreckage of Eve and Harmonie's life spilled out over the deck and into the sand below, giving him a hint of what he'd find inside.

There was nothing left intact or in place. The couches and piles of pillows had been sliced open. The loungers had been turned over, their cushions shredded, the coir filling pulled out.

He wandered awhile, lost in the small pile of vivid memories he'd made in that house, on that deck, but the likelihood that someone would be back, sooner or later, forced him to turn away. He wasn't leaving Eve, only her ghost.

On his way past the driftwood folly, Jack grabbed the jade Buddha he'd first seen in Eve's threatening hand. The heaviness in his muscles and the slow drag of his breathing made hauling anchor and raising sail a torture, but he had to get back to the mainland.

Eve might need him.

CHAPTER SEVENTEEN

Eve's lawyer had counseled that Eve not say a single word more than necessary, but she didn't want to simply endure questioning without digging her own grave. She wanted to control the situation and shift the ground, put the agents on the defensive. They made it difficult, of course. That was their jobs. Eve reminded herself that they had nothing. Jack had gotten away with the only pieces of evidence that could convict her.

The beige room and the metal table could have been taken right off a movie set. Even the smell—burnt coffee and sour sweat overlaid with ammonia-based cleaners—matched her expectations.

The agent went back to a question he'd asked a half-dozen times. "What was on the servers before you wiped them?"

A pang hit. Her new album. Had Harmonie backed her tracks up to the hard drives she'd given Jack or was all that work lost? If it was on the drives, she'd get it back sooner or later. If it was gone…a miscarriage might feel like that.

The interrogator must have seen a shadow of her painful thought. He leaned forward. "We will be able to get something from them, you know. Our techs are better than you can possibly know."

"My servers were ready for loading with my music creating program."

"You don't need magnets like we found for loading data into a computer."

"The servers weren't new. I thought it best to give them an absolute wipe before loading my programs and data. When creating an artificial intelligence, any scrap of code could corrupt the effort."

She and Harmonie had giggled over their cover story. It sounded just as demented in the featureless interrogation room as it had while they rolled around on pillows in the den. If she couldn't sell it, at least she could stick to it.

Planting the idea that she'd bought used servers also gave her another level of deniability in case some data did manage to hang in there against the magnets. *Why, officer sir, I didn't know that was there!* She resisted the desire to drum her fingers on the table but glanced at her lawyer. Shonda stared at the agent, as she'd done throughout the hours of questioning. Eve wouldn't be as confident of her cover story if Shonda hadn't grilled her mercilessly in private before the questioning began. She'd taken the first flight back from Mexico when the news had reported Eve's arrest. Eve had hired her a decade back, when she realized that there would always be someone suing her for something, and though their relationship had remained professional, she trusted Shonda as much as she'd ever trusted a lawyer.

"What happened to your head?"

Nope, not going to bring Jack into it. "Just clumsy, I guess."

"Why did you need high-speed connectivity?"

He was pretty clumsy too. Offbeat question, hammer her with the real stuff. Yawn.

The agent displayed his quirks rather openly for a government-issue kind of guy. He wore his suit and those horrible FBI shoes as though they were fine couture, sliding his fingers up and down his lapel, carefully arranging the crease in his trousers when he sat.

He spent very little time in the chair across the empty table, though. Special Agent Will Smith, who tolerated no jokes about his name, had a frenetic energy to him. Eve's automatic response had been to slow her speech patterns, push a little drawl into her voice, and drape her arm across the back of her plain chair as though she were lounging in the comfort of her own home. Smith's back straightened a touch every time she smiled at him, so she did it often. He was so tight he'd bend over backward before too long.

She studied him for weaknesses as they fenced. Attack, parry, riposte. He was conventionally attractive, but not enough so to have learned to use it. No ring, but that could be a defense against exactly the kind of attack she might have made. Not easily frustrated or distracted.

Eve had been arrested in her robe, but the arresting agent had been easier to manipulate than Special Agent Smith. He'd allowed her to dress, perhaps not realizing that she was donning armor for the battles ahead.

She wore a flower-print dress that Donna Reed would have been comfortable in, and her hair curved around her face before it disappeared in a tidy bun. Her makeup was subtle but effective for widening her eyes and softening her mouth. Her arrest photos showed a woman who had no idea why she'd been taken from her home in the middle of the night.

The look didn't match her mood, of course. Vicious anger pressed her to strike out at Smith and all the others who'd arrived to paw through her things. Only the knowledge that her house was clean helped her maintain a semblance of calm. She'd been paranoid enough about her pirate activities to keep meticulous books, pay all her taxes (though not one penny extra, which would be just as suspicious as hiding income), and require that the entire island be a no-drug zone. Much as she missed the occasional stoner evening, they would never be able to jail her for offenses unrelated to those named in the warrant.

Over hours of repetitious repartee, she and Smith had developed a rhythm, with Shonda providing the grace notes. He pressed for details, trying to catch her in a lie or make her improvise. She trotted out the story she and Harmonie had spent months developing. They'd become so enamored of it that Harmonie had written a short story and submitted it to a science fiction magazine. They hadn't heard back yet. Perhaps it would end up being published.

He wouldn't find any holes.

Her connectivity was suspiciously powerful. Her servers were suspiciously capacious. Her retreat was suspiciously complete. None of that could possibly lead to a conviction.

On the other hand, she hadn't lived in a bubble. The torrent aggregator who gave them her identity wasn't the only person with an idea of what she'd been up to. Her emails had come through a friendly Internet service provider and Integrated Music, though hosted independently, was registered with a domain name server. Neither was based in the US, but the FBI had connections. It was only a matter of time before they got some portion of her communications.

"Who took the backups away? Did they have a boat? A seaplane? How were the backups stored?"

Eve lost some of her disdainful bravado, but masked it with a slow blink. "I don't know what backups you mean, but hordes of boats pass my island every day."

Shonda's jaw tensed for a split second.

Eve fought off a shiver. She uncrossed and recrossed her legs to hide her sudden tension. Too many words. She should have stopped with questioning the very idea of backups. A sloppy attempt at misdirection.

Smith's eyes followed the crossing of her legs and she was relieved when he chased her up the wrong tree. "Your island? I thought it was owned by a Haitian citizen, one Harmonie Bonheur."

She shrugged and let one hand rest lightly on her knee. A leg man, was he? "A simple subterfuge. There is always someone hoping to invade my privacy."

"And what did Ms. Bonheur have to do with your server operation? Was she also...uh, programming...this AI?" The disbelief in his voice slid toward insulting. Even though the AI was a complete fiction, his insinuation that neither of them were that smart brought a snarl to Eve's lips.

She turned it into a light sneer. "Harmonie is excellent company—" She drew out the words, giving them a sexual connotation that even the stiff Special Agent Will Smith couldn't miss. She added a light stroke of her hand over her knee, absently, as though in remembrance of Harmonie's touch, and his eyes dropped again, "—but she won't be revolutionizing computer sciences." Preposterous to erase Harmonie's skill, but necessary.

"So you're claiming that it was all your idea, all your doing." Smith paced on the other side of the table but watched her face.

"Of course." There. Nice balance of pride and defensiveness.

He stopped and leaned over the table. "You are a liar and a thief, Ms. La Sirena. Your ridiculous story about the AI won't last. It certainly won't shield you once we finish running the fingerprints at your house. You didn't have many guests, but you're no computer programmer and I bet I can get someone to talk."

Jack's prints were all over the house, including on the ladder that descended to the server room. She could only sit and sweat and hope that they'd been obscured by the team that had taken her and Harmonie unawares.

Eve rolled her eyes and took a deep breath as though reaching for patience. "I've told you. Programming became a hobby of mine a few years ago. I find it soothing, much like music in its mathematical intricacies. Your rude insistence that I couldn't possibly be good with computers is quite simply off base."

She delivered her lines smoothly, selling them well, but inside she wanted to scream.

If Harmonie managed her bimbo defense and Eve maintained the AI fiction, it was possible Jack wouldn't be on the hook for anything at all. No crime, no criminal liability. On the other hand, Eve had no intention of waiting around and letting the government write the end of her story.

❖

Sandpaper rasped across his chin and Jack woke suddenly. Tigger's cat looked at him from inches away and then licked his chin again.

Guess it was time to get up.

Any minute now.

Instead, he stroked the long-haired ginger cat and scratched behind her ears. The queen of the couch had been miffed when he'd settled in for the night, but his stillness had coaxed her from hiding. He'd woken several times in the night and she'd been closer each time. The last time, he'd gotten up to pee and she'd curled in the warm spot left in the cushion before he'd made it back. Lying back down, he'd scooted her over but hadn't pushed her away.

What was her name? Oh, duh. Winnie.

Jack cuddled with Winnie until he heard Tigger stirring. Winnie's ears turned like satellite dishes, and she abandoned him to pad across the tiny living room toward the kitchen. He wished he could have a cat, but the charter business was hard enough without bringing allergens aboard. Of course, his charter days might be over. He didn't even know whether or not he was being hunted.

The Marshals were bound to figure out that he'd been at Eve's house. If they took fingerprints, they'd find him right away. The process for getting a captain's license included fingerprinting and a background check. He was definitely on file.

They'd search the boat. Whether they could deduce it or not, he'd removed the very evidence they wanted, sailed it away from their reach in the dark of night. He wished the story felt as exciting and valorous as it sounded. He couldn't stop being overtaken by waves of fear. Fear for himself, for his boat, for Harmonie and Marie. Fear for Eve.

When he'd returned, his locker struck him as the worst possible place to hide the hard drives. Without any experience in running from the law, he wasn't sure what place would be better. He'd gone low-tech and stashed them among a pile of pallets that had been in a nearby boatyard since well before he'd moved to town. Now he only had to fear rain.

His fitful napping hadn't made up for the long night—and day—under sail. Paranoia had sent him off the boat after the first night, and Tigger hadn't hesitated to take him in, even with the possibility of risk.

The smell of coffee gave him enough energy to sit up. He lowered his head into his hands, though. Was he going to fuck all his friends over? Marie first, now Tigger. If the FBI showed up, they wouldn't give a shit what Tigger had or hadn't known. They'd tear her place apart either way.

A knock at the door startled him into standing. Tigger came to the open passage between the kitchen and the living room. She raised an eyebrow at him, questioning, and he pointed at himself and then at her bedroom. He almost tripped on her feathered mules but reached her room without making a sound. He watched around the edge of the door as she slipped on the mules.

Tigger sipped her coffee and waited until the knock came again. She wore youth pajamas covered with space invaders and jagged word bubbles that said things like pow and zorp. Her light, fine hair puffed a couple inches from two ponytails, one over each ear. She looked like a kid, but her calm demeanor showed her true colors.

"I'm coming." She clomped over to the door and rose on tiptoe to look through the peephole. She opened the door and Jack jerked out of sight. "Hi."

"You must be Tigger. I'm Harmonie."

Jack peeked. Harmonie was alone. The momentary rise of hope left a void in his chest. He came out of Tigger's bedroom. "Where's Eve? How did you find me?"

Harmonie and Tigger eyed each other. Oh, great. Not the best time for chemistry.

"Harmonie, where's Eve?"

"She's okay," Harmonie said. She put down her bags and rolled her shoulders. "Can I get something to drink?"

Tigger nodded. "Coffee, tea, or me?"

Jack wanted to smack her. No, that was Tigger all over. Irrepressible, even in the face of danger. "Where is she?"

"I'll have coffee regular, please. Light and sweet. But if you have any juice, I'd love some of that too. Water, if not."

"Oh, you're thirsty-thirsty. I'll see what I have." Tigger disappeared. Winnie sat with her fluffy tail wrapped over her paws and stared at Harmonie.

"Harmonie…"

"She's somewhere in the FBI offices. I'm sure she's being questioned, but the last information I have is that her lawyer arrived late yesterday."

"How did you get out?"

Harmonie grinned. Tigger returned with orange juice and Harmonie thanked her before tipping the glass and downing half. Tigger went back to the kitchen. "Bimbo defense."

That brought an unexpected smile to Jack's face. "Seriously?"

"Oh, yeah. We'd prepped it pretty well. Eve has a cover story and I'm sure she'll stick to it. It's just a matter of time before they give up on questioning her and take her to holding. They'll expect to frighten her and soften her up, but it'll never get that far."

Jack waited a beat, but Harmonie watched for Tigger to return with her coffee. "What's the plan?"

"There's no reason for you to know the details. Suffice it to say that there's a fan."

"Guess there would be."

Tigger returned and handed Harmonie a mug. "What kind of fan?"

Harmonie looked at Jack, surprised. "You haven't told her?"

He shook his head. "No. I didn't feel like I had the right."

Harmonie's face softened. She sat on the couch and patted the seat next to her. Before Jack could take her invitation, Winnie jumped up and sniffed Harmonie's arm. A much needed laugh lightened the mood.

Jack sat on the cat's other side and their fingers met in Winnie's fur. He let Harmonie grip his hand and squeezed back. "Jack here has had the fortune—both good and bad—of falling in love with Eve La Sirena." She grinned. "I guess her loving you back tips it toward good."

He swallowed, but he couldn't suppress the lift in his chest. Tigger whistled, eyes wide.

"Eve won't be in custody much longer, but when she leaves, it'll be alone. I need the hard drives so I can arrange the series of flights and identities we've scattered around the world. She'll have a long way to go before she settles anywhere."

"How can I meet her along the way?" Jack feared Harmonie's answer.

"You can't. We didn't plant identities you could take over. All the ID and passports and tickets are tied to her and me. If we were more alike..." Harmonie smiled wryly. "On the other hand, you aren't in the clear. While I was being as dumb as a box of rocks, they showed me satellite photos of the cove with *Lysistrata* anchored there. I admitted to having seen that boat a few times and babbled about people swimming and making beach fires and sun tanning. It was all I could manage, without setting up something more detailed with Eve in advance. It's best to tell the truth, mostly the truth, and as much of the truth as is useful."

Jack's chest squeezed. His instinct to hide had been valid. "They'll find out about Marie. She's on my muster list. I've never tried to stay on the down-low, so they'll find you too, Tigger." He frowned. "How did you find me so fast, Harmonie?"

"Not with any methods the cops can use. I went to Puss'n'Boots and convinced some folks to talk to me."

Jack nodded, but he hoped the cops would be stupid enough to identify themselves before they asked. The BDSM community was still on the sharp edge of the laws around assault, pandering, prostitution, domestic abuse, and public nuisance, and anything that looked like police pushing a community member over the wrong side of that edge wouldn't get much assistance.

Tigger brought the coffee pot and refilled his cup. Harmonie shook her head and Tigger sat on the floor to listen. Winnie slipped from the couch and crawled into her person's lap. Jack missed the warm softness, but the vibe was probably pretty harsh between him and Harmonie. He couldn't help but feel that she was keeping him away from Eve.

"What are you going to do?" He turned on the couch to face Harmonie.

"Start a new kind of record label, try to reshape the industry instead of dynamiting it. Eve and I agreed that artists were maneuvered into terrible agreements, but we disagreed on the best replacement."

"Eve is going to be all alone, then? Alone and on the run around the world."

"Less alone than I'd prefer. There are a lot of people tied into these plans we set up. Fans in a dozen countries who've kept the documents she'll need and the costumes she'll wear. There will be people to pick her up at airports and drive her to train stations. That kind of thing gives her tremendous invisibility but also an enormous chance of being turned in by someone along the way. It doesn't matter if they tell the authorities or the media. Any word of her travels might unravel the whole ball of string. Eventually, she'll settle in one of a few places." Harmonie finished her juice and set the glass down with a click. "I need to be going. Lots of work to be done activating all those plans. Tigger, thank you for your hospitality. Here's my card. Call me."

Jack restrained a snarl. A hookup, really? He coached himself to be understanding. His world felt like it was coming to an end, but that didn't mean people could do without comfort. Harmonie had just lost her girlfriend of years—he didn't know how long they'd been together—and his unachievable desire to be with Eve didn't have to poison his hopes that his friends would find happiness. But...she would stop running at some point. Where?

What was that island in the Azores?

"Jack, the hard drives?" Harmonie held his gaze. She put enough command into her voice that he frowned. Did she think he might hold out on her?

"They're hidden nearby. Want to come with me or wait here?" He looked at her feminine linen business suit. "Your heels might come out worse for wear."

A smiled played around Harmonie's lips. "I'll stay here then. Tigger and I can get to know each other."

Jack rolled his eyes and pulled on his shoes. "Great. It'll only take me about ten minutes." His warning brought smiles to both Tigger and Harmonie's faces.

CHAPTER EIGHTEEN

Eve hated the chair, the table, and the one-way mirror. She hated the women who escorted her to the toilet. Even the satisfaction of refusing to be humiliated was blunted when the officer was unfazed by Eve's exhibitionist stripping at the sink for a quick wash.

When the original escort returned, she figured she'd been in the interrogation room a full day. Without windows or changes in lighting, it was hard to tell. Shonda had come and gone twice, leaving her alone for painfully long stretches. They were treating her with the cop version of kid gloves and it strained her nerves. They wouldn't be so gentle for long.

No lawyer was going to get her out of custody. They'd had enough for the warrant and they'd hold her the full three days allowable by law on that basis alone. Didn't matter what the charges would be, eventually, they'd try to break her in the rough atmosphere of a holding cell.

The plain door opened, and she didn't bother looking over until a gasp reached her. Harmonie's scent hit her at the same time, and her spirits made a disorienting leap. Time started moving again, and her numb mind ground into gear.

Harmonie sat on the opposite side of the desk and looked over her shoulder at the strange agent who stood at the door. "Like this, sir?"

The breeze off her batting eyelashes might have stirred the agent's hair if it hadn't been cut Marine-short. Eve swallowed a laugh, relieved to find some humor in the situation.

"Yes, miss. Please keep your hands on your side of the table and don't attempt to pass anything to Ms. La Sirena." Did the guy know how using her name put him at a disadvantage? His gruff tone couldn't pull all the music from it, though he seemed to try.

"Like this?" Harmonie rested her fingers on the table, caressing it in tiny motions.

"Yes, miss." His face went stony and he said nothing more.

"Eve. Hi."

Eve set herself to pay close attention. They had a certain rhythm planned for any conversation that might be overheard, but they'd also have to communicate as well as they could nonverbally. "Hey, Harmonie. How have you been? Did they give you any trouble?" *Are they buying the cover story?*

"No trouble, but they asked so many questions about the computer lady you were making. I didn't understand half of what they said." *The bimbo defense worked perfectly, and they haven't been able to disprove the AI story.*

"I bet you were mobbed by the media on the way out." *Who knows about the arrest?*

"Nope, I was all by my lonesome. Well, except I did find my handsome friend from Greece and met some people he's been hanging out with for a couple days. They had so much to tell me that I haven't been able to absorb it all. We should have come and partied more often." *The arrest hasn't made the news. Jack's hiding out, but he gave me the hard drives. Some of the people who were part of the plan haven't gotten back to me. It would have been a good idea to contact them periodically.*

"Maybe we'll have more time to party when I get out." *How long will I have to be here?*

"Don't they have to let you out soon? We give them money and they let you out, right? Or is it about who you know?" *Do you want to see if you make bail or should I set in motion the other plan?*

Eve knew the question would be coming. She had no intention of sticking around through a trial, if they managed to indict her, and taking the chance of prison. They had two plans. The patient one involved Eve making bail before she got out of Dodge. Besides the passive torture of being left alone in a room that never changed, she wasn't being tested so hard that she simply had to get out as soon as possible.

Safer, simpler, and less frightening than a jailbreak.

That could change for her in holding. It had been a long time since Evrim Nesin had fronted such an attitude that the girls in her dorm had rolled over and made her top bitch. The rich and famous rarely came out well when envious and violent people had a chance to bring them down a peg or twelve.

She'd bottomed enough to know that she had a high pain threshold. A savage beating in a jail cell had nothing to do with the consensual brutality she'd courted, though, and she didn't know how fear would affect the experience.

The arguments stacked up on the side of getting out sooner rather than later, but she faced her real reason. If she left as soon as possible, if she didn't wait to make bail, there was a slim chance that Jack would remember their conversation about the Azores. If he remembered, he could sail out of the country before the government had anything on him at all. There was a chance, she had no idea how thin, that Jack might be in the port at Lajes das Flores when she arrived. With the Marshals hunting him and the possibility that they might be able to reunite in a new island paradise, she had to take the chancier option.

"I think it's about who you know. Will you ask around and see if anyone can make this whole thing go faster?" *Break me out. As soon as possible.*

"Well, sure, Eve. I don't see what I can do, but someone should be able to help." *Will do. I won't be there, but I'll arrange it.*

"Perfect." Eve's eyes filled with tears for the first time since the agents had broken down her door. "I'll miss you, Harmonie."

"I'll miss you too, Eve. I better get going."

"Love you." The somber tone wasn't in character, but Eve hoped that whoever was watching would assume she was on her way to being broken. She couldn't let Harmonie walk out the door, for what could very well be the last time, without saying the words.

"I love you too, Eve. Be well."

Here's hoping.

❖

Had he gone completely insane? Jack dropped yet another twenty-pound bag of rice on the floor of his storage unit. He'd spent all day and every penny in his checking account hitting every grocery store in town, stocking up a little at each one so he wouldn't attract any attention. He bought enough food to get him through even the slowest possible trans-Atlantic passage.

Charlie lifted the last case of canned tomatoes from his trunk and passed it to Marie. "This is a lot of food."

She handed it over to Jack, who set it next to the rice.

"Six weeks' worth." Jack's quick-and-dirty navigational math said he'd need three weeks of food to get to the Azores. He'd stocked twice that, since he didn't know what would greet him on the other end of the trip. Would the Portuguese authorities know that he was being sought for questioning by the FBI? Would they turn him away and force him to make the rest of the trip to Africa?

"Shit. Which countries on the west coast of Africa don't have extradition treaties with the US?"

Marie sat on the tailgate of Charlie's station wagon. "You're going to Africa?"

"Maybe. I shouldn't say anything that'll force you to lie."

She tapped at her phone. "Cape Verde. Ten islands with black-sand beaches and a lot of green. Hey! They speak Portuguese!"

"Now if only I did too…"

Would Eve even show up? They'd talked about the Azores, about having a place to run and a home no one knew about. He couldn't remember the name of the town, but he knew where it was. Southern coast of the westernmost island. He hadn't dreamed that he could ever be brought so low as to head into the open ocean, running from US Marshals and FBI agents, for the mere chance that she would eventually join him on the other side of the sudden journey. Eve had plans, identities all worked out. People to help her run and hide, people to keep her safe.

He had a boat and a ton of rice.

Eve loved him. He just needed to remember the tone in her voice and the feeling of being in her arms.

He sat on the pile of rice bags. "I always dreamed of sailing wherever the wind blew, bouncing off coasts and islands. Exploring the world at an easy walking pace."

Charlie leaned against the wagon. "Who doesn't?"

"It always revolved around some shadowy figure. I wanted a lover who would join me at the rail." A knot stopped his throat. "Looking behind me in fear wasn't part of the dream."

Marie stopped pecking at her phone. "I didn't know. I thought you were happy here."

"I hadn't been working very hard on leaving. I paid off *Lysistrata's* loan last year. The release-of-lien letters are with my other official documents. But when it came down to it, I liked the passengers." He looked at Marie. "I like you. With you as crew and life going along so comfortably, sailing away started feeling like a mirage, never getting any closer."

"It's as real as it gets, now. And you haven't had much time to prepare." Charlie's worry added to Jack's fright. If an old sea dog thought he wasn't ready…

"I have been preparing." He made his voice firm. "I just hadn't put a timeline on it."

Marie came over to sit next to him. She hugged her knees, her shoulder brushing his. "Are you going to tell anyone else you're leaving?"

"No." He made a grab for his water bottle and tried to swallow the lump in his throat. His friendships had also created a certain inertia, though not one of his friends would like hearing that. Coming out as trans and using his rightful pronouns hadn't changed him, fundamentally, but it had removed a barrier to intimacy. The first level of getting to know someone had taken on new stakes, with the trans-rejecting bounced out of his life pretty quickly. Once he felt comfortable with someone, though, he'd found a real freedom in being himself. His close friends—sailors and gender warriors alike—never questioned or pressured him on what his transition would look like. The community at large wasn't always so accepting, and he'd parried more than one question about when he would be having a mastectomy or starting hormones. Still, he'd found a home, *built* a home that pulled together disparate aspects of himself and let him be the kinky trans sailor he knew himself to be.

Eve was everything he wanted in a sailing partner. Her daring and passion overmatched his own, spurring him to new heights. Eve, who might never make it out of police custody.

He couldn't bear to think of her in prison. Harmonie didn't believe it would happen, and he would toss his trust in with hers.

In his sailing fantasies, he never thought of leaving forever. It never occurred to him that his country could become dangerous to him. With the Marshals on the hunt and the FBI slavering for a chance to question him, Jack only saw two options. Either he left the US for good, hoping that Eve would be part of his expatriate future or he turned into the arms of authority and tried to outwit them. He didn't know enough to help them find Eve, but he could destroy Harmonie.

So. Only one option.

Charlie took Marie's place on the tailgate and gripped the edge with both hands. "Do you have to go transatlantic? What about heading south? Cuba isn't far at all."

"Right? Assata Shakur's been there for decades." Marie turned toward him, her eyes brightening. "Why go half a world away? What if this whole thing blows over without bringing you into it at all?"

"Sure, it would be easier to return to my life from the Caribbean or Central America." His lips twisted. "But that's not where Eve will be."

Silence took over as Marie and Charlie exchanged a long look.

Jack stood and held a hand out to Charlie, who brushed it aside and grabbed him in a big bear hug. "Fair winds and following seas, Jack."

"Thanks, Charlie. For your friendship and your help. For being someone I can count on."

"Let me know if there's anything else I can do for you. Email me or something."

Jack made a mental note to get a new, anonymous email address. So many details, so little time. "Will do."

Marie's worry vibrated like a struck bell. "Jack. I'm scared for you. Please be careful."

"I will. Once I'm out on the water, the danger is minimal. Just the usual. Wind and waves."

"It's hurricane season, Jack. Are you sure you have to go? Maybe they aren't even looking for you."

Jack took Marie's hand and squeezed it. "I know they are. Staying here means putting everyone I know in the target. If I leave before they have any proof I helped Eve, they won't be able to hassle you and Charlie and Tigger. I've got to go."

Marie pulled him into a hug. When she released him, she rubbed her eyes and said, "Well, I don't have to do anything for a while. That was a lot of money, you know."

"Yeah, I figured." He wished Eve had given him some. Mercenary, maybe, but he was broke all of a sudden, and it made him uncomfortable.

"I think I'm going to save the money for tuition. Whenever I decide what to study. Charlie says I can sign on to crew with him. We worked well together last week."

Jack shook his head. Had it only been a week since he'd taken Eve sailing and fallen irretrievably in love? "Whatever you decide to do, you'll be great at it. Best of luck."

Charlie and Marie lingered another minute before they drove off. Jack watched the taillights fade, then disappear when they turned a corner. He was on his own.

The storage unit at the pier usually held his spare bedding, the non-perishable foodstuffs he bought in bulk, and a complete set of tools. With the additional food—plain fare as opposed to the fancier stuff he served passengers—it was stuffed full. He closed the door and started walking, planning how to pack it all aboard *Lysistrata*.

No reason to leave anything behind that might be useful in the long run, and no boat worth the name lacked capacious storage compartments.

The mile to Justin's house passed quickly under his feet. The last light flirted with some low-lying clouds on the horizon. Second thoughts about refusing help for the final loading nagged at him, but he wanted to provide as much distance as he could between his escape and his friends.

He turned down the walkway through Justin's front yard, heading to the path leading behind the house.

Justin came out of the front door with his arms wrapped tightly around his ribs. "What the fuck, man?"

Surprise brought Jack around, and dread tensed his muscles. "What?"

"I don't know what you're into, but you can't be doing it here. I don't need The Man poking around in my business, dude."

A sharp spike of fear went through Jack's skull. He turned, though Justin continued complaining, and ran to the back of the house.

The small dock was horribly empty and Jack doubled over. He fell to his knees and put his hands flat on the weedy ground, struggling to push back the darkness that threatened his vision.

"No." He couldn't say anything else. Couldn't think anything else.

Justin appeared beside him. "Whoa, dude. Are you okay?"

Jack shook his head and pushed back to sit on his heels, hands clenched on his thighs.

"Whatever you got going on, you can't stay here. Marshals came and seized your boat. They had papers, man. There was nothing I could do." Justin's voice shifted from accusatory to defensive as Jack glared at him.

"You didn't think to call me? It didn't occur to you that I might want to know my boat was gone?" His voice grated in his throat. He struggled to his feet, pushing Justin away when he tried to help him up.

"I don't know, man. I figured I should stay out of it."

"Good move. Just stay the fuck out of it." He struggled with the desire to punch Justin in the face. He wanted to break something, anything, and he grabbed a plastic lawn chair. He heaved it across the crab grass, but it just bounced and rolled into the weeds.

He'd lost everything. He thought he'd hit rock bottom when he'd returned to Lysistrata Cove to find the authorities had beat him there. Then Harmonie telling him that he couldn't go with Eve had ripped his last hope away. He'd nurtured the unlikely and impractical dream of meeting Eve in the Azores, but...

He couldn't get there without a boat.

CHAPTER NINETEEN

E ve sat quietly in the jolting vehicle. Four women, including her, sat on flat benches along the sides of the enclosed bed. They looked terrible, one and all, but Eve had done what she could to keep her spirits up. She'd managed to braid her hair neatly and her dress was creased but still fairly clean. A smile pulled at her lips. It was all about the smudge-hiding floral pattern.

Who knew she had such good sartorial instincts for the proper arrest clothing?

The real butch-looking person—Eve hadn't made any conversation and wouldn't be willing to assume their gender identity based on how the cops sorted them—was her best guess on which of them would start the whole thing. Their forearm tattoos moved smoothly over ropy muscle and Eve could imagine them pulling a shiv from some intimate place.

The woman sitting next to the butch wore makeup and sported a cheap perm. She kept staring at Eve, her head moving sinuously in the rocking vehicle. Eve got antsy about being recognized and having some kind of scene play out before it was time to go. She tried not to sneer back, tried to keep her head down, but it felt dangerous to take her attention off someone who was so focused on her.

Just when Eve reached her breaking point and glared at her, as she opened her mouth to express some version of "Fuck you looking at?" the woman pulled something out of her hair. Eve froze and couldn't help glancing at the guard. She'd kept her eyes scrupulously off the guard to that point, because she didn't want the other prisoners to gather they had something going. The guard met her eyes with a tiny smile, then turned around in order to present her back to the prisoners.

Perm lady gathered her body into a springy ball, then surged across the butch toward the guard. The butch almost scotched the jump out of pure instinctual reaction, clearly unused to anyone crossing their lap unless they were being attacked. The restraints saved the day, and possibly her life, by leaving the perm lady free to grab the guard and start rapping out orders.

"Down on your knees. Get down! Radio, hand me your radio. Put your gun on the floor and slide it to the other end." The whole time, the sharp point of the shiv pressed just under the guard's eyeball. She'd paled and darted a look at Eve as though to say, "How realistic is this going to be?"

Eve froze in shock until the perm lady forced the guard onto her belly. Eve scooted down next to the guard and squeezed her hand until the guard responded with a small squeeze back, then reached for the cutters in the guard's belt. She freed the butch first and handed her the cutters, then turned around and sent a commanding look over her shoulder.

Perm lady sat on the guard, crooning to her and poking her hard in the neck. The guard hid her face, and her fear, by turning her head away, but that angered the perm lady. As Eve's arms came loose, she stumbled purposefully into the perm lady and knocked the shiv loose. The guard didn't move, except for one hard shiver, but the perm lady screeched. Eve stuck the shiv in the guard's sock. Perm lady, still constrained by the zip tie handcuffs, struggled awkwardly until the butch pulled her up by her hands and held her eyes. "Shut the fuck up." They pushed her down to the bench without freeing her hands.

The butch looked at Eve expectantly. "How do we get out of the van?"

Eve cleared her throat and looked at the perm lady. Not the best conspirator, but it couldn't have been easy getting someone into the same transport. The butch seemed ready to follow her lead, as long as they believed she would be leading, so Eve took her seat back and crossed her legs elegantly. The nonchalance of the gesture was somewhat weakened by her compulsion to rub her bare wrists, as though the ties could spontaneously reappear.

"Someone will open the door from the outside at a traffic stop along the way. Simple as that."

The butch shrugged. "I like a simple plan." They elbowed the perm lady. "Let's keep this simple, eh? No need to put any special damage on this guard here, or they'll burn the city down to find us. Unless the guard changes her mind about keeping this peaceable." The butch put a boot on the guard's kidneys.

Being locked in a vehicle with a woman wielding a weapon hadn't sounded scary until perm lady had started jabbing the guard with such glee. A couple moments too long, and the plan might have gone sideways.

She owed the butch for taking control. "You got email?"

"You think I'm stupid? Everybody's got email."

Not quite true, but good enough. "Write it down and I'll make sure you get something for helping."

The butch frisked the guard and found a notepad. Meanwhile, the fourth woman in the vehicle spoke up timidly. "Are we escaping?"

Eve and the butch exchanged amused looks. Eve said, "We are, sweetie. You can stay here if you want. I'm sure you won't get in more trouble if you do."

She swung her thick black hair back and her sudden smile packed a vicious punch. "Fuck that. Get these off me."

The butch clipped the zip ties after a quick look at Eve. They leaned back, still signaling the guard to stay down with a boot on her back.

Eve looked around the group. One big happy family.

Before anyone could get more antsy, the vehicle stopped. Everyone looked at Eve, and she snapped, "I don't know."

The back doors opened and a pale-skinned man in a suit waved impatiently. "Come on, hurry."

The women poured from the vehicle, the butch jumping out as it started driving off again.

"We couldn't get the driver, so I don't know how much time we have. Ladies, please set off in any direction except ours." He gripped Eve's elbow and tried to hustle her away. Perm lady scurried down the cross street, and the quiet one slipped away after her.

The butch stood, boots planted. "Sure you wouldn't like some company, Eve?"

Appreciation for their discretion up to that point and a swift tug of attraction had Eve pulling away from the strange man. "What I'd like and what I get aren't always the exact same thing. Thanks for keeping the blood in everyone's bodies."

Eve reached out for the paper with the butch's email address. She followed up by nestling close and pulled the butch's head down. With a fleeting thought for how long it had been since she'd brushed her teeth, she nipped.

Hard arms wrapped around her waist and pulled her to her toes. The clinch got out of Eve's control, but a tap on their arm had the butch releasing her. Red-faced and breathing hard, they stood their ground. The butch was still watching when Eve looked over her shoulder before disappearing behind the first turn.

The man who'd let them out put on a cap that turned him into a chauffeur. Eve twitched at her clothing and patted her hair. She didn't want to be the one to spoil the impression. She didn't have a bag to swing from her elbow.

The little inconsistency nagged at her hard. Way too hard for its relative unimportance. She took a deep breath, then another, manufacturing a calm she was far from feeling. She'd been freed, but she wouldn't be able to relax until they were out of the country.

When the chauffeur stopped at a town car and opened the back door, Eve slipped inside as though nothing could be more natural. She lowered the screen as the chauffeur went around the car. As soon as the door closed, she said, "How are we doing?"

"No reason for anyone to notice us."

"Except this is a very expensive car for this neighborhood."

"There's underground gambling on this block. They've seen fancy cars driving people who want anonymity."

"Ah." She settled into the comfortable seat and crossed her legs.

"It's more important we fit in on the other end of the drive."

Forty-five silent, nerve-wracking minutes later, the car pulled up to a gate and the chauffeur had a brief conversation through the intercom. The heavy wrought iron swung out of the way slowly, ponderously, while the nearness of escape brought Eve's tension to a fever.

A small jet sat at the end of the private runway. The house's owner was not home and would hopefully never know his runway had been part of her route. A trim uniformed pilot, rather on the short side, waited by the hatch. She waited until the car had stopped and the chauffeur opened the door, then stepped forward to offer Eve a hand.

"Ms. La Sirena, I'm Michelle Adams. Please call me Mick. I'll be your pilot until you tell me otherwise."

Eve shook Mick's hand and assessed her quickly. Neat, quick, and calm. Three things Eve prized just then, especially the parts she couldn't quite manage. "Call me Eve, Mick. I'm hoping we'll keep each other company a bit on the flight."

Mick grinned. "Not sure I'm very entertaining, but we'll manage."

"Shall we?" Eve schooled herself to hide the jitters that threatened her cool image.

"Let's." Mick led the way to the plane but waved Eve along to board first. The chauffeur got back in his car and drove away before Mick had the hatch closed.

Eve worried about him. He'd given her no reason to trust him, not a single vibe that put her worries to rest. She'd have to hope he was in it for the money and that the money had been good. She wasn't in any position to tip.

In a flash, Eve was seated and buckled in. Her hunger and thirst would have to wait until they were off the ground. Mick sat in her cockpit and said, "You can listen in on the radio chatter if you want. There's a headset next to your seat."

Eve pulled the headset on for the distraction, and she found the smooth, repetitious call and response patterns soothing. They took off without incident and left the controlled airspace in very little time.

Mick spoke in her ear. "The air looks smooth between here and Cartagena. If you want to talk, you can use this channel or you can come sit next to me. There's food and drink in the fridge at the back. We didn't bring an attendant. Best to keep this operation as small as possible."

That answered one question. Mick knew where she stood in the big picture. Eve was glad—those who helped her leave the country were in greater danger than those who would help her stay out of it. She didn't want anyone sucked into her troubles unawares. Of course, she hoped they would all protest their ignorance if it came down to it. She'd be happy to take the blame as the exploitative employer.

Eve said, "Thanks, Mick. For everything. I'm going to eat, so call me on the speaker if we need to talk."

"Roger that."

Eve pulled the headset off and let her head fall back against the seat. Tension drained from her body, though they weren't out of US air space yet. She felt safe, and there was nothing she could do about it if she wasn't. She sat up, then stood, feeling ten years older than she had before she'd been arrested. She kicked her heels off and stretched. Before looking through the refrigerator, she went to the toilet.

Luxurious. A small shower drew her across in a trance. She unzipped the dress from armpit to hip and pulled it off over her head. Wrinkle-resistant, yes, but she hung it anyway. When she removed her bra, she moaned with the relief of it and pulled her squashed nipples. Like a little mini-orgasm, that release from bondage. She stepped out of her underwear and let them fall to the floor.

The shower's hot water beat away some of her fatigue. Good water pressure for such a tiny plane. She wouldn't question her good fortune. Once she felt up to moving again, she scanned the plain bottles in the soap holder. She sniffed the one marked shampoo and tears came to her eyes.

Only Harmonie would supply a getaway vehicle with Eve's favorite toiletries. She lathered her hair and cleaned her skin, tears mixing with the shower water the whole time. By the time she turned off the water, Eve had come to a tender, delicate calm. She dried with a thick towel, wrapped her hair in another, and slipped on the light robe hanging on the back of the door in front of a garment bag. She lowered the zipper a few inches to reveal the collar of a shirt she'd never seen before.

She'd lost all her clothing. A long moment passed as she struggled with the thought. All her things. The ridiculous and the sublime, the gorgeous and the comfortable. All gone. She was down to whatever Harmony had given her.

Speaking of...She looked and, sure enough, there was toothpaste and a toothbrush in the vanity. She stroked the box lightly, but she wanted food first.

The refrigerator held maki, wakame, and a microwavable bowl of miso soup. By the time Eve had hunted down the very last scraps of seaweed, she was sated, sleepy, and sore. Hours and hours of tension, days to be accurate, had left her muscles weak. She checked in with Mick, who said they had at least an hour before landing, and decided to take a power nap.

A chime sounded, then sounded again. Eve felt like she'd just fallen asleep, but a glance at the clock confirmed she'd slept for an hour. Mick's voice came over the cabin speaker. "Sorry to wake you, Eve, but we're coming down for landing. About five minutes until you need to be buckled in. I thought you might want to make another bathroom trip."

Eve stretched, achy even with such a comfortable seat to sleep in. She picked up the headset and said, "Thanks. I'll make it quick."

After using the toilet, she dressed in the slacks and blouse from the garment bag. She checked herself in the mirror and realized she hadn't done anything with her hair. It waved from her crown, long and wild, framing the bright red line of her scar-to-be. She shrugged at it and used her little time to brush her teeth. Nasty.

The landing and disembarking went smoothly. Another man awaited her, this one obsequiously accommodating. He took a piece of luggage from Mick, and Eve thought again about how wonderful Harmonie was. He whisked her away as soon as she'd thanked Mick, took her to a hotel, and gave her the address at which she should meet her next ride, a hired car.

After he left, she looked around the bland hotel room, smaller by far than any she'd seen in the last decade. Size didn't matter; anonymity did. Whether or not she was safe, she was well out of the country. Tomorrow she'd start running again, but for one night, she would sit in peace.

Thoughts of Jack badgered her. Was he well? Had he run or did the FBI have him? Would he be able to get to her in the Azores?

She wanted to get a message to him, reminding him of the plan and confirming that she was on her way, but it was impossible. She couldn't even contact Harmonie to find out if he was free without endangering their entire plan. Their first check-in call was days away.

The weeks of travel ahead of her brought her mood low. She couldn't simply brood all day, every day. She'd get sailing books and study up. She'd plan her revenge on the lawyer who sicced the cops on her.

Jack, Jack, Jack. She longed to press him under her body, to match their limbs and feel him along every bit of skin. A snatch of music appeared and disappeared. She stood in front of the television she had been about to turn on, but she turned away instead and grabbed the hotel stationary.

Eve sat cross-legged on the bed and played an imaginary piano. Too bad they'd taken her harmonica. Eyes closed, whispering words and humming, she transmuted her yearning into song.

CHAPTER TWENTY

Jack walked away from Justin's house, a scream filling his mind.

Lysistrata was gone. His life, his livelihood. Everything he'd ever wanted and shocked himself by getting. His clothes, his mementos, even the very documents proving the boat was his. All gone.

He'd heard about Marshal seizures. They could confiscate anything that might have been paid for with illegally acquired funds, but he'd paid for *Lysistrata* with his own hard work, all aboveboard. He could have done cash sales off the books, but he'd played by the rules. See what that had gotten him?

He might eventually get her back, but not until they'd disassembled every cabinet, tossed through or broken everything he had aboard. One of the guys who fished off the pier had gone to an auction for boats they'd seized. He'd said they weren't worth the price of moving them by the time the cops got done searching them.

Lysistrata was dead. Whatever happened, he would never get back the same boat they'd taken from him. He didn't know if he'd feel the same about her, even if he could find her right that moment. Could he put his things back in their places, clean up the broken pieces, and feel comfortable and confident aboard?

Did it even matter? He couldn't get the boat back without facing the authorities and convincing them he'd had nothing to do with Eve and Harmonie's pirate activities. Of all the things Jack had joked about, piracy suddenly seemed to hold very little humor.

Homeless, helpless, and broke. He might have had enough money to get to the Azores before provisioning to sail there, though he doubted it. Signing on as freighter crew might get him there. The spark of hope guttered and died. That would take way too long. How many ships would hire him? How many of those would be going there? What would happen when he jumped ship there? The last thing he wanted was to be hunted at his final destination.

Jack's steps had taken him back to the pier. He sat on a piling and looked out over the marina. All those boats, and not one of them his. Most of them never left the marina, or went out only on the big holidays. Father's Day, Memorial Day, Fourth of July, Labor Day. The holidays of summer brought out the "captains courageous," those foolhardy folks who tossed themselves upon the waters in boats that hadn't been started or run in months. Liveaboards scoffed at those who owned boats and hardly ever saw them. Racers scoffed at liveaboards who rarely went sailing. Those who lived aboard *and* sailed regularly were a small group, and Jack figured he knew every one of them on that stretch of coast.

Some made their living from their boat, like he did. Like he had. Pain twisted his belly. Others made their living on their boat, using it as a mobile workshop for fixing other people's boats. Most of his friends were one of those types. Workers of some stripe.

Then there were the travelers, the lightly employed or retired, like Steve on *Reliant*. Steve's union career as a master welder had set him up quite nicely with solid retirement pay and a chunk of savings. His wife had died a decade before him and his kids hadn't figured much in his stories. Jack had gotten the impression they didn't exactly like each other. When Steve had died, Jack tried to get a message to his kids through the marina office. He'd been willing to show them the boat. Explain how things worked.

He kept *Reliant* aired out and afloat, but when he asked again, the marina manager told him the kids had made out like bandits on Steve's life insurance and savings. They had no interest in taking on a home-built boat and the expenses involved in keeping it up. By the time Steve's will had gone through probate, the boat had represented more debt than value—or so the older kid had said when the manager had contacted them, trying to get paid for months of past-due dockage. He told the manager to torch the boat for all they cared.

And so it sat.

Jack stared at *Reliant*, lips pursed. Mold spread over the sail covers and sprouted from the scuppers. The wheel, Steve's only bit of varnished brightwork, had tiger stripes where the varnish had peeled away and the wood had gotten wet.

Jack wondered.

He sat on the piling, his hands loose in his lap, and wondered. Could he?

Was there anything lower than a boat thief?

He thought of *Lysistrata*, stolen from him legally and gone forever. Anger returned, and a desire to send a big fuck-you to the authorities grew in him. If they were going to treat him like a criminal, he'd show them what real piracy looked like.

Jack's pulse pounded and his mouth went dry. He couldn't move.

It was a way out of the pit. He could raise himself from the abject helplessness that had frozen him.

He could sail to the Azores.

Eve.

Turned out he could move, as long as he had something to move toward.

Jack's practical side screamed at him not to throw his lot into a boat that had sat, abandoned, for months. He clicked through the issues in his mind, one after another, as he walked down the gangway to the floating docks of the marina. His mind not yet made up, he stepped aboard *Reliant* and ducked under the awning. He opened the companionway doors and pushed back the hatch cover.

From one moment to the next, between taking his hand off the hatch cover and grabbing the handhold inside, Jack gave up all his pretenses. If the boat would make the trip, he was going to steal it.

No law but his own judgment. No court but his conscience.

His conscience was clear. No one wanted *Reliant* but him. No one needed it or used it or cared about it in the least. He could do this.

Jack tore through the boat, system by system. Electrical, plumbing, cooking, engine. The engine was a diesel, but Jack would simply have to deal with that horrible technology until he could arrange to replace it. He changed filters, filled the water tanks, rinsed the watermaker and prepped it for action. The fuel tank was full and Jack realized he wouldn't have been able to add any had it been empty. He was still fucking broke.

He couldn't figure out how to do a subtle check of the sails in the dark, but Steve had laid in plenty of extra sail fabric when he'd built the sails originally. Jack could practically make new sails if it came down to it. When he found a brand-new sewing machine in a purpose-built box, he realized that was more accurate than he'd known.

He didn't think about what he was doing or why. He simply went through the steps of commissioning *Reliant* and provisioning her for a trans-oceanic journey. He moved fast, clearing the clothes that wouldn't fit him and filling the lockers with food from his storage unit. He saved whatever he would be able to wear, including Steve's foul weather gear. It was all too big, but once he was out on the unforgiving ocean, he couldn't be caught without the layers that would stave off hypothermia.

Steve's decades of meticulous work habits showed themselves in the tidy, labeled plastic bins of spare parts. Jack sat, staring into the storage area under the main settee, and almost wept with gratitude. He pressed his hands to his face, shook the emotion back, and closed the hatch.

A dozen trips to the storage unit with the big marina cart, and *Reliant* was loaded. Jack had worked through the night, hoping to beat the sunrise, but the job was too big. He couldn't wait any longer. The marina workers would arrive in an hour or so, and several fishing boats had already putted their way out of the dock. He looked around at the last bags of groceries sitting on the cabin sole and shrugged.

The engine started hard, chugging and blowing a great cloud of black smoke. He didn't know what he would have done if it hadn't. Sailed out of the dock? He would have tried. He tested the transmission, putting it into forward, then reverse, pulling on the dock lines. It worked.

He let the engine warm while he disconnected the shore power and coiled the water hose. He packed them into the last space in the lazarette, then untied the boat. He jumped aboard and shoved her into slow reverse, easing out of the slip into the fairway, then slow forward. At that moment, the nerves he hadn't had time for beat against his heart and lungs. His hands trembled on the wheel.

A man stood fishing on the pier—the guy who'd told him all about the auctions of seized boats. He watched, incurious, as Jack floated by, but then recognized him and raised a hand. Jack waved back and fought the urge to hit the throttle. Full speed just wasn't that fast in a sailboat. The Coast Guard Defender-class response boats could do ten times the speed of *Reliant*. More if *Reliant*'s bottom was covered in barnacles or the propeller had been eaten away by galvanic corrosion.

Any vague thought Jack had about using the boat to get south, to any of the dozens of countries within a few days' sail, exploded in the vision of that one guy who knew him. Knew him, knew his boat. Knew that he was on another boat, an unmistakable design.

Once the cops talked to that guy, they'd know what Jack had done.

There was no coming home.

A DEA boat zoomed toward him and he froze. *Reliant* continued along its course, impervious to the fear that spiked through Jack. The agents aboard didn't even look at him as they went by.

Jack firmed his will and set the tiller minder. He went forward and raised the sails, overwhelmed with gladness to see that they were just fine.

Everything was just fine.

CHAPTER TWENTY-ONE

E ve brushed her wig out, the dark red of the hair lending a rich tone to the skin of her hands. Her little house nestled between two fields, potatoes in one and grass in the other, for the sheep. Their shepherd was Leonor Crespo, a shy girl who spoke no English. Eve's Portuguese was a mess, her pronunciation far better than her vocabulary. They'd managed to get friendly anyway, and Eve pulled on the wig so she could share a few warm words when Leonor came through later with her charges.

She tidied the long bangs over her forehead. The wound she'd sustained on *Lysistrata* had long since closed up and the vividness was fading, but it was still the most immediately recognizable aspect of her appearance. It had almost gotten her caught in Bruge, of all places, when a punctilious member of their police had recognized her from an Interpol poster. They'd gotten plenty of photos when she'd been arrested and the news footage had used her arrest photo liberally. Everyone who watched celebrity news, business news— hell, any kind of media at all—had seen her face with the livid red line. She applied makeup with a quickness born of practice, flattening the curve of her eyes, building up her eyebrows in a straight line, and fading her nose's bridge while fattening her nostrils.

It helped her confidence, if nothing else, to feel disguised.

After four weeks of bouncing from place to place so quickly that she wasn't sure she could list them all from memory, she'd alighted in Ponta Delgada on the island of Sao Miguel in the Azores, then taken a ferry to Flores. At first, she'd searched the ports eagerly, taking ferries from island to island, hope filling her with energy. She visited every place a boat could anchor or dock, but there was no sign of *Lysistrata*.

She hadn't given up hope. She'd returned to Flores, rented the little house for a week, and walked through fields bounded by low, hydrangeas-covered stone walls to the cliffs over Lajes. As she would do again later that day.

No one knew where she was, except Marc's family. They'd arranged the rental, saying only that she was a friend of Marc's who needed quiet time to herself. They'd implied perhaps she was mourning a lost love, but she'd overheard talk in the village guessing that she cried for the lover's return. They watched along with her, wondering which boat would be his.

She wandered from the bedroom to the living room and ran her fingers over the guitar. Someone had seen her playing her fingers over a rock and singing, and Narciso, Marc's father, had found it for her. She treasured it as the gift it was, and it had smoothed her way to completing a new album. Raw, chilling and heated by turns, full-hearted love songs had spilled from her, one after another, during her travels, and she used her waiting time to smooth them, to let the songs take on their own lives. She wandered the cliffs for a second week, singing love songs over the ocean's crash.

The nerves built, day by day, as Jack didn't come. She believed, stubbornly, that he would, that nothing would keep him away from her. She knew her power over him, knew that his love would answer hers. But as the third week passed, she worried that she'd be caught and taken away before he could find her.

She resisted the urge to pick up the guitar and lose herself in a world wholly shaped and controlled by her will. She'd never imagined such helplessness as knowing that Jack had disappeared and fearing that he may never make it back to her arms. The ocean's wild strength could have overpowered him.

She shook off the thoughts that hung about like ghosts.

Eve stepped out her doorway when she saw Leonor approaching her gate. She nodded and wished her a good morning. That much

Portuguese she'd mastered. She showed Leonor a simple book and asked if it were a good book to learn from. Leonor giggled and said it was for babies. Eve tried to say she was no better than a baby, but Leonor giggled again. "I will bring you something better," she said in Portuguese.

Eve thanked her and waved as Leonor walked away. The air felt thick with humidity that the ocean breeze did its best to fling away. The idea of staying long enough to master the language both attracted and repelled her. She couldn't live like that forever. Waking. Making coffee. Cleaning. Reading instructional books on sailing, boat maintenance, and living aboard. Going for her long daily walk along the coastline to the port in Lajes. Up and down, cliffs and valleys. Returning, disappointed again. Using her emotions to perfect the songs she'd written from the depths. Preparing food and reading herself to sleep.

English language books hadn't been too hard to come by. The British, American, and Canadian boaters who came and went, avoiding the larger yacht port at Horta, had set up a book trade in the coin laundry. When she wasn't trying to master the art of sailing by reading about it, Eve gravitated toward the romances and cried, night after night, at the torture love put the couples through.

The romances of past centuries held tales like hers, the guarantee of a happy ending forfeited through character weakness.

Eve kicked a stone on the path and blinked in the sun. Holy shit, this place was getting to her. She'd always been good at taking on a role, but fuck this.

She was there because of her strengths, not her weaknesses. She waited for her love because she knew he wasn't in Miami anymore. He'd left within a day of her, but the news was vague and confusing. He'd stocked up on food for a long sea journey— that much Harmonie had been able to learn from the friends who'd helped him—but there was an arrest warrant out on him for grand theft.

The newspapers hadn't covered Jack's story, though they'd chewed hers to bits. A sharp irritation prodded her at the way they'd hounded Harmonie. The sensation pleased her in a way, banishing the sticky lassitude of her last few days. As lovely as the rocky island was, she wouldn't grow old as the One Who Waited.

Where the fuck could he be? She'd avoided the American boats that came through, but the grapevine told her that boats leaving after Jack had made the trip in three or four weeks. Junk rigs were better on some points of sail than others, sure, she got that, but show the fuck up, Jack.

She topped the hill and strode to the end of the land. Far below, the water dashed itself to rainbowed mist against the rocks. Out to sea, she saw sails.

It was early in the season for crossings, so every boat could be *Lysistrata*. There wasn't enough traffic for her to be blasé about seeing sails. Even that surging hope pissed her off suddenly.

How long could she wait? Every stranger who saw her was another chance that the authorities would find her. Portugal was not a country to hide in, not even this westernmost little nub surrounded by the Atlantic Ocean.

She hadn't made any alternate plans, but maybe it was time to start. She could leave some kind of contact on the island. She could buy a SIM card and use random phones to check the voicemail. She should work out a destination, someplace she could spend a few months in safety while she figured out what to do with the rest of her life.

Without Jack, she didn't know where to go.

If she picked a place he could sail to from here, she'd be looking at going back toward Central America or heading farther east to Africa. Oh, for the days when Turkey and the US had been at loggerheads. She would have loved to go home.

As she pondered, the sailboat drew closer. From the hill, she had over fifteen miles of visibility over the water. Even at a good clip, it would take three to five hours before that boat would round the point she stood on and make for the harbor.

Long before then, she realized that the boat sailing toward her was the wrong color. Not *Lysistrata* black, but silver. The boat's sails also leaned differently somehow.

A junk rig, but not *Lysistrata*.

Eve walked back to her little house.

She had barely reached it when fury overtook her. She wanted to ruin that fucking lawyer all over again, but she could only send her to jail for corruption once. The usual pleasure of knowing she'd turned the tables on the lawyer failed her and the very walls of the simple two-room house felt like a prison. She wanted to break dishes, rend the sheets and blankets, and burn the rugs.

The things she wanted to destroy were not hers. She snatched the guitar and slung it over her back. She walked out of the house without a second look, wishing she would never return. She struggled back up the hill and sat overlooking the water with a rock at her back.

Her fingers moved on the strings. For the first time, she let go of composing the songs and simply played them.

Chapter Twenty-two

J ack leaned toward the island as though he could arrive faster that way. The strong breeze blew him toward it faster than he'd gone for weeks. He was almost there.

And just in time. His food was almost gone, except one huge bag of rice that had gotten wet and swelled with mold. He couldn't bring himself to throw it away with so much else going wrong.

He'd ducked under the low pressure zone of storms that moved up and down the Atlantic every year, but he'd miscalculated and gone too far. Days of doldrums had turned into weeks, and the infuriating diesel engine had refused to save him.

For a while, it had turned over and run when he needed a bit of a push or extra power to run the watermaker. One day, lurching over slick waves seven feet high, it had weakened, strengthened, weakened again, then died. He cursed the technology that had catapulted the world into runaway heating and tried everything in the engine's shop manual. In the end, it looked like water and solids had fouled the fuel, clogged the filters, and starved the engine. Changing the filters and pushing more fuel through the system until new stuff reached the injectors helped until, eventually, the injectors became clogged. The manual specifically forbade sticking anything into the holes to clear them. The tiny hole couldn't take the smallest scratch or bend.

So he'd washed around at the mercy of large waves kicked up by wind elsewhere in the Atlantic, trying to control his drift with a big parachute anchor Steve had bought cheap at a military surplus store. Setting that up had kept him busy for a couple days, then figuring out how to spill the water out of it for retrieval had taken most of another day. By the time he felt hopeful that he wasn't going to drift in circles forever, he'd realized that the battery system wasn't designed to handle the electrical load of the watermaker.

Since most of his provisions were dried rice, beans, and lentils, he couldn't do without water. He didn't wash anything except his face in fresh water, and still he used frightening amounts. He started putting canned vegetable into everything so he could use the canning liquid. He didn't want to think what it would taste like to cook beans in fruit juice.

He wasn't proud that it took him so long to realize that he could run out of food. He'd focused so hard on his water problem, hoarding power for the watermaker by only running the chartplotter once a day, that he'd burned through most of his canned goods before he thought about it.

The trip that was supposed to take three weeks stretched into six and kept going.

Once he'd gotten a bit more wind, the wind generator had supplied a strong, day-and-night charge for the batteries. Good thing, too, since he had no experience navigating by the stars. Good old Steve had a book about celestial navigation and a cheap plastic sextant, but the whole process called for charts and worksheets Steve hadn't thought to buy.

Jack's respect for Steve had gone through dramatic ups and downs along the way. High quality construction gave way to the strangest fixes in places. Jack imagined him thinking he'd get back to it, but he'd never had the chance. One system that never failed was the bilge pump. When Jack was on deck one day, raising the last sail panel for the seven hundredth time, he had heard the surge of bilge water leaving the boat and been glad he didn't have to worry about sinking.

Then it had occurred to him to wonder how all that water was getting in.

Fixing the leaking seacock had been straightforward compared to struggling with the diesel engine. Jack came abovedecks after that project with a new confidence and found that *Reliant* was sailing well for the first time in weeks.

From that point on, it had been a race between him and his food supplies. The leak had soaked a bag of rice, and he had fears of psychoactive compounds at best, fatal ones at worst, lingering in the bulging bag.

The chartplotter could stay on more often as sun and wind power did their jobs. He knew exactly where the island was as he approached it and stared for long minutes at a time in that direction. He was bruised all over from bouncing around the unfamiliar cabin, exhausted from sleeping in stretches of no more than an hour for fear of a cargo ship overrunning him, and weak from eating short rations for the last five days.

When the island finally appeared, he didn't recognize it at first. He thought it was another ship and almost changed course to miss it. A second later, his throat seized up and he cried.

He was going to live.

His celebration was the last can of chili, eaten like a greedy child, cackling laughter and everything.

Four hours later, he studied the port through binoculars and picked out a nice, wide-open spot for him to anchor under sail. He brought *Reliant* in gently, but sheeted her tighter as the wind started to die behind the cliffs. He tossed off the sheets and stumbled to the bow to drop the anchor, then let the boat's own motion pull the chain over the roller. The anchor stuck hard in thick mud and whipped the boat around. The sails banged on the masts and Jack dropped more chain overboard until he was satisfied.

He dropped the sails and placed his hands flat on the mast. He lowered his forehead to the mast and let his relief overwhelm the fear that he'd made the trip for nothing.

It didn't take him long to wash and put on fresh clothes, even his own clothing too big by far after weeks of barely eating. He launched the dinghy and climbed in, but when he took up the oars, malnutrition and exhaustion caught up with him and dragged at his arms. He forced himself to row steadily, if not swiftly, and came ashore in the rich light of late afternoon.

Green bombarded his eyes and red shouted its flowery accompaniment. Blue had dominated his world for so long that other colors almost hurt. At his first attempt at walking, his legs trembled and he sat on the little dinghy landing. The world was too still for his ocean-adapted muscles and his stomach surged into his throat.

Within minutes, a gathering of silent people stared down at him from the seawall. Island people knew the look of one who'd been out too long and come too close to death.

He heaved himself to his feet and turned. Hoping someone spoke English, he looked up at the assembled faces and said, "I'm looking for a woman."

When someone repeated his words in Portuguese, smiles blossomed from one end to the other of the people-hedge. An old woman made a pulling motion, come, come, and he climbed the ladder. She was tiny, less than five feet tall, and brown as a walnut. Maybe they were related. He could use some loving care.

She took his hand and patted it as she led him toward land.

He followed blindly, aware of the procession behind them but unable to think about anything except putting one foot in front of the other.

The whole crowd stopped when the old woman did. She pulled his arm, and he looked at her, focusing as best he could with dazed eyes. She pointed up a hill track, just a little trail that made a fairly straight line to the top of the cliff he'd rounded to enter the harbor. She pointed again, then pushed him forward.

Jack succumbed to the eagerness of the old woman and her people. They wanted him to go up the hill, so up the hill he would go. How many millions of times had people been faced with one more hill when all they wanted was to lie down and give up? Sometimes, the only thing that kept a body going was the impetus provided by other people who'd decided they had some stake in the matter.

The ground was loose under his feet, hard dirt overlaid with small stones, with sharp green bordering the black and gray track. He concentrated on setting his feet under him, one after another, until the hill began to flatten out. He heard a hint of sound, then the wind slacked a moment and music filled his awareness.

He stumbled, wanting to run, but too weak to carry it off. He topped the hill and saw burnished red hair on the other side of a rock. Confusion made him falter, then stop. With the flowing ache of guitar music stroking his wind-whipped hearing, he stood, uncertain, until her voice rose to join the intricate weaving of notes played by her fingers.

Ocean feels not love nor hate
And weather won't pursue you.
But my love's lost and the moon won't wait.
Just draw the tide to drown you.

Jack breathed, finally. A song he'd never heard in a voice he'd never forget. "Eve."

A stumble in the music and he said it again. "Eve."

The guitar stopped and he heard it hit the ground. The red hair turned and eyes peeked over the rock.

As Jack struggled to know, struggled with the changing shapes and colors he saw—were those her eyes? Straight across, but exactly the right black—the wind ruffled her bangs and he saw the scar forming on her forehead.

"Evrim." At his shout, she stood and there was no doubt. She skirted the rock and raced at him, caught him up in an embrace that nearly bowled him over.

"Where have you been? What have you done to yourself?" She groped his whittled down body with racing hands, and he trembled in her arms.

"I love you, Evrim. I made myself believe you'd be here, but I was so scared..." Tears filled his nose and throat, then streaked his dry, hot cheeks.

"I love you, Jack. I love you so much. I waited for you. I've been here for weeks, but I waited for you." Her words lost coherency, and Jack stopped fighting gravity, pulling her down with him.

"Sing to me, Evrim."

She sang a new song, a hopeful, joyful song, and Jack dropped off to sleep with his head in her lap.

About the Author

Captain Dena Hankins writes aboard her boat, preferably in a quiet anchorage. She spent eight years as a sex educator, soaking up the most stimulating stories of human sexuality, and is honored to provide some tales in return. She is a queer, poly, kinky, adventurous sailor with so much left to learn!

Being a military brat, wanderlust is deep in her, and she has been sailing since 1999, covering waters from Seattle to San Francisco, across to Hawaii, and from North Carolina to Maine. Whether traveling in the physical world or ranging far in her imagination, she is happiest accompanied by her partner since 1996, James Lane.

Books Available from Bold Strokes Books

Basic Training of the Heart by Jaycie Morrison. In 1944, socialite Elizabeth Carlton joins the Women's Army Corps to escape family expectations and love's disappointments. Can Sergeant Gale Rains get her through Basic Training with their hearts intact? (978-1-62639-818-4)

Before by KE Payne. When Tally falls in love with her band's new recruit, she has a tough decision to make. What does she want more—Alex or the band? (978-1-62639-677-7)

Believing in Blue by Maggie Morton. Growing up gay in a small town has been hard, but it can't compare to the next challenge Wren—with her new, sky-blue wings—faces: saving two entire worlds. (978-1-62639-691-3)

Coils by Barbara Ann Wright. A modern young woman follows her aunt into the Greek Underworld and makes a pact with Medusa to win her freedom by killing a hero of legend. (978-1-62639-598-5)

Courting the Countess by Jenny Frame. When relationship-phobic Lady Henrietta Knight starts to care about housekeeper Annie Brannigan and her daughter, can she overcome her fears and promise Annie the forever that she demands? (978-1-62639-785-9)

Dapper by Jenny Frame. Amelia Honey meets the mysterious Byron De Brek and is faced with her darkest fantasies, but will her strict moral upbringing stop her from exploring what she truly wants? (978-1-62639-898-6E)

Delayed Gratification: The Honeymoon by Meghan O'Brien. A dream European honeymoon turns into a winter storm nightmare involving a delayed flight, a ditched rental car, and eventually, a surprisingly happy ending. (978-1-62639-766-8E)

For Money or Love by Heather Blackmore. Jessica Spaulding must choose between ignoring the truth to keep everything she has, and doing the right thing only to lose it all—including the woman she loves. (978-1-62639-756-9)

Hooked by Jaime Maddox. With the help of sexy Detective Mac Calabrese, Dr. Jessica Benson is working hard to overcome her past, but they may not be enough to stop a murderer. (978-1-62639-689-0)

Lands End by Jackie D. Public relations superstar Amy Kline is dealing with a media nightmare, and the last thing she expects is for restaurateur Lena Michaels to change everything, but she will. (978-1-62639-739-2)

Lysistrata Cove by Dena Hankins. Jack and Eve navigate the maelstrom of their darkest desires and find love by transgressing gender, dominance, submission, and the law on the crystal blue Caribbean Sea. (978-1-62639-821-4)

Twisted Screams by Sheri Lewis Wohl. Reluctant psychic Lorna Dutton doesn't want to forgive, but if she doesn't do just that an innocent woman will die. (978-1-62639-647-0)

A Class Act by Tammy Hayes. Buttoned-up college professor Dr. Margaret Parks doesn't know what she's getting herself into when she agrees to one date with her student, Rory Morgan, who is 15 years her junior. (978-1-62639-701-9)

Bitter Root by Laydin Michaels. Small town chef Adi Bergeron is hiding something, and Griffith McNaulty is going to find out what it is even if it gets her killed. (978-1-62639-656-2)

Capturing Forever by Erin Dutton. When family pulls Jacqueline and Casey back together, will the lessons learned in eight years apart be enough to mend the mistakes of the past? (978-1-62639-631-9)

Deception by VK Powell. DEA Agent Colby Vincent and Attorney Adena Weber are embroiled in a drug investigation involving homeless veterans and an attraction that could destroy them both. (978-1-62639-596-1)

Dyre: A Knight of Spirit and Shadows by Rachel E. Bailey. With the abduction of her queen, werewolf-bodyguard Des must follow the kidnappers' trail to Europe, where her queen—and a battle unlike any Des has ever waged—awaits her. (978-1-62639-664-7)

First Position by Melissa Brayden. Love and rivalry take center stage for Anastasia Mikhelson and Natalie Frederico in one of the most prestigious ballet companies in the nation. (978-1-62639-602-9)

Best Laid Plans by Jan Gayle. Nicky and Lauren are meant for each other, but Nicky's haunting past and Lauren's societal fears threaten to derail all possibilities of a relationship. (987-1-62639-658-6)

Exchange by CF Frizzell. When Shay Maguire rode into rural Montana, she never expected to meet the woman of her dreams—or to learn Mel Baker was held hostage by legal agreement to her right-wing father. (987-1-62639-679-1)

Just Enough Light by AJ Quinn. Will a serial killer's return to Colorado destroy Kellen Ryan and Dana Kingston's chance at love, or can the search-and-rescue team save themselves? (987-1-62639-685-2)

Rise of the Rain Queen by Fiona Zedde. Nyandoro is nobody's princess. She fights, curses, fornicates, and gets into as much trouble as her brothers. But the path to a throne is not always the one we expect. (987-1-62639-592-3)

Tales from Sea Glass Inn by Karis Walsh. Over the course of a year at Cannon Beach, tourists and locals alike find solace and passion at the Sea Glass Inn. (987-1-62639-643-2)

The Color of Love by Radclyffe. Black sheep Derian Winfield needs to convince literary agent Emily May to marry her to save the Winfield Agency and solve Emily's green card problem, but Derian didn't count on falling in love. (987-1-62639-716-3)

A Reluctant Enterprise by Gun Brooke. When two women grow up learning nothing but distrust, unworthiness, and abandonment, it's no wonder they are apprehensive and fearful when an overwhelming love just won't be denied. (978-1-62639-500-8)

Above the Law by Carsen Taite. Love is the last thing on Agent Dale Nelson's mind, but reporter Lindsey Ryan's investigation could change the way she sees everything—her career, her past, and her future. (978-1-62639-558-9)

Actual Stop by Kara A. McLeod. When Special Agent Ryan O'Connor's present collides abruptly with her past, shots are fired, and the course of her life is irrevocably altered. (978-1-62639-675-3)

Embracing the Dawn by Jeannie Levig. When ex-con Jinx Tanner and business executive E. J. Bastien awaken after a one-night stand to find their lives inextricably entangled, love has its work cut out for it. (978-1-62639-576-3)

Jane's World: The Case of the Mail Order Bride by Paige Braddock. Jane's PayBuddy account gets hacked and she inadvertently purchases a mail order bride from the Eastern Bloc. (978-1-62639-494-0)

Love's Redemption by Donna K. Ford. For ex-convict Rhea Daniels and ex-priest Morgan Scott, redemption lies in the thin line between right and wrong. (978-1-62639-673-9)

The Shewstone by Jane Fletcher. The prophetic Shewstone is in Eawynn's care, but unfortunately for her, Matt is coming to steal it. (978-1-62639-554-1)

A Touch of Temptation by Julie Blair. Recent law school graduate Kate Dawson's ordained path to the perfect life gets thrown off course when handsome butch top Chris Brent initiates her to sexual pleasure. (978-1-62639-488-9)

Beneath the Waves by Ali Vali. Kai Merlin and Vivien Palmer love the water and the secrets trapped in the depths, but if Kai gives in to her feelings, it might come at a cost to her entire realm. (978-1-62639-609-8)

Girls on Campus edited by Sandy Lowe and Stacia Seaman. College: four years when rules are made to be broken. This collection is required reading for anyone looking to earn an A in sex ed. (978-1-62639-733-0)

Heart of the Pack by Jenny Frame. Human Selena Miller falls for the domineering Caden Wolfgang, but will their love survive Selena learning the Wolfgangs are werewolves? (978-1-62639-566-4)

Miss Match by Fiona Riley. Matchmaker Samantha Monteiro makes the impossible possible for everyone but herself. Is mysterious dancer Lucinda Moss her own perfect match? (978-1-62639-574-9)

Paladins of the Storm Lord by Barbara Ann Wright. Lieutenant Cordelia Ross must choose between duty and honor when a man with godlike powers forces her soldiers to provoke an alien threat. (978-1-62639-604-3)